Fit for You

Also by Cynthia Tennent

The Bookshop on Autumn Lane
Skinny Dipping Season
A Wedding in Truhart

Fit for You

Cynthia Tennent

LYRICAL SHINE
Kensington Publishing Corp.
www.kensingtonbooks.com

LYRICAL SHINE BOOKS are published by

Kensington Publishing Corp.
119 West 40th Street
New York, NY 10018

All Kensington titles, imprints, and distributed lines are available at special quantity discounts for bulk purchases for sales promotion, premiums, fund-raising, educational, or institutional use.

Special book excerpts or customized printings can also be created to fit specific needs. For details, write or phone the office of the Kensington Sales Manager: Kensington Publishing Corp., 119 West 40th Street, New York, NY 10018. Attn. Sales Department. Phone: 1-800-221-2647.

Lyrical Shine and Lyrical Shine logo Reg. U.S. Pat. & TM Off.

First Electronic Edition: July 2017
eISBN-13: 978-1-5161-0318-8
eISBN-10: 1-5161-0318-1

First Print Edition: July 2017
ISBN-13: 978-1-5161-0319-5
ISBN-10: 1-5161-0319-X

Printed in the United States of America

To my three daughters, who are proud of their mixed heritage . . . and to their poor knees (all four of them), wounded on the soccer fields of glory.

LESSON ONE

The Hardest Part Is Getting Started

A garbage truck covered in mud-spattered stuffed animals sprayed sludge in its wake as it coasted down the two-lane highway straight for me. I wobbled on my crutches, trying not to fall in a snowbank. I was either in a teddy-bear zombie apocalypse, or the Vicodin was still screwing with me.

The truck slowed and a million beady eyes zeroed in. I planted myself in the icy gravel next to a bus stop sign that quivered in the wind. Other than a small building and the bleak frozen landscape at the intersection of a deserted county road and a state highway, my options were limited.

I could hobble across the street and seek refuge in a place called Flo's Bait Shoppe. They might have a harpoon I could use on the little critters. On second glance, that was out. A sign in the window read CLOSED WEDNESDAY AFTERNOON.

I could call the nice man who said he would pick me up at the bus stop. He should be here by now. But my cell phone reception had been spotty since Saginaw.

I could make a break for it and run into the woods. But I'd never get far on my bad knee.

It was already too late. A dingy stuffed bear with piercing yellow eyes laughed at me from the front bumper. My skin crawled as the truck came to a stop beside me.

I balanced on one good leg and one gimpy leg that was secured by Velcro straps in a black leg brace. I was going to have to modify the lessons I had taught in my self-defense classes. Squeezing my hand around the crutches, I prepared to strike. I would work my way up, attacking every vulnerable part of my foe.

Knees. Groin.

Button nose.

I had sparred with high-caliber athletes before, but I wasn't sure I knew how to brawl with a teddy bear.

"Hi there!"

It took me a moment to figure out which mammal was talking, the bearded man leaning out the window or the sad-looking fluffy whale on the door beneath him.

I waved a crutch in the air. "No, thanks, I don't need a stuffed animal!"

"What?" His furry chin wavered.

"Thanks for saying hello. Have a good day!" My whisky voice sounded even more hoarse than usual. "I'm going to call my friend at the police department now. He's picking me up."

He sent me a lopsided smile. "The sheriff? I just saw him at the Family Fare. You don't want to interrupt him on double-coupon days. Besides, I'm the one giving you a ride."

Over my dead and broken body. There was no way the last thing I was going to see in my twenty-eight years of life was the bug-eyed smile of a plush toy.

"Let me help you into the truck," he said.

I turned away and stumbled down the icy gravel of the shoulder, searching for anything that might resemble civilization. Two steps into my short journey, I heard a door slam and the thud of boots running to catch up with me. I limped faster and almost fell.

"Lady . . . calm down, will you?" Two log-sized arms reached out and he caught me. I looked up into a set of captivating gray eyes. My mouth went dry.

They say some of the most notorious serial killers look like the guy next door. Ted Bundy. Jeffrey Dahmer.

And now this guy.

The low-lying winter sun shimmered off the blond highlights in his wavy brown hair. He wore a red plaid camp shirt that reminded me of the brawny lumberjack on the wrapper of paper towels. Instead of clobbering him with my crutch, I wanted to burrow in his flannel. He made sure I was stable, then he stepped away and checked me out. Not really "checked me out" like a guy at a cheap bar. Given my appearance, that wouldn't be possible. I was wearing a puffy white down coat that ended midthigh. The thick dark hair I had inherited from my Korean mother was hidden in a pink knit ski hat. And my face was makeup free. To him I was nothing but a lump with a pink pom-pom on top.

Oh God, to him I probably looked like I belonged on the truck!

I had a mental image of myself splayed across the side of the truck beside the faded blue elephant dangling near my hip. Little Dumbo had big black eyes and a half smile underneath his long trunk. Without thinking, I tucked him back under an elastic tie that held him in place.

I turned back to Hercules. "My ride should be here any minute. So you and your furry friends are free to mush along."

The giant scratched his head. "Are you making fun of the truck?"

"Not at all," I replied with a straight face. Then I ruined it by saying the first thing that came to my unfiltered, exhausted mind. "I didn't realize I was on the island of misfit toys."

His lips quivered. "Good thing Uncle Pete isn't around to hear you make fun of his truck. He gets awfully sensitive when people laugh at him."

I didn't want to make things worse. "I love the look. Very, uh, creative."

He bent over and started laughing. A cross between a hoot and a deep bark. I didn't get the joke. Staring at his wide, shaking shoulders, I wondered if I was still capable of performing a neck lock.

Over his head I glimpsed an older model silver sedan heading our way. I raised my hand to wave it down. The driver slowed and lowered his window.

Still smiling, "Brawny man" straightened and grinned. "Hey, Doc!"

"Edge! Are you going to start scooping anytime soon?"

"I'm starting up the freezers next week. As soon as I get a forty-five-degree day, I'm ready for the kiddos."

"Can't wait."

Kiddies? Freezers?

I was so horrified, the driver was halfway down the road before I could hail him. "What do you do? Lure the kids in with Care Bears and then put them in the ice box?" I mumbled.

"You have a sick mind, lady," he said with a chuckle.

Not really. Just two older brothers who loved making me watch horror movies when I was little.

I ran my hand across my eyes and tried to clear my head. I still felt fuzzy from sleep deprivation and the general fogginess of a long day of travel. The Vicodin before bed last night wasn't helping.

I should have taken my mother up on her offer to let me recuperate at her Santa Monica home. Right now, I could be lying on a couch watching a shopping channel and eating ramen noodles with the wooden chopsticks she collected from the Golden Dragon.

The burly man stared at my luggage and my sports bag. "You *are* the lady who is here for that health grant, right?"

I raised my chin. "You know about me?"

"Not very much," he said, staring at my knee encased in the large black brace.

A group called the Triple C's was sponsoring me, and I had been forthright about my injury. Sort of. At the very least they understood that I had a condition that prevented me from performing some of the fitness exercises myself. It wasn't going to impact my ability to work with the residents of the town. At least not in theory.

"I appreciate your help, but my ride should be here any minute."

His lip twitched as if he thought that was funny. He extended an arm toward the truck. "And it is."

"You must be mistaken. Yesterday I spoke with a lady who told me a nice older man was picking me up from the bus stop. I just texted him."

"That nice old man is my Uncle Pete. His back gave out on him again. So, you're stuck with me."

"No offense, but no one mentioned a lumberjack and a truck that functions as kiddy bait. How do I know you aren't some crazy serial killer?"

His gray eyes twinkled and I thought I could see the pucker of a dimple peeking through his unshaven cheek. "I forget how Uncle Pete's truck might seem to outsiders. I assure you it's perfectly safe."

I wasn't buying it yet. "How about you find me a nice cab and I'll get there on my own. An Uber ride is fine, too." I heard a car behind me and I stuck out my thumb. But it was too late, a silver minivan passed us.

"Are you trying to hitchhike?" The man beside me made a clucking sound with his tongue and whipped out his phone. "Look. Here's the text from Uncle Pete." His short, spotless fingernails and clean hand clutching the latest iPhone seemed oddly out of place with the rest of him.

Keeping my distance, I balanced on one crutch and pulled my own phone out of my pocket. I scrolled through my recent texts. I held it up next to his phone. Same number.

He shifted to the text. *Shit mybackwent out again canyou cover for me until Friday also I promised Mayor's wife Ide pick up the new health knot hired at 5 at the bust stop*

I raised an eyebrow. "Bust stop and health knot?"

He shrugged and put his phone back in his pocket. "Uncle Pete can't text very well."

A gust of wind penetrated the Gore-Tex of my coat and made me shiver. "There is no such thing as being too careful nowadays, you know."

"Right you are," he said as if I had commented on the weather. "I'll get your suitcases and then let's get you inside the truck."

I followed him in a three-and-a-half-legged hop. "I can help."

Ignoring me, he reached for my suitcases.

"Be careful with those." The Greyhound bus driver had given me a hard time when I asked him to help with my two bulging red suitcases. He had made quite a show of grumbling that they were over the weight limit. But hunky man didn't seem to care. He lifted both bags and threw them in a well behind the cab as if they were feather pillows.

He turned to me and held out a long flannel arm. "Ready?"

I hesitated. This was mortifying. Almost as bad as sobbing in front of the whole post-op staff after surgery. Or trying to pee while the nurse patiently waited for my urinary tract to get on course again. Or having my mother wash me like a baby while I sat with my leg propped on the side of the tub.

Or injuring myself in the first place . . .

He waited patiently, as if he knew I needed a moment to accept the inevitable.

A muscle wiggled behind his beard. "Before I take you in my

arms, I should introduce myself." He held out his hand. "I'm Edge Callahan."

"Edge?"

"That's what everyone calls me. Except my mother. She calls me Edgar when she's mad."

He had a mother?

I let out a deep breath. "I'm Lily Shue."

Keeping my weight on my crutches, I raised my hand in my best businesslike handshake and stared at the way his big fingers encased my own. They were warm. And slightly rough. I ran my eyes up his shirt to search for muscles. The human body was my profession and he had a bicep worth inspecting.

At least that's what I told myself.

When he released my grip, I raised my tingling hand to my fuzzy hat and removed it. I was suddenly hot.

Edge didn't notice the odd way I slapped the air behind my neck with my hat to get rid of my sweaty goose bumps. He was busy looking back and forth at the truck and my knee.

Nodding as if he had made a decision, he held out his hands for the crutches. I lifted my arms and let him take them.

I felt the need to explain. "Last week my doctor cleared me to put weight on my right knee. This is just for the trip."

"Hmmm." He threw the crutches in the truck behind the passenger seat and turned back to help me.

A spark of my old self flared. "Thanks for the offer, but I think I can do it."

If I was going to be on my own for the next few months, I needed to learn how to do things myself again. I hopped to the truck and put my hands on the wheel well, trying to vault myself up. When that didn't work, I grabbed the open door. If only my body hadn't grown so weak in the past three weeks. After hanging for less than two seconds, my toes were still on the ground. Embarrassing.

I put a finger in the air as if I had just remembered what I was doing. "I'll just pull myself up backwards."

I turned around and put my hands behind me. Unfortunately, there was nothing to use for leverage.

Edgar, Edge Callahan, aka teddy garbage man, had been waiting patiently while I worked out every angle. But he had had enough. "I'm thinking we should try to get going before dark, maybe?"

"Sorry, I just have trouble with steps . . . and giant trucks." Fatigue added bite to my voice.

He stilled. "Steps? Do the Triple C's know this?"

"If I go up backwards, I'm fine." Total lie. I had been forced to move out of my wonderful multilevel condominium because of the stairs and my . . . well, my financial situation. "I'm getting better every day. I can go up and down from a seated position."

He leaned his head to the side and asked, "And you can shop for yourself and cook three square meals?"

I was feeling defensive from all the questions. "I don't eat anything complicated."

"Breakfast?'

"Cereal."

"Lunch?"

"A granola bar and an apple."

He looked down at his watch. "And at dinnertime you eat beef jerky?"

All right. So I wasn't the best at taking care of myself, right now. It certainly didn't impact how I could handle the job. Getting the town of Truhart in shape had nothing to do with my own miserable failures. I could help others just fine. Kind of a *do as I say, not as I do* kind of thing.

"Can we just go? You said it was going to be dark soon." I blinked away frozen moisture. At least the cold prevented my frustration from running down my cheeks.

Edge looked at the truck and said softly, "I'll try not to hurt you."

It was demoralizing for a woman who prided herself on being an athlete, an advocate for healthy bodies, to be picked up like a frail grandmother. He placed one hand on my back and another under the upper part of my thigh and lifted me.

He might look like a cuddly flannel toy, but now I knew I was right about him. The man was volcanic rock. I wouldn't have found a love handle if I'd spent an hour searching his midsection.

And his scent . . . I was expecting him to smell like trash. But when I breathed in I was met with a fragrance that was like pine trees and winter mint.

He raised me high until we were nose to nose, as if searching my face for any sign of pain. There were flecks of green and blue in his eyes and a hint of dimples underneath his beard when he broke into a grin.

He settled me in the passenger seat in one slow, smooth movement. "Okay?"

"Yes." I may have purred a little.

"You sure?"

I bit my lip and summoned my inner feminist. "I could have done it myself."

"Sure you could have." I looked back to see if he was teasing me. Nice smile. Even teeth. Either I was in the clutches of the kindest garbage man in Truhart, or I was another gullible victim of a serial killer.

When he shut my door, I mourned the returning chill. What the heck was wrong with me? Was I really falling for a hairy man who drove a furry truck? I reached down and grabbed the top of the brace, settling my knee until I was comfortable.

I had never been in a garbage truck before. Beside me was a console with several complicated-looking switches and toggles. Despite all the switches in the cab, there was, surprisingly, a lot of room. I looked for a nonexistent seat belt and sniffed. An air freshener hung from the mirror. Another one was tucked into an air vent. And yet another, stranger-looking air freshener was plugged into an outlet on the dashboard. I guess odor was a hazard for garbage men.

Edge climbed into the driver's seat in one fluid motion. "Comfortable?"

"I am." I had to admit, it was nice to be sitting down again. I granted him my first smile of the day and his eyes grew wide. Did he think I didn't know how to smile?

When he came out of his stupor he asked, "Do you want a snack? Uncle Pete keeps his candy—" He opened a compartment in front of me and out popped a snake. To my credit, I only squeaked.

"Aww, sorry!" He gathered the coiled, flowered snakes and threw them behind the seat. "April Fools' Day isn't for a few weeks, but Uncle Pete is always early with his jokes."

I waited for my breath to return and finally said, "The apartment I'm going to be living in is at Sixteen Main Street. I hope it isn't out of the way for you."

He shifted the truck into gear, checking his mirrors at the same time. "Sorry, Lily. There has been a change in plans."

I felt the blood drain from my face. "A change?"

"We are going to talk to the Triple C's," he said.

A band of panic cinched my chest.

Harrison County had been awarded a grant from Fit4You for two trainers. One trainer was going to live and work in Harrisburg and one was going to live and work in Truhart. That was me. I was being hosted by the Community Center Committee. The Triple C's, as they called themselves. I knew I had to face them sometime, but I was hoping I wouldn't look quite so tired and helpless when they saw my bum knee.

I held up my palms. "No need to talk to them right now. Just yesterday the mayor's wife said the apartment would be unlocked and ready for me."

He stared out the windshield and said one word. "Complications." A tick in his furry beard gave him away.

Suddenly the minty air and the bumpiness of the road, combined with the unexpected change in plans, gave me a major bout of nausea. I clutched my midsection and ran my hand over my eyes. The truck turned and I almost lost it right there. The window next to me lowered. The fresh air erased some of the minty smell and settled my stomach.

Several minutes later I was capable of raising my head. "Thanks."

He pretended I hadn't almost puked all over the interior of the truck. "We're almost there."

With misery building in my chest, I waited for any signs of town. I hoped for a quaint gazebo or a cute church with a white steeple. A boardwalk along a pristine lake. Victorian homes fronted by wraparound porches in pastel trim. But everything was gray, white, and empty. The late March sun was low in the sky, sending spindly shadows of the bare tree branches across the road.

Edge tapped his hand on the steering wheel. "Did you have far to come?"

Had I come far?

Two months ago I had been in sunny California, teaching Pilates and CrossFit to beautiful people who paid me an enormous sum to make them even more gorgeous. I lived in a modern condominium on the beach in Santa Monica. I drove a convertible. I worked hard to afford that lifestyle.

Then my big break happened. An opportunity to be on TV's *Just*

Lose It as a trainer with my own team. Quitting everything, I prepared myself for prime time. I wrote my diet plans down to the last detail. I researched every way to motivate people to lose the weight that had kept them from living their dreams. I even mixed my own protein powders and created a nutrition plan that guaranteed weight loss. With weeks to go before taping, I was ready for success.

Who knew a treadmill could cause such damage?

To my knee and my career.

I ended up where I started many years ago. On my mother's yellow floral couch with a hairy dog at my feet, eating noodles and watching TV.

"Not far," I told him.

Five minutes later, we were closer to some kind of civilization. Along the road was a building marked HARRISON COUNTY SHERIFF'S OFFICES, and a neon sign for COOKEE'S DINER.

Edge pulled up in an illegal parking zone and stopped. "Hang on a minute. I'll leave the window open. I am going to let the Triple C's know you're here."

Before I could say anything he jumped out and headed through the front door of Cookee's Diner. It was the quintessential small-town gathering place. Full of people and homey looking.

Through the large front window, I watched Edge enter the diner. A half a dozen ladies gave him a hug and more gathered around him. He said something and the women shifted their focus to me. I slouched down and pretended I didn't notice their stares.

They turned back to him and I breathed again.

While they spoke, I searched the frozen tundra ahead of me for any sign of a gym or the apartment building where I would be staying. Other than a huge pile of snow in the middle of the street, an auto garage, and a few vacant-looking buildings, there was nothing.

A large young man walked toward me. His hands were stuffed in his coat pocket, his mouth was turned down, and his shoulders were slumped. Tough day. I felt the same way he looked. Suddenly a ball of white hit his head, knocking his hat off.

Down the street, a group of teenagers laughed. "Too fat to run, Mountain?"

He picked up his hat and kept walking. Another missile fired.

I leaned out the window, "Hey! Stop that . . ."

A third snowball hit him squarely between the shoulder blades.

Without thinking I grabbed a brown bear off the truck below my window. I threw it toward the kids. "Stop!"

The little bear didn't make if far, but it did its job. The kids took off down the street. The young victim was halfway across an open field, safe from the bullies. I watched his retreating back, wishing kids were kinder and I had better aim.

Edge came out of the diner followed by three women. A curvy blonde wearing an expensive-looking pair of fleece-lined boots and a bright red vest, a large woman wearing a smock with rainbows of some sort, and a pretty, curly-haired younger woman wearing jeans and a Vassar sweatshirt.

When Edge pulled open my door, three pairs of eyes went directly to my injured leg, then traveled slowly to my face.

I smiled at them. "It sure is a cold day, huh?" None of them seemed concerned about the temperature. I held out my hand. "I'm Lily Shue."

"We're so excited you are here, Lily." The curvy blonde wearing expensive clothes extended her hand. "I'm Regina Bloodworth."

"Nice to meet you." I shook her hand and couldn't help my usual checklist. Buxom. Poor hand strength . . . Needs core and weight training.

"And this is Marva O'Shea," she said, pointing to the large lady, who adjusted a pair of pink-rimmed glasses. She was quite overweight, but her strength was surprising . . . Cardio, definitely.

"And this is Elizabeth Lively." The younger woman in the sweatshirt waved. Energetic. Lean . . . Might need yoga and breathing exercises to relax, though.

I forced myself to focus. "Edge, here, was just taking me to the apartment you have arranged for me. "

The ladies shot glances back and forth. The larger woman, Marva, put a hand on her fleshy throat. "The thing is—the apartment is up a set of rickety steps."

The younger woman bit her tongue. "It's nowhere near a store or a pharmacy."

Regina stared at my knee. "Living on the second floor would be dangerous for you with your . . . injury."

"I will be fine," I said, putting my hand over my knee, trying unsuccessfully to block their view of the brace.

Edge gazed at me over their heads. "What they're trying to say is—"

Regina and Marva spoke at the same time.

"There was a fire—"

"We had a flood—"

"Plumbing issue!" Elizabeth Lively said loudly, giving them each stern looks.

Edge ran a hand over his eyes.

"I'm sorry?"

Elizabeth giggled nervously. "You know how it is when disaster strikes. Complete confusion! First there was a fire, and that made the pipes burst, and then there was a flood."

Regina clarified things. "In any case, the whole thing is a bit of a mess. We think it will be better if you stay somewhere else for now."

Would it be rude to call my employers liars a minute after meeting them?

"I know you probably think I can't take care of myself because of my knee, but I assure you I can."

Regina smiled. "Of course you can. But the apartment is a mess, like we said."

This new development made things more complicated for me. One of the perks of the job was the proximity to the gym. I wouldn't have to worry about the fact that I couldn't drive. I could simply limp next door to the gym for work.

I started to argue, then stopped myself. I was in no position to complain. At least someone had hired me. I could deal with a change of plans. Fortunately, they hadn't changed their minds the minute they saw my knee.

"Should I stay with the other trainer the county hired? The one in Harrisburg?"

"Do you know her?" Marva, asked.

I shook my head.

"Then you would never suggest it." She patted my leg and then pulled her hand away quickly, as if she was afraid she had hurt me.

Regina glared at Marva's gesture and changed the subject. "We thought about the Amble Inn, but they are booked for the next two weekends. So, we've made other arrangements. There won't be an issue with stairs and it will be much easier for you to get around."

"And a ride to the gym each day will be available," Marva said, nodding at Edge.

I was feeling queasy again. When was the last time I had hydrated?

Elizabeth grabbed my hand. "You will like it better anyway."

"Edge will take you now so you can rest, honey," said Marva, reaching toward my knee again.

Regina grabbed her hand and scowled. "We'll meet you at the gym tomorrow. Then you can tell us all about your plans for the fitness program. I've got all sorts of ideas on ways we can get this town in shape—"

Elizabeth interrupted. "The grant from the Fit4You Foundation is going to do a lot for our town."

The three women said their goodbyes and waved me on, practically running back into the building. A swarm of women surrounded them when they entered. I could practically hear the chatter from where I sat.

I took a deep breath, feeling like I had been blown over by a strong wind. It had been a long day. A long month, actually.

"All set?" Edge asked, closing my door. I stared at the little bear on the sidewalk. It was ridiculous, but I couldn't leave him.

I angled my head out the window. "Can you . . ."

He glanced around. "What?"

I pointed to the little guy on the sidewalk. "He, uh, fell off."

It was a sad testimony to my throwing arm that it only took two long strides for Edge to reach the little guy. He swept up the bear and turned back to the truck.

"It was here." I patted the area beneath my window.

He reattached the bear. "That's odd. I can't imagine how he came off."

He sent me a speculative look before climbing back in the cab.

"What is the name of the hotel?"

Edge picked up an old iPod that was plugged into the dashboard. "Do you like classic rock?"

Before I could say anything, the high-pitched, wailing voice of Robert Plant singing "Black Dog" filled the truck. Edge shifted the truck into drive and we took off. He bobbed his head to the beat, completely oblivious to my question or my concerns.

"Where are we going?" I repeated.

"You'll like it. Free food, comfortable bed, nice people."

He turned up the music.

While he tapped the steering wheel and played air drums, I debated rolling down the window and sticking my head outside in order to save my long-term hearing. We were on a road that bordered a lake, with houses on the left and the right. Every once in a while we passed a vacant lot and I could see the lake clearly. It was covered with a layer of snow and ice and dotted with dozens of small shacks. We passed a plump lady snowman wearing a polka-dotted scarf and a straw hat rimmed with pink flowers. Warm weather would melt off her fat. Too bad losing weight wasn't as easy as that.

That's where I came in. My job was to improve health and fitness in the county. An important job. A little inconvenience and a tough day weren't going to make me forget my mission.

We made a left turn into a long driveway and Edge honked the horn. "Here we are."

I ducked my head to see out the front windshield. The drive sloped upward. A two-story green-shingled house built into the side of a gentle hill was nestled among the trees. A separate two-story garage stood to its right.

"I appreciate all the space, but I don't need a whole house."

Edge seemed to think that was funny. He turned off the music and jumped out.

A woman appeared from the corner of the house, followed by three small dogs of indistinguishable breed. I caught part of her greeting. "—finished with the route already?"

His voice was too low for me to hear. But she looked my way and nodded her head as he spoke. I opened my door and considered whether getting down would be any easier than getting in the truck. Before I could do anything, Edge and the woman were beside me.

With her light brown, closely cropped head of hair, she could have been anyone's mother. But she was tall, in blue jeans and a long, bulky sweater, and when her gray eyes smiled, and dimples appeared on her cheeks, there was no mistaking the resemblance.

"Lily, this is my mother, Louise Callahan."

Just like the ladies at the diner, her eyes went straight to my knee. But there was more than open curiosity in her face.

She ran her hand up and down her neck. "You're not a skier, are you?"

"No. I'm a fitness trainer. I was hired for the new community center grant."

"Community center? Oh, of course. The Triple C's. Kreapps. I've been so out of the loop recently that I forgot all about that."

"The Triple C's are creeps?"

She laughed. "Not like that."

"Lily was supposed to live over the old booksto—I mean above the community center."

"How can she manage—" She glanced at Edge as if she had just put two and two together.

"It sure was strange timing when the fire and plumbing caused a flood in the apartment," I said, arching a brow Edge's way. I don't know why we kept talking in half truths.

"What flood?" Louise said, turning to Edge.

Edge ruffled a dog's head. "Big mess over there. Nasty. That's why we're here. Lily is staying with us."

Louise pasted on an overly cheery smile, one that I had seen my own mother wearing for the past few weeks. "Of course you should stay here."

"With you?" I looked from Edge to his mother. He suddenly seemed fascinated by one of the dogs, who was holding a stick in his mouth. He grabbed the stick and played tug-of-war.

Louise stepped away and picked up a dog with wiry hair. "Don't worry about a thing, Lily. Years ago, before we had kids, we rented out the downstairs. It has a separate entrance, a bathroom, and a kitchenette on the same floor. Help her down, Edge. Then we'll get her settled inside."

Edge was back, ready to help me down. I sank back into the seat. "Wait a minute. I can't stay with your family. Surely there's another place I can go where I won't impose on anyone."

Edge leaned closer and lowered his voice. "Mom gets her feelings hurt really easy, Lily. Don't make her feel like you don't want to stay here. I hate to see my mother cry."

"I wouldn't want anyone to feel bad," I whispered back. "It's just that I wasn't—"

Edge put a finger to my lips and whispered, "Shh. Don't upset her. The last time someone refused her hospitality I had to get her a dog. As you can see, we don't need any more."

"Oh, come on—"

Edge spoke under his breath again and shifted his eyes to the side rather obviously. "Is she crying? Sometimes it looks like she's going to laugh. But it's really crying."

Behind him, his mother was biting her lip and staring at the sky. She blinked rapidly as if she might be ready to burst into tears . . .

"Look, Edge—"

"You two coming?" Mrs. Callahan shoved her head in front of Edge's.

He stepped behind her and sent me a warning glance over her head.

"Just until my knee is better and I can stay in the apartment in town," I said to Edge. I wasn't going to play the game everyone else had started. I knew the apartment was perfectly fine.

"I am so glad to have you here. I love guests. It's extremely distressful for me when the house is quiet."

He raised his eyebrow at me over the top of her head and mouthed, "*See.*"

"Come on, dogs." Mrs. Callahan turned up the driveway and the furry dogs followed her as if she were their mother hen. The dogs yipped and barked at each other, almost drowning out the sound of her laughter.

LESSON TWO

Stick with It—No Excuses

I waved Edge off and tried to disembark on my own from the teddy truck, as I was beginning to think of it. He stood by the open door, scrolling through his phone as if he hadn't a care in the world.

After a long minute of repositioning my leg and grasping the door frame, I sighed and raised my arms, signaling for him to lift me down like I'm sure he was planning to do all along.

Without a word, he reached in and plucked me out of the cab. Once I was on firm ground, he grabbed the crutches from behind the passenger seat and handed them to me. Then he lifted out my suitcases as if they were marshmallows.

"Shall we?" He nodded to the driveway.

I cautiously planted the tips of the crutches. It was going to be more difficult to come down in the morning. The thought pulled me to a stop.

"Wait a minute. How am I going to get to the community center tomorrow?"

Edge didn't even bat an eyelash at my question. "I'll take you."

I stomped my crutches. "This whole thing is a ridiculous inconvenience for everyone."

The whole point of coming to this place in the middle of nowhere was that I would have a certain amount of independence. I would be able to work. I would have my own apartment. And I would be able to nurse my wounds without my mother hovering or my brothers making jokes about my knee.

Very little had been in my control for the past two months. Not my career. Not my body. Now, in the space of an hour, my plans to be independent had fallen apart. I wanted to cry over the change of plans, but damn if I would do it in front of teddy bears and a man who thought his steering wheel was a drum set.

"Are you all right?"

"Why wouldn't I be?" I clenched my teeth and moved on, grumbling under my breath. "I love being helpless . . ."

I clodhopped my way up a virtual mountain and dug the crutches into the slushy ice, wishing it were a certain spunky blond trainer's face I was smashing with every step.

Edge followed behind me. "Just watch yourself. It gets slippery when the sun starts to go down."

I moved up the driveway, feeling sorry for myself every hobble of the way. Then I hit a particularly slippery spot and my good leg started to slip.

Two hands reached out and grabbed my waist. "Whoa. Steady there."

I twisted away. "I'm good."

Edge reached down and picked up the luggage he had dropped "Course you are."

I should have thanked him. He saved me from a face-plant that might have cost me years of dental work. "I don't want to be a bother. I can find my own ride tomorrow."

"It's not a bother. I'm heading into town anyway."

"You have your, uh . . . garbage work to think about."

"The trash can wait."

"I don't want to make the teddy bears mad," I said before turning up the driveway.

He laughed behind me. "Humor. Glad to see you handling this change of plans so well, Lily." Actually, I wasn't being funny. Sarcastic, yes. However, unlike Edge Callahan, everything wasn't a joke to me. I hated people who made everything in life a stand-up routine. They reminded me of my brothers.

He opened a door and we entered a large room. A flat-screen television dominated one wall and several video game consoles and controls cluttered the floor. A futon covered with pillows and blankets rested opposite the television and a Ping-Pong table was folded in half against the wall near a sink and a refrigerator.

My older brothers would have died for a room like this when they were younger.

Edge put the suitcases down and removed his boots. He took my coat and hung it on a peg while I sat in a chair near the door and struggled to remove my boots. Without a word, he knelt down and helped me, making me feel a million times worse. I stared at the top of his curly head and wondered what kind of man would drive a teddy truck and help a lame woman with her shoes.

Louise's voice called out from somewhere upstairs. "Edge, you can put Lily in your bedroom."

I almost fell off the chair.

"You should see your face right now," Edge said with a wicked grin before heading down a back hallway with my luggage.

I followed, struggling to recover from the image of Edge and me sharing a bedroom. "Uh, Edge, your mother didn't mean we would share . . ."

We passed several doors. One was closed and had signs across the front that said KEEP OUT! The other room had a trail of clothes that led from the door to the bed and posters of teen bands taped to the walls.

Edge put down my luggage and waited for me beside a door at the end of the hallway. I stepped inside the room. The curtains were open and the late afternoon sun painted pink squares on the blue carpet. A bed that may have been half of a bunk bed at one time sat against the wall. A dresser, and a desk with pictures and a stack of old textbooks, were the only other furniture in the room.

Confused, I asked, "Is this your room?"

"You don't mind sharing the bed, do you?" What kind of back-woods humor was he trying on me?

I sent him a withering gaze and he picked up the bags and placed them in the room. "Almost had you."

"Not funny."

"I thought it was," he said, tilting his mouth up. He signaled toward the front of the house. "I live across the street in Grandma's old ranch, nowadays. This used to be my bedroom. The sheets are clean and the closet is mostly empty."

He opened the closet door and pushed several hangers toward the back. "You'll have to share a bathroom with my sisters. I can't guarantee that there isn't makeup and other girl stuff all over the counter. But I'll tell them to leave you some space."

All of this was happening so quickly.

"Why don't you wash up and get comfortable? Dinner will be ready soon."

When he left, I closed the door and leaned back. I wanted my condo in L.A. back. I wanted my career at the Pacific X Gym back. I wanted sunshine and my BMW and the job I lost.

What the hell had I been thinking? This new job was already a disaster. Stuck in a town full of strangers who thought trucks covered in stuffed animals were normal.

I felt like a little girl at camp all over again, assigned to a strange cabin with people I didn't know. I wanted to write home to tell my parents to come and get me. This wasn't what I wanted after all.

What was it Dad had said when I called home from camp once? *Take it one day at a time. Wash up. Get a good night's sleep. Make a friend tomorrow.*

I caught a glimpse of myself in the mirror over the desk. My large brown eyes had circles under them and my golden skin looked paler than normal. My knee throbbed. All the travel today made it feel like it had grown ten sizes since this morning. Trying not to think about anything but the task at hand, I unpacked as much as I could. I made my way to the bathroom with my toiletry bag.

The bathroom was cluttered, but there was no need for anyone to go out of their way for me. My needs were light these days. Soap. Shampoo. Even clothes-wise, I dressed simply. Loose yoga pants and Lycra tops, most of the time. My taste had always been sporty. I was much more at home in Lycra than linen. Even when I did dress up, I gravitated toward Title Nine and Athleta dresses. It drove my mom crazy. For years all she talked about were her friends' beautiful daughters who wore makeup and high heels. *Too bad for them*, I told her. Not only was I the comfortable one, but at the end of the day, I could still run five miles on feet that weren't sore.

I washed my face and applied gloss to my dry lips. Morphing back to my normal self made me feel better. I brushed my straight dark hair and kept it loose where it fell just below my shoulders. I double-checked my image in the mirror. To me my Korean heritage dominated my features. But some people mistook me for Hispanic. Or Greek. Or even Middle Eastern. My *imo*, Aunt Julie, called me "interesting" looking. There wouldn't be many Koreans in Northern Michigan. I guess people would think I was just one of those crazy California mixes.

I was going to stand out like a palm tree in the woods here.

When I was finished cleaning up, I wandered into the recreation room. Edge lounged on the futon with a remote control in his hand. The talking heads on ESPN were breaking down the upcoming basketball tournament in Indianapolis.

Sports. I almost felt at home.

USC, my own alma mater, wasn't anywhere near the top of the rankings. But my brother's was. North Carolina was favored to win the tournament and I never heard the end of it when Chip was around. At least my other brother Ned's team sucked. Stanford was better at football than basketball these days.

A player for North Carolina raced across the court and pivoted before passing the ball.

"Traveling!" Edge and I called out at the same time. The referee thought so, too. He blew his whistle.

"Do you think they're going to take it again?" I asked, referring to the blue-and-white Tar Heels on the screen.

"Naw. I think the Spartans have a chance. O'Roarke gets those rebounds faster than—" He glanced my way and stopped midsentence, as if he forgot he wasn't talking to one of the guys. His eyes traveled from the tips of my striped socks to my head. His nostrils flared and he took a deep breath as he forced his eyes back to the screen.

"O'Roarke . . . you were saying?" I prompted.

"He's really good on the rebound." His lips curved as if he was pleased with his choice of words.

He unfolded his body and stood up. He took two short strides and was across the room. I felt like a twig next to a skyscraper.

"You can take the chariot upstairs." He pushed a button on the wall and down floated a chair.

I didn't know whether I should be pleased or embarrassed. "You have a stair lift in your house?"

"Sure do. Handy, isn't it?"

After the chair glided to a halt, Edge flipped a lever and the chair pivoted toward me. Now, I really felt stupid.

"I can make it without this."

"You could. But why bother when you can use the chair?" He leaned down and held out his arms as if he was prepared to lift me. "Or I could carry you."

"Oh no. I can sit."

I fell for it and he chuckled.

Stairs had been one of the things my mother had been most worried about. Besides being upset that I insisted on taking the job before my knee was stronger, every few minutes she asked me how I was going to live alone. I ended up lying through my teeth. I told her that I was living in a flat with another woman who was going help me manage until my knee was stronger.

Ironically, my lie had caught up with me. Now it was practically true.

I sat down in the stair lift and Edge reached down to help work the controls.

I raised my elbow to block him from hovering over me like a nursemaid. "I can do it."

"Suit yourself." He was distracted by the sound of car doors slamming and raised voices in the driveway. He stepped outside and left me sitting alone. I settled myself and my crutch and pushed the button. The chair made a slow ascent.

The next level of the Callahans' house came into view, bottom first. A powder-blue carpet with haphazard vacuum tracks. Chair legs that hid a half-eaten dog bone. A pair of fuzzy blue socks perched on the footrest of a wheelchair.

When I reached the top, the owner of the wheelchair and the fuzzy socks stared at me from behind her gold-rimmed glasses with the sharp eyes of an owl. "Turn."

"What?"

She raised a bony finger and pointed at the bottom of the lift chair. "Turn."

I looked down the stairs for help. Edge was nowhere to be seen.

I rose out of the chair. The old woman slapped the armrest of her wheelchair. She shouted, "Turn . . . lock . . ."

Giggles erupted from the nearby dining room table. A set of identical little people pointed at me as if I was the most hilarious thing they had ever seen.

The old owl with a shock of white hair moved her lips and I was pretty sure her teeth were missing. "Do!"

"Turn . . ." She shook her wheelchair with her body.

"Ma!" Louise rounded the corner, a dishcloth still in her hands. "Lily is our guest. Don't scare her before you even meet her!"

The older woman deflated right in front of me. She lowered her hand, and her shoulders slumped. Her eyes grew hazy.

Louise reached for a lever I hadn't seen at the side of my chair. She flipped it. My chair spun and locked, making it safer for me to disembark without falling down the stairway.

"Thank you." I felt ridiculous. Of course, Louise's mother had been warning me to do it right.

Edge's reason for offering his own family's home as my new lodgings became clear. It was already equipped for handicapped access. A chair lift, easy pathways for a wheelchair (and crutches), and a family who was used to dealing with a semi-invalid.

I adjusted my crutches and moved into the living room. A large set of windows with a panoramic view dominated the room. The tips of the bare branches stretched out, making me feel like I was in a tree house. Beyond the trees and across the road was a one-story house and a large lake beyond.

"Lily, this is my mother, Ivy Adler." Then Louise piped up in a louder voice, "Ma, this is Lily Shue."

"Shoe?" Ivy looked at her feet.

"Her name is Lily Shue, Ma," Louise explained. Ivy pressed her lips together and stared at me.

I held up my hand and waved. "Nice to meet you, Mrs. Adler."

"Feel free to call her Ivy, Lily," Louise said. She turned and pointed behind us to the kids who watched the show from a dining room table covered in Play-Doh. "And those are my grandsons, Justin and Jason."

The boys smiled as they smashed a handful of dough in each fist, letting it seep out between their fingers. My heart did a funny nose-dive. It hadn't occurred to me that Edge was married with children.

"The boys and their mom, my daughter Tracy, live over the garage," Louise added.

"Oh." Was that relief? Why would I care about a man who looked like he could be on *Duck Dynasty*?

A door slammed downstairs. Angry voices carried to the second floor.

Louise rubbed her hands on the towel and nodded toward a couch, as if screaming girls were an everyday occurrence. "Have a seat, Lily. Can I get you something? Juice? A glass of—"

"Bourbon!" the older woman in the wheelchair said loudly.

"Ma, stop asking for a drink. You know what the doctor said." Louise sighed and retreated around the corner to the kitchen.

Ivy mumbled under her breath again while I navigated my way to the couch. A series of yips erupted below us and three hairy fur balls vaulted up the stairs. I limped toward a blue skirted sofa with a crocheted throw blanket, trying to avoid the flurry of wagging tails.

The voices downstairs grew louder. "I waited more than twenty minutes for you. And all you were doing was talking to a bunch of your stupid friends."

"You weren't supposed to be there until five thirty."

"Mom said five fifteen. Next time get your own ride!"

"You're such a b—"

"Take it somewhere else. We have a guest upstairs." The authority in Edge's voice surprised me.

A female voice moaned. "Oh no. Don't tell me Aunt Addie is visiting again!"

I was adjusting the angle of my brace to accommodate a sitting position when a streak of orange flew up the stairs and shot into the kitchen. I ended up falling, more or less, into the sagging cushion of the couch.

"Mom, she did it again." While the girl continued to vent, I shifted, trying to get comfortable.

Ivy motored her chair until it was facing me. She crossed her hands in her lap and stared, as if I were the nightly news.

"Nice house," I said, pretending keen interest in the room around me.

Meanwhile, the argument in the kitchen continued and was joined by a disruption at the dining room table. "I was going to use that color!"

"You already took all the blue!"

From the corner of my eye I saw one boy reach over and smash his fist on his brother's creation. His twin reacted with his own weapon. He put his knuckles to his eyes and let out a piercing scream.

No wonder Louise didn't mind a guest. What was one more person in this wacky household?

I was tempted to stand up and make everyone do breathing exercises to calm themselves down. Or maybe I should just do it myself. I breathed through my nose and out my mouth, remembering how I used to love the large family gatherings on my mother's side of the family. The chaos, the constant bickering and teasing, the food that never stopped coming from the kitchen.

I preferred a quiet, more mature life style now. My adults-only condominium allowed no pets, no children, and no parties. And even though I sometimes left the TV running all night and put my mom on speakerphone when I ate dinner, it didn't mean I was lonely.

Footsteps stomped on the stairs. "She could have at least texted me that she was there. Instead she sat in the car and purposely counted the minutes so she could complain."

I shifted my attention out the window, feigning fascination at the ice-covered, barren lake.

The lanky girl with a red ponytail was halfway through another complaint when she stopped in the middle of the living room and stared at me. "Who are you?"

Edge appeared behind me. "Lily, this is my little sister Olivia."

"Hello," I said brightly.

Olivia waved. "Hi there . . ."

"Everyone calls her O-loud-ia," he said, pulling an ottoman away from a nearby chair and pushing it in front of my leg.

"You're so funny . . . Edgar!" his sister taunted. She stopped when she saw my leg. "How did you hurt your—"

"Sports injury," was all I said. My canned answer for anyone who asked.

"But how—"

Edge cut her off with a single glare and she bit her lip. He gently lifted my foot and propped my leg up on the ottoman.

Louise walked in from the kitchen and clapped her hands at the two rascals still fighting at the dining room table. "Time to clean up, boys. Dinner's soon."

The streak of orange I had seen a few moments earlier emerged from the kitchen. Older than her little sister, she was also tall, but had long auburn hair. She grabbed the Play-Doh from both boys and jammed the blobs back in the containers. The little guy, the one who had been doing such a good job with his pretend cry, jumped off the chair. He ran toward Edge, practically tackling him from behind.

Edge swept him up in the air. "Not so fast, Justin. Get your butt back to the table and help clean up."

The little boy giggled when Edge set him down. Edge roared like a bear and pretended to go after him.

Both boys screeched and Olivia rolled her eyes. "Grow up."

Louise waved toward the girl in a bright orange sweater. "The angry chauffeur over there is my other daughter, Sarah."

"Hi." Sarah nodded and returned to her original gripe. "I should just become an Uber driver. At least then I could charge a late fee for ungrateful little sisters."

I could have used her earlier.

"You're such a baby—"

"Enough," Louise said, cutting them both off. "As long as I pay for the gas, and the insurance, you two need to share the rides. Honestly, you girls should be grateful to have a car."

"Mine!" Ivy said, pounding her fist on the arm of her wheelchair. "I drive!" For a moment the room was quiet.

"Sorry, Grandma," Sarah said, coming over to give her grandmother a hug.

Ivy moved her feet restlessly. "I pick up . . . the . . . one."

"Mom, you can't do that anymore. Remember what the doctor said."

"Sh . . . sh . . . shove." The older woman looked at me and then at my knee. We were both in the same boat.

Louise turned back to the kitchen. "I hope you like spaghetti, Lily. Just like the old commercials, Wednesdays are spaghetti night around here."

She left me in the living room with Ivy, Olivia, and Edge.

I was rusty with kids, old people, and men with dimples.

"Are you the reason we have to clean our bathroom?" Olivia asked.

Sarah called out from the dining room. "Olivia, you are so rude!" She grabbed the hand of each little boy and walked them down a hallway beyond the kitchen. The sound of water running and the toilet flushing reached the living room.

I adjusted my knee. "Sorry to be such an inconvenience."

Edge sat down at the far end of the couch. "You're not the inconvenience. My sisters are. Have been since they were born."

Ivy's face bent into a hundred tiny lines. It took a moment to realize she was smiling. "Good . . . one."

"Thanks, Grandma."

The boys were back. They spotted Edge and flew across the room.

I braced myself for a possible collision that would take my knee out. But Edge was faster. Which was surprising for his size. He jumped forward and caught them before they reached the couch. "Easy, boys. You've gotta go slower around Gram and Lily, here."

Edge settled down with both boys on top of him. Boy number one, as I labeled him, surveyed my knee brace with intense interest. "Is that a fake knee?"

"No. I just injured it."

That disappointed him. Boy number two's eyes lit up. "Did you get it caught in a shredder?"

"What?"

The other one leaned across Edge's lap. "Or did you blow it up by a land mine?"

"How old are you two?" I asked.

"I'm six," announced number one with only five fingers up. "And he's ten minutes older than me."

I took a stab. "Justin?" One raised his hand. "Then you are Jason." A second hand went up. I tried to look for some distinguishing feature that would help me tell the difference between the two.

"Birthmark," said Edge.

"What?"

"Justin has a birthmark on the left side of his nose. Jason has one on the right."

"Now all I have to do is try to remember Justin—left, Jason—right."

"Of course, if you are facing them, it would mean the opposite."

Jason, I think, dangled his head to the ground. "Or if we're upside down . . ." Thinking about it made me feel dizzy.

Justin was back to my leg. "Hey, Jason, maybe her leg got caught in the toilet."

"Ooo, gross!"

I twisted my lips, not sure whether to laugh or stay serious. I should understand their humor. My brothers still acted that way. Instead of joking back, I usually just got mad. Or defensive.

"Who's talking potty talk up here?" The sound of a woman coming up the stairs prompted the boys to hide behind Edge's back, giggling the entire time.

A young woman carrying a computer case came into view.

Edge threw himself backwards, smashing the gigglers into the couch. "Grandma! How many times do we have to say it. Enough of the potty talk."

Ivy shook her head and snorted. "Ha."

Edge waved toward the newcomer. "Lily, this is my sister Tracy. The mother of these two poopers."

The woman stood at the top of the stairs and sent me an apologetic look. "Sorry. My family has a weird sense of humor." That earned him another cluster of giggles.

Tracy came over and shook my hand, pretending not to notice the boys plastered against Edge's back. When she saw my knee, she asked, "Are you a skier?"

"She's the new fitness instructor at the new community center," said Edge.

"Can I play with your crutch?" interrupted Jason.

His brother squirmed from behind Edge. "Yeah! Let's pretend we got our legs blown off in a bomb and we have to use it to walk."

"And there's a secret gun inside!"

"Yeah! Cool!"

"Not today, SEAL Team Six." Edge stood up and grabbed a boy in each arm, tucking them tightly against his side to keep them still as if they were two footballs. "Go see what you can do to help in the kitchen."

Tracy asked, "Is it spaghetti night?"

"It's poopy night," Justin said, making the other boy laugh hysterically.

I watched them stumble into the kitchen and wondered if it was too early to take another Vicodin.

The spaghetti was good, and I was hungrier than I thought I would be. I forced myself to move part of the pasta to the side and add more salad to my plate. Being a fitness and health instructor meant I was always "on."

When I tried on my old winter coat before coming, my mom said in her accented English, "You look like a snowman in that jacket. Ha. Be careful, you might blow up like one if you eat too much." She was always joking about my awkward stage. Just like my brothers used to. The three of them had the same sense of humor.

Edge seated me at the end of the table, where he could prop my knee up on a vacant chair. No one remarked about my knee again. Like potty humor, the Callahan family took handicap issues in stride.

The dining room had long ago lost its battle with the family. The china cabinet was full to the brim with dishes and teacups in random arrangements. Stacks of paper sat on an empty chair. A laundry basket full of toys sat in the corner. A counter separated the dining room from the kitchen. It was strewn with a toaster, a coffeemaker, and canisters with cows on them.

After we said grace, Louise nodded at the empty chair next to her and the one my knee inhabited. "We have two empty seats. My other son, Peter, is a sophomore at State. My husband left earlier this month. He works on a lake freighter and they just started running in the lower lakes this month."

"They haul iron ore," Tracy added.

I had little knowledge of the Great Lakes and the shipping industry. In fact, the only freighter I had ever heard of was the *Edmund Fitzgerald*. But I did know something about having an empty seat at the table. My own father had been gone since I was twelve years old. I mostly remember his gray hair and smiling eyes. And the way he cheered like a fool at my soccer games.

"Grandpa is going to let me steer the freighter next time we visit him," said Justin . . . I think.

Jason, or the other twin, shifted to a kneeling position and decided to educate me. "Did you know that Grandpa steers from the front of the boat because it goes through the lakes. If it was an ocean freighter he would steer from the back."

"I never knew that." I was changing my mind. Maybe the kids were kind of cute.

Justin proudly let a noodle hang out his mouth before sucking it up with a whoosh. Not to be outdone, Jason did the same.

"Stop," Tracy told her sons. She shouldn't reprimand them for my benefit. Slurping was normal in my half-Korean house. My mother would have outslurped them both. It was perfectly polite in Korea.

"Where are you from, dear?" asked Louise as she poured a glass of milk for each of the twins.

"Los Angeles. But I was born in Connecticut."

"Then you know a thing or two about winter," she said.

"I moved to L.A. when I was twelve, but I don't remember Connecticut being as cold as this."

"Are both your parents from America—" Olivia started. She jumped as if she had been kicked under the table. Sarah sent her a dirty look. I remembered the nickname O-loud-ia, and understood now. It was about more than just the volume of her voice.

I put her out of her misery. People were always curious anyway. "My mom moved from Korea to L.A. when she was fourteen. She's a citizen now. She was working in Connecticut as a translator when she met my dad."

My father, eighteen years older than my mom, met her in a business meeting. Dad was the old guy in a young office. The kind of man everybody liked, but who was more comfortable watching television and putzing in his garden than socializing with large groups of people.

Mom took one look at Dad and decided to make him her project. She cajoled him out to dinner with the rest of the staff, and by the time midnight rolled around Dad was singing the chorus at a karaoke bar. If the match seemed odd to anyone, they kept their mouths shut. Mom's family liked the fact that Dad had a secure job. Dad's family was beyond grateful to the tiny Asian girlfriend who pulled Dad out of oblivion.

The Callahans were fast talkers. Olivia talked about the girls in her high school, Tracy mentioned a test she was studying for, and Louise reminded an unhappy Ivy to eat more. They passed the rest of the meal teasing, arguing, and interrupting at lightning speed.

When the meal was finished, I told everyone I had work to do and headed toward the lift at the stairs. The girls were telling stories of their day, and I felt out of place. The heat of Edge's gaze rested on me as the chair drifted down to my bedroom on the first floor. He was probably regretting his decision to have me stay here as much as I was.

As the sound of the family faded, I swallowed past a lump in my throat. A remnant of my mood. And the drugs, of course.

I closed the bedroom door and tried to ignore the muffled sounds of the Callahans talking. Occasionally someone laughed and voices rose. The atmosphere around the table tonight reminded me of the holidays with my mom's family. Mom and her sisters would gossip in Korean. My brothers and cousins would leapfrog over each other, comparing their successful careers. And I would hide in the corner of the couch and watch sports on TV.

I pulled a resistance band out of my suitcase and lay on the floor. Wrapping the band around the heel of my foot, I forced myself to do the exercises the physical therapist had taught me. He had been opposed to my insistence that I could handle my own rehab. But Lord knows I had rehabbed my other knee once already. I was practically an expert.

"It isn't the same when you rehab yourself," he explained. But I argued that I had no choice. There were no physical therapists in Truhart. And driving a half hour to Gaylord was out of the question for me. He felt better when I promised him that every month I would make sure to check in with the orthopedic physician affiliated with Gaylord Central Hospital. In the meantime, I had a dozen earmarked pages of pictures and directions to help me strengthen my knee on my own.

I tried to fire the quad muscle on my shrunken right leg. Compared to my left leg, it was feeble. As tired as I was, it was important to keep up with my exercises every day. I had no tolerance for people who gave up on their goals. Quitters were always losers. I had learned that for myself years ago. I hadn't been a natural at sports, like my brothers. I was awkward and heavy. In fact, the first time I ran out onto the soccer field, I scored a goal . . . for the opposite team. Mom laughed at me on the car ride home. But Dad said a goal was a goal. It made him just as proud.

When I first started working as a trainer at the local YMCA, I had clients who felt they would never succeed. I understood their frustration more than they knew. Those early years taught me the importance of fighting through the insecurity and self-defeating habits that kept people from reaching their goals. I missed those days. In some ways, they were the most satisfying times of my career.

I ran my finger over the old scars on my other knee, and rolled down the compression stocking I wore to help with circulation during a long day of travel. Everything healed, given time. Even the ugly new scars and the swollen knee that was bigger than the quadriceps I used to be proud of.

After a short shower, I lay in bed doing my best to ignore my throbbing knee, resisting the urge to take a Vicodin.

Someone knocked on the bedroom door. "Lily?"

Too tired to get up from where I had collapsed on the bed, I called out, "Yes?"

Louise Callahan's face appeared through a crack in the door. "We thought you might like a little ice on your knee."

I started to refuse, but she was already through the door with a box and hose in her hand. I almost cried in relief.

Ice machines were one of the most useful aids for any knee after surgery. It provided a constant circulating coolness all night. Because of its bulk, I had decided to forgo bringing mine with me across the country. Mom said she would ship it if worse came to worst. But seeing the familiar-looking machine in Louise's hands made me grateful that Mom wouldn't need to go to the trouble.

Louise stood beside the bed. "Tomorrow is going to be a big day for you. You'll probably meet half the town. No need to start with a swollen knee."

"Half the town?"

"The Triple C's have been waiting for this day to arrive ever since they got the grant. Don't let them overwhelm you too much. Especially my aunt Addie. God, I love that woman, but she is like a steamroller made of Jell-O. Now let's see if we can get this on you."

I sat up and adjusted my leg. "You are an angel, Mrs. Callahan."

"Louise." She unwound the cord and tube from the box, and moved toward the wall to plug in the machine. "With five kids in sports over the years, we've had our fair share of knee injuries . . . Some knees more than others." She looked down at both my legs.

"I—just . . ."

"No need to explain, Lily. If there are war stories to be told, we can save it for another day. Right now, let's get you comfortable."

I helped her wrap the cool padding around my knee and secure it with an ace bandage. Then I watched as she attached the hoses that ran from the padding to the ice chest. I could feel the immediate cool water running from the ice chest to the pad on my knee. I closed my eyes and sighed.

"Better?" Louise asked.

"Heavenly! I can't thank you enough."

"Thank Edge. He's the one who scavenged in the attic to retrieve this."

"He did?"

"We hoped we would never have to use it again. But you know how it is when you get rid of things like this. It's a jinx. Before you know it, you need them again. We figured if we kept everything, we'd never need it again. Ha! But here we are . . ."

"Well, at least I'm not one of your kids, Louise."

I lay back and she patted me on the shoulder. "Doesn't matter. It still hurts my heart to see anyone need one of these."

When Louise left, I closed my eyes and tried to forget about Edge and his gray eyes that saw more than they should. Even so, I drifted off to sleep, buried in a soft bed and fluffy comforter that made me feel like I was being hugged by a teddy bear.

LESSON THREE

Set Reasonable Goals

The next morning I sat across the dining room table from Ivy, who stared at me as if we hadn't met the day before. The girls had already left the house for school, yelling at each other about being late. And the twins were on the bus to elementary school.

Louise placed an egg in front of me, even though I told her I was happy with just coffee. "We always have a big breakfast around here. It's the one meal of the day I know my kids will eat. The girls are terrible about meals, and Edge is always on the run somewhere. And Mom"—she nodded at Ivy—"I try to give her a good breakfast before we go to Lakeview every morning."

"Lakeview?"

"The adult day care that I manage." She ignored the grunt that came from Ivy. "In between nursing school classes, Tracy works there, too."

Ivy spoke up. "Don't."

"Mom, I know you have fun when you are there. You heard music yesterday. And you love making flowers." She nodded to an arrangement of paper flowers on the counter behind me.

"Don't. Like!"

Louise shook her head and reached for the coffeepot on the counter behind her. She poured me a cup and explained, "Since Mom's stroke, she's lost a lot of mobility and some language skills. But she has no problem understanding."

Ivy fed a piece of her toast to the dogs.

"Mom used to live across the street. Having her here makes life easier for both of us, right, Ma?"

Ivy pinched her lips together. When Louise left to get dressed, Ivy lifted the remaining piece of toast to her mouth. She bit into it and then spit it back on the table.

"Are you okay?" I asked.

"Too . . ." Her voice trailed off.

"Too hot?"

She shook her head.

"Too hard?"

She dropped the toast for the dogs, who scrambled at her feet.

I shifted in my chair and tried to make small talk. The weather was always safe. "Nice day. Have you had much snow this winter?"

Ivy frowned at the table. Maybe she wasn't a morning person.

My mom's parents were relatively young and healthy, but my dad's parents passed away many years ago. My clientele were mostly under sixty. This type of interaction was new for me.

I decided to focus on my egg and my plans for the day. A door downstairs opened, and the dogs barked. A few moments later, Edge pounded up the stairs wearing another flannel shirt, loose jeans, and a baseball hat.

"Good morning, Grandma," he said, giving Ivy a kiss on the cheek. She smiled at him and patted his jacket. The first smile I saw her give today.

"Morning, Lily." He waved, his eyes scanning my work clothes. I was wearing my yoga pants and a gray quarter-zip pullover. My hair was in a ponytail, and I had taken the time to put on mascara.

"You ready to go soon?"

I took one last sip of coffee. "Just give me a minute to get my bag."

"No rush. I'll just sit here with my favorite girl and talk about the weather." Edge sat down next to Ivy, putting his feet up on the nearby chair.

Fifteen minutes later, Jack White's "Lazaretto" wailed in the cab of the teddy truck as we plowed through a patch of snow. I assumed spring in Michigan would be different. I had visions of cherry trees blooming and green grass sprouting. Not this barren land of gray slush and crusty snow.

I clutched the pen and paper in my hand and tried to steady the shaky scribble of notes I was writing down for my fitness training plan. "Do you mind turning that down a bit?"

Edge lowered the volume from earsplitting to loud. "What are you doing?"

"Making notes in my training planner."

"Your training planner?"

"Yeah. This morning I'll need to take stock of the equipment at the gym. Assess the space."

He fixed his eyes on the road ahead of us and said something under his breath. Jack's guitar drowned him out.

"What was that?" I shouted.

Turning the volume all the way down, he said, "Don't you think you might want to see the place first?"

"Of course. But it doesn't change the way I work. I'm meeting with the Triple C's and looking forward to checking out the facility so I can fine-tune my plans."

A muscle beneath his beard tightened. "Well . . . we're just a small town, you know."

"Oh, don't worry. I'm not expecting a cutting-edge gym like we have in L.A. I don't need a lateral elliptical or zero-gravity, open-stride machine to get people in shape. Thirty minutes on a stationary bike works just fine."

"Stationary bike?" He coughed.

"Cardio isn't the only thing, of course. I will promote resistance weights and free weights as well. All really important to overall fitness."

"Lily, you're going to have a problem—"

I lowered my planner. "I know I may not seem exactly like an athlete right now. But I know what I am doing." I didn't mean to sound so irritable. I had been battling my mother and brother about this very issue. They thought I should stay on Mom's couch and slurp noodles.

"It's just that I don't want you to be disappointed."

We were passing the diner where we stopped yesterday. I ran my hand over my ponytail and craned my neck to see down the street. The community center must be close.

"Give me a few weeks and I'll prove to you that any town can get fit and healthy given a little time and training."

Edge eyed my notebook and shook his head. "No offense. But I don't think that a few weeks can change years of behavior."

I hated it when people talked that way. Just because something was difficult didn't mean they should quit. "Getting in shape has to start somewhere. Your county received the government grant because you have one of the highest obesity rates in the state. Should I tell everyone to eat, drink, be merry, and enjoy the diabetes?"

"I'm just saying that you shouldn't be upset if those plans you are writing down in your little diary there might not be as effective as you think. It takes more than happy words of encouragement and a written plan to get people healthy."

"You're right. It takes a lot of work. People need to rethink how they live."

Edge tapped the wheel. "That can be tricky when you—"

"Behavior change is difficult. I know." We were passing an ice cream store with a large image of a cow with ice cream cones underneath its udder. I pointed. "The Dairy Cow? That's a perfect example of the problem."

He looked in his side mirror. "It's just an ice cream parlor."

"At the center of town. Look, a putt-putt golf is attached. It figures."

"Sounds like fun to me." His eyes crinkled in the corners.

I pointed my finger back toward the Dairy Cow. "That's a trap. Like cartoons on sugary cereal boxes. It starts the kids out on bad habits early."

"An ice cream cone is a treat. Not a bad habit."

"Ha. No one ever thinks of attaching a putt-putt golf course to a fruit and vegetable stand, do they?"

A muscle twitched in his cheek. "Who wants to eat a stick of celery while they play putt-putt golf?'

"I do. And besides, I wouldn't call miniature golf the most optimal form of exercise. See that?"

"What?" He lowered his head to gaze out the window to where I pointed.

"Those tennis courts. The fence is half down. It looks like it was built when the Beatles were still together."

"You know, now that you say that, I think it was."

"Why doesn't someone keep it up? Tennis is a great way to encourage families to stay in shape."

"Well, it's winter right now. Someone will probably string a net out by the Fourth of July."

"The Fourth of July? The summer is halfway gone by then." We turned the corner and came to a stop.

"It was a joke. Forget what I said about your sense of humor yesterday."

"Don't take it personally, Edge. I'm sorry if I sound like I'm on a soap box. I am just pointing out that bad habits form everywhere. We don't see them most of the time. But if we question them, make changes, motivate, we can find a way to bring about healthy options."

He took a deep breath. "I can't wait to see what kind of healthy options you come up with after you visit the community center."

I gathered my bag and looked around. "Thank you. Now where exactly is the community center?"

"Right here."

I looked behind me, then in front of me. All I saw was an empty storefront with the faded words BOOKS FROM THE HART and a larger store that abutted it with crooked letters that read GROCERY. A cluster of larger buildings on a street beyond and a vacant lot were the only other visible signs of life.

"I don't get it."

The corner of his mouth twitched. "I guess they didn't have a chance to put up a sign that says 'Healthy Options Place' yet." He opened his door and jumped down.

I scanned the street around me. Regina Bloodworth had told me on the phone that the community center was in the center of town. A huge pile of snow sat in the middle of the road, obscuring what looked like a frozen lake beyond. I was all turned around and couldn't figure out if it was the same lake that the Callahans' houses were on.

Edge opened my door. I grabbed the single crutch I was using today out of the backseat and lowered it to the ground. I attempted to use it as a brace instead of Edge's shoulders. When I almost fell, Edge caught me and lowered me to the sidewalk. Once again I was struck by an overwhelming heat that made me wish I had applied a second coat of antiperspirant. I stepped away, fanning my face, and started toward the larger buildings on the street beyond.

Edge cleared his throat. "Ahem. Lily. The community center is here."

Before I could say anything, the grocery store door opened and a familiar figure stepped out.

"Good morning, you two!" Regina Bloodworth beamed at us.

Edge backed toward the truck, one step at a time. "Good morning, Mrs. Bloodworth."

Regina wore a fuchsia Lululemon Lycra jacket and fitted yoga pants that looked like they had never been worn for anything that involved sweating. Her perfectly matching lipstick and purple eyeliner looked like they had been applied by a professional.

"Just give me a call when you want me to come back and get you, Lily," Edge said, tipping his baseball cap my way.

"It might be a long day. I've got a lot of things to do as I check out the gym."

Something I'd said made the corner of his mouth turn up. He took one look at the building and then glanced back to me. "Don't tire yourself out with all those plans and that motivation, now."

Was that sarcasm? "And don't you tire yourself with all those stuffed animals either, you hear?"

He had the audacity to wink at me before he hopped in the truck. The last thing I heard was the ominous beat of The White Stripes' "Fell in Love with a Girl" as Edge headed back down Main Street.

"So . . . this was a grocery store once?" I pasted a smile on my face and tried not to let Regina see my disappointment as I swept my eyes across the building where I would be working for the next few months.

"Kreapps," she said with a flick of her wrist as if it wasn't that important.

"Creeps?"

"That was the name of the family that owned the grocery store. They still live around here."

Well, that explained it. I had been so confused when people kept calling the grocery store creepy. "Are the Kreapps retired, then?"

"Actually, no. You might say they're making their name in fresh produce and such nowadays."

"Really?" I loved supporting local businesses that sold healthy fare. "Do they sell in any markets nearby?"

"Umm, they're kind of independent . . . they specialize in roadside stands." She held open the door. I limped in on the crutch, acting for all the world like it was the most normal thing in the world to be a disabled trainer.

I looked around the room and blinked. Something was off. Unless exercise equipment suddenly came in holiday-theme decor, we were in the wrong building.

"Is that a sleigh against the wall?"

Regina broke out in a nervous giggle. "Yes, but it's fake. There was a real one, the one Grady Fitzpatrick, the handyman at the Amble Inn, used for Charlotte Adler's wedding. But it was heavy and too difficult to get in the community center, so we didn't use it last year."

"Use it . . . ?" I let the words trail off as I turned to face the other wall.

Regina came and stood beside me. "Now, I know you might be a little surprised—"

"What is that?" I pointed to a large square structure against the wall. "I know it's a fireplace, but what is the red thing coming out of it?"

"That's Santa's, uh, rear end. He's coming out of the chimney on Christmas Eve. We were really lucky that we could use the fireplace for double duty. Both Halloween and Christmas. "

"And in that corner? Is that what I think it is?" I pointed to the only other object in the room.

"It's a coffin. But not a real one. We made it for Bridget."

"She died?"

"No, she was supposed to be dead, but she kept opening her eyes."

The ends of my fingers tingled the same way they had when Edge pulled over in the teddy truck yesterday. If this were a horror story, eerie music would be playing in the background and all the camera angles would start shifting. I looked longingly toward the door just as two women walked through it.

"Lily! How wonderful to see you this morning," said Elizabeth Lively, holding a cardboard container with several Styrofoam cups.

"Did you sleep well?" asked Marva O'Shea.

Elizabeth passed the cups around. "You look like you need a good jolt of caffeine this morning. You must still be tired from traveling."

Just dazed and confused and wondering when I had fallen down the rabbit hole.

"I was just explaining to Lily how we used this space for Santa's Attic at Christmas and the House of Horrors at Halloween," Regina said.

Is that what she was doing? Now that she put it that way it made sense. This room was used for holiday activities.

The hair on the back of my neck settled and I propped myself on my crutch to remove the lid from my coffee. I was more partial to herbal tea. But what the heck. It had been a rough twenty-four hours.

"So, where is the gym?" I asked.

They darted nervous glances at each other. "The gym?"

I nodded to my sports bag. "I've been making plans for the past week or so. But of course, it all depends on what equipment you have and how old it is."

"We thought someone told you about the gym." Elizabeth tucked a stray piece of curly blond hair behind her ear and glared at Regina.

They were embarrassed, of course. "Don't feel bad if the equipment is old. The industry is crazy these days. Almost as bad as technology. A new phone is outdated before you can even get it home. Sports equipment is the same way, right?"

"Regina?" Elizabeth's blue eyes were wide. Secret eye messages between the ladies sucked the air out of the room and I shifted uncomfortably on my crutch.

Regina put her arm around me. "The thing is, Lily. We don't have any exercise equipment or a gym."

The last few words echoed in the room. Maybe I didn't hear her right.

"I'm sorry. I thought you said—"

"We did," Elizabeth said. Her words hit me like a block of ice.

"Just a room? No gym?" They nodded.

"Not even barbells?"

"No."

I had an absurd image of people hitching up the sleigh so people could work on their abs by pulling Santa out of the chimney. The room was tilting a bit. "Do you have anywhere I can sit down?"

Elizabeth and Marva immediately ran for the coffin. They dragged it across the floor until it was right next to me. "Here you go."

I sat down on my cryptic chair and let the information sink in. "So let me get this straight. You used your grant money to hire a trainer, but you don't have a single treadmill? No StairMaster?"

They nodded.

"What is the other trainer hired by the fitness grant doing?"

"I have everything I need in my end of the county," a commanding voice announced from the doorway. A tall figure posed, her hands on her hips and her legs spread apart like Wonder Woman.

I swallowed, and choked on my dry mouth. I took a quick sip of coffee. "Who's that?" I asked under my breath.

Marva sighed. "Aubrey." It was impossible to miss the regret in her voice. It was the kind of tone that was usually followed by three notes in an old B movie. *Duh, duh, DAH!*

"Aubrey" was a specimen of intimidating power. She was statuesque. Her tight-fitting leggings enhanced her glistening muscles. Her high-arching eyebrows were so pronounced they looked like tattoos. Her long black hair was pulled up to the very top of her head in a single long ponytail. It could double as a whiplash.

A smaller woman followed her into the room, trailing like a little mouse seeking crumbs. Her heels clicked on the wood floor as she extended the hand that wasn't holding a clipboard, to greet me.

She stopped short of the coffin as if she were afraid a dead body might pop out. "I'm Marie Joiner, project manager for the Michigan Department of Health and Human Services. And you are Lily"—she looked down at her clipboard—"Shue?"

I put down my coffee and hid my crutch against the side of the coffin. Standing carefully on my one-and-a-half legs, I held out my hand. "Yes."

Her limp hand reached out for mine. Weak. Marie needed strength training. Ironic, considering she was in charge of administering a fitness grant.

Aubrey's gaze wandered around the room and then to my knee. "I didn't believe it when I heard the news. But now I've seen it with my own eyes."

"Just a temporary sports injury," I said with a laugh. I straightened to keep myself from losing my balance and knocked my crutch off its perch. It crashed to the floor.

Elizabeth picked it up and handed it to me. "Silly injuries. Just last week I jammed my thumb reaching for a bag of potato chips."

Aubrey walked around the room with slow, deliberate steps. "So this is your gym? An empty room with nothing but leftover carnival props?"

Marie made a nervous squeak in the back of her throat. "Lily, this is Aubrey Vanderbeek."

Aubrey mistook my nod for familiarity. "You've probably heard all about me? The gym opens in West Bloomfield in two months. And yes, it is going to be as amazing as they said it would be in the *Detroit News*."

She reminded me of another trainer I knew in L.A. Every sentence out of his mouth had been either a jab or a boast. He had made life on the *Just Lose It* set unbearable.

Marie lifted several papers on her clipboard. "Aubrey and Lily, I've sent you most of this information already. As you know, you've been approved for your salary, travel, and lodging."

Aubrey held out her arms and twisted back and forth. Then she touched her toes and jumped at least three feet from a squatting position. Her strength was amazing.

"Is anything else included in the grant?" I asked, trying to keep my envy off my face.

"Unfortunately . . . no." Marie handed us each a stack of papers. "This grant has several components that are outlined in these documents."

Aubrey added, "I take the western half of the county and you take the eastern half."

"Do we share your gym then?"

"Why would we do that?" asked Aubrey.

"You have equipment, right?"

"State of the art. Your gym has . . . Santa." She cracked herself up. "I guess you will just have to use that creativity you mentioned in your résumé."

How would she know what was on my résumé? I had mentioned my creativity to illustrate that I could work with an injured knee. "Why not let everyone use your gym, then?"

Her eyes ran over Marva. "And risk breaking our equipment?"

I couldn't believe she'd said that. I shuffled in front of Marva to keep her from noticing Aubrey's rude stare.

Elizabeth came to stand beside me. "The Vanderbeeks built the gym for Harrisburg residents only. They are very active contributors in their town's community center."

"Too bad Truhart doesn't have generous donors, too," Aubrey said, flicking her ponytail my way.

I reached for my coffee and tried to keep my smile in place. "Should we go over a plan for evaluation?"

Aubrey flexed to the side with her hands over her head. "No need." She leaned down and touched her head to her shins. "Marie will be evaluating us separately. I just came along today to meet you."

"Even so, we might benefit from sharing our knowledge and working together to motivate the whole county."

She glanced at my knee and shrugged. My cheeks were burning. I had the sudden urge to stick my face in the pile of snow in the middle of the street.

Marie bit her lip. "I do have concerns about parity between both programs."

Aubrey raised her arms and flexed her shoulders. She stared at the wall and said to herself in a singsong voice, "Seems to me there might be some other things to worry about."

Marie ignored her. "I am evaluating both programs every month. The forms you need to use for evaluation are in your packets."

I was familiar with the information already.

Elizabeth put her hands together. "This is going to be a great opportunity for our community."

Marie's gaze wandered around the room and settled on the fireplace where Santa's bum was protruding. "I can see that."

Aubrey finished doing her impromptu stretching routine, and handed her card to me. "In case you need me."

"Wait a moment and I'll get mine—"

"That's all right. I know where to find you. The Callahans', right?"

News traveled quickly.

She pulled her tight shirt down with embarrassing slowness and smoothed it over her chest. "Give my regards to Edge. We had a sort of *thing* once in high school."

Visions of her contorting herself naked in front of Edge made me wish I hadn't eaten that egg this morning.

Marie shook my hand and turned toward the door. "I look forward to seeing how things go."

Aubrey added, "Me too." She threw back her head and laughed at her own sarcasm.

* * *

A blast of cold air rushed through the room after they left. I took a deep breath and let it calm my battered pride. I knew this would be a tough challenge when I took the job.

My gym in L.A. was shiny and state-of-the-art. Almost every piece of equipment had a flat-screen television. The treadmills looked out over a tropical garden. A juice bar stood in the lobby. Even my clients were different. They panicked when they gained two pounds. When I thought I was going to be working on *Just Lose It*, I looked forward to being able to follow my client from the time she woke up in the morning to the time she let herself collapse into bed. I was going to measure her carbs and proteins, chase her away from the soft-serve ice cream machines, and discuss all her emotional baggage that manifested itself on the outside.

Now I had a different strategy to consider.

It took me a minute to find my ragged voice. "This changes things a bit."

"It isn't as bad as you think. We have two hundred and thirty-three dollars left from our fundraiser last Christmas," Marva said.

That would buy a few resistance bands at most. Maybe some foam rollers. Something occurred to me. "Wait. My lodging is free, right? Does that leave you extra cash from the grant?"

"Actually, we were never going to need that money for the lodging. That was the best part of the grant for us," Elizabeth said. "Last summer the new owner of the bookstore claimed her inheritance, Books from the Hart."

Marva pointed to the wall next door. "At first we all thought she was crazy. She lived in her car and wore the strangest clothes."

"And she was a vegan!" said Regina.

Elizabeth shook her head. "A person's eating habits are their own business. We shouldn't judge anyone."

"You're just saying that because you don't want us to criticize you," said Regina. "In any case, the point we are trying to make is that because of Trudy, the bookshop and this grocery store belong to the Triple C's now."

I was so confused. "Trudy?"

Marva looked at me like I hadn't been paying attention. "The niece who inherited the bookstore! She and Lord Darlington—"

"He's not a lord, Marva."

"He will be someday, that's what all you people are forgetting."

Elizabeth patted my shoulder. "I'm sorry, Lily. All this must seem very strange to you. What Marva is trying to say is that these two buildings came into our possession free and clear, thanks to Trudy's generosity."

"And his lordship's," said Marva. "They didn't have to do that. That pawnshop guy, Logan Fribley, would have been more than happy to buy the place from Trudy."

"But she gave it to us," Elizabeth finished up.

They stared at me as if the story made perfect sense. I sipped my coffee—pretending to understand. The only thing that was clear was that the buildings belonged to the Triple C's. I might have a good budget after all.

"So . . . if the county gave money for my salary, my travel, and my lodging, there is money left over from the lodging."

"Yes. Plus the extra two hundred and thirty-three dollars from the Santa's Attic at Christmas."

"Great." I started a mental list of basics that would get things started.

"Yoo-hoo!" The door swung open and more than a half dozen women walked in. They wore yellow T-shirts with bold letters that made them resemble giant bumblebees.

A woman pushed herself to the front of the crowd. "The boxes arrived! We were so excited, we decided to show you." The halo of hair on her head was not quite gray. More like light blue. She wore her T-shirt over a floral dress and light panty hose that bunched at the ankles. If *The Brady Bunch* were still on the air, she was Alice forty years older and sixty pounds heavier.

She walked over and gathered me in her arms for a hug. "You must be Lily!"

"Careful, Addie, don't hurt her knee," Marva said as if she had never slapped it herself yesterday.

The older woman jumped back with amazing agility. "Oh my Lord, I am so sorry. I just got carried away, honey. You're staying with Ivy's family."

Elizabeth put her hand on Addie's shoulder. "Lily, this is Addie Adler, Ivy's sister."

The "Aunt Addie" Louise had told me about last night.

I looked closer and saw a resemblance around the chin. "It's so nice to meet you, Mrs. Adler."

"Oh Lord, call me Addie. Aunt Addie. We're practically family."

A frail woman with a fishing hat covered with either lures or an insect infestation poked me in the shoulder. "Is it true you're from Hollywood?"

"I lived in L.A."

"But you were on the show *Just Lose It*, right?"

"Very, very briefly." I didn't want to go into the details of that right now, or ever.

"Did you ever meet George Clooney?"

Was she joking? "Ahh, no. He didn't really need to lose weight. And I am pretty sure that he has his own trainer—"

"What about Oprah? Or that comedian? The one who is so rude?"

I glanced longingly at the door, where more bees—I mean, women—buzzed in. The devil on my left shoulder was telling me I could limp out right now and catch the bus back to Lansing. I edged away from the group. But then a tall, bleached blond woman with dark eyebrows planted herself right in front of me. She was rail thin, and had lines around her mouth. Smoker. Or maybe past smoker. She smelled like French fries, not nicotine.

"What do you think?" She stretched her T-shirt out with both hands so that I could read what was written across the front. I wasn't interested in rating T-shirts at the moment. But I did what she asked.

AIM HIGH,
WORK HARD,
DON'T QUIT!
—LILY SHUE

My words. My slogan. On every single T-shirt in the room. I clutched my chest and lost hold of my crutch.

A hand reached for me. "You okay?"

It took a second to find my breath. "I just never saw myself quoted on a T-shirt before."

Regina Bloodworth beamed. "That's where we spent the eight hundred dollars we saved on your lodging."

Marva put a hand to her chest. "It was my idea."

"I thought it was my idea," said the bug-hatted lady.

"No, Flo. You came up with the idea to quote Lily from her blog! But I had the original idea. We needed to motivate the town. Everyone who gets involved in the fitness challenge will get a free T-shirt."

"My husband, the mayor, got a deal at Lakeside Printers. We have boxes of them," Regina said.

"A box for smalls, one for mediums, two larges, two extra-larges, two extra-extra-larges," fly-lady Flo said. "That gives you an idea of how much we need you."

Aunt Addie took a seat on one side of the coffin, oblivious to the fact that the other side left the floor. Two of the younger ladies jumped on it so she wouldn't tip over. I was startled to see the lid beginning to bow under their weight.

"We want to hear all about what you have planned for us, Lily," said Addie.

I had a schedule of workouts in my planner that would help chisel away the pounds. I had scores of recipes and dieting tips. The thing was, I had imagined all of it happening in a different setting and with people who didn't think coffins were armchairs and T-shirts were the answer to losing weight.

I stared with regret at Addie Adler's shirt and tried not to picture all the things I could have done with a budget.

The words, my words, jumped out at me.

AIM HIGH,
WORK HARD,
DON'T QUIT!

I had coined the slogan a couple of years ago. The banner, along with a cute picture of a woman running up a hill, was boldly displayed at the side of my *Lily's Lessons* fitness blog. The one I hadn't written since my ACL tear.

I looked around the room. Really looked. There was nice light from the window. A wood floor that might clean up well. There was no reason I couldn't run the gym without equipment. Body-weight workouts were quite effective.

And if I was honest with myself, the T-shirts were amazing.

My little catchy marketing phrase stared back at me, challenging my willpower and fortitude. I felt the first glimmer of an emotion I hadn't experienced for weeks. Not since my injury. Hope.

I had to start somewhere.

And "here" was as good a place as any.

No. That was wrong.

"Here" wanted me. "Here" needed me.

A hive of expectant faces waited for me to explain what I was going to do for the town of Truhart.

I ignored the dull ache in my knee and responded to Addie Adler. "I have a lot of great plans."

Aunt Addie bobbed up and down in excitement, sending the ladies on the other end of the coffin up in the air like a seesaw.

"I need a day or so just to gather some information about the town. The space here. And your local food options."

Marva O'Shea raised her hand. "I can help you with the food options. I am the manager at the Family Fare."

"Lily means restaurants. Right?" the tall, French-fry-smelling woman said.

"How do you know what she means, Corinne? And last I heard the restaurants had to get the food from somewhere, and that means me—I mean the Family Fare."

The two started bickering and I tried to explain to them that I meant both, but they were too far gone.

Elizabeth whispered in my ear. "Don't worry. They're best friends. They do that all the time."

Regina raised her voice. "Since my husband is mayor"—a short woman behind Regina rolled her eyes—"I can get you all sorts of information on the demographics of the region."

"Thanks. You can help me to publicize events, take a leadership role in the program."

I pulled out my notebook and started taking notes. "Can we have a meeting with the participants in a day or so?"

"Tomorrow before the fish fry at the Elks," Regina said.

A fish fry? Oh Lord, there was so much to do . . .

"Please tell us if you need anything," said Elizabeth.

I wanted to say *money and equipment*, but I clutched my notebook and smiled instead.

One by one, the yellow T-shirts left the community center.

"We need to get moving. The Harrisburg Community Association has flyers up and classes scheduled. They already have a head start," Regina said.

Marva snapped her fingers. "It makes no difference. They're still on this year's list of most obese towns in the state."

"Yeah, but they're fifth on the list," said Elizabeth.

"And Truhart?" I asked.

"First." All the ladies said it at the same time.

"It's the only thing we beat them at," Marva said with a grin.

Elizabeth walked toward the door. "That isn't a good thing, Marva. Stop acting like you're so proud of it."

Marva opened the door and sent me a thumbs-up. "Gotta start somewhere."

LESSON FOUR

Measure Before You Start

Regina gave me a key to the community center and reminded me to lock up. Did she seriously think someone was going to break in and steal Santa's rear end and a sarcophagus?

I grabbed my planner and sat down on the pine box. Leafing through the pages, I searched for anything usable. Each detailed plan included something the community-center gym didn't have. One by one, I ripped out my notes and wadded them into a ball. I took aim at the big guy coming out of the fireplace and hit my red target eight out of fifteen attempts. Hopefully, I wouldn't be on the naughty list next Christmas.

When I came to the first blank page I stopped.

Other than walking on icy streets, there were always dynamic and isometric exercises. And yoga. None of which I could do. It brought me back to the question that had plagued me from the moment I took the job. How could I teach something I couldn't do myself? I could explain the movement. I could show videos. I could ask for volunteers. It still wasn't ideal. I had a new appreciation for disabled athletes.

No wonder Edge had been so amused by my note-taking this morning. I had gone on about plans and equipment and he never said a word about the actual state of the community center. He must have thought I was the most naïve person in the county to prepare the details for something I had never set eyes on.

Like a compass that couldn't find true North, my mind spun in circles. Maybe instead of true North I should just head west again. I kicked my doubting self to the curb. No quitting.

I jumped when my phone erupted with the theme from *Mission Impossible*. My big brother, Chip, had changed my settings the last time he was in L.A. He said he deserved a ringtone more dynamic than "marimba." It was just another reminder that he was on par with an action hero.

"Hi, Chip."

"Hey, how's my favorite cripple doing?"

I sighed. "Do you let your patients hear you use that kind of language?"

"They love me anyway. So, are you bored out there in the middle of nowhere?"

"Not at all. It's gorgeous. I am living right on a lake. There's lots of open spaces and enthusiastic people. Couldn't be happier." I drew a sad face on the blank page in front of me.

"I'll be darned. I have a friend who lives in Charlevoix and they said that Truhart was basically the armpit of the state."

"They must be thinking of another town. This is really a . . . quite a tourist attraction . . ." I tapped the pine box I sat on. "Especially at Halloween and Christmas."

"Sure it is."

I never had been able to pull one over on Chip. He was six years older than me. Overachieving brother number two, he'd gone to UNC Chapel Hill undergrad, Cal Tech for engineering, then on to Harvard for medical school. Now he traveled the world bringing new medical technology to every corner of the earth.

My other superhero brother, Ned, was two years older than Chip. He was the CFO of a Silicon Valley microchip company that had just gone public. Every time I saw him he reminded me that I should have invested in the IPO of his company instead of creating my own protein-powder brand with a shelf life that was about to expire.

"Mom wanted me to check on you and make sure you were doing all right." I wouldn't be surprised if she was listening in on another line. "Have you managed to nag anyone to death yet with your froggy voice, Lardo?" I was going to be eighty years old and Chip and Ned would be calling me "Lardo Lil," like I was ten. They still thought a noogie to the head was the same as a kiss. Every time I complained, they told me to lighten up. Stop taking life so seriously. Easy for them to say. Mr. Perfect numbers one and two.

"Everyone here is alive and well," I said.

"Knee all right?"

"Getting stronger."

"Food?"

I thought about the spaghetti dinner. "Practically gourmet."

I couldn't remember the last time I had eaten spaghetti that wasn't changed up with tofu, or turkey, or zucchini noodles. Surprisingly, I had enjoyed it.

"Well, go easy on the helpings, Lil. Extra weight is a risk on your joints. You don't have any more healthy knees to spare. Haha."

I held my fingers up and played the punch-line end beat, *da, da, dum, DA!* Edge didn't have a corner on the air drum market.

"Mom also wanted me to let you know that a letter came from *Just Lose It* yesterday. She opened it. It's just another reminder that your contract is terminated." Chip had the decency to lose the funny-man routine. His tone was gentle. I put the air drums away.

Years ago, when I tore my left ACL, Chip had flown in to be with me for the surgery. It was all very touching until I saw him afterwards. As I woke up, groggy and disoriented, he held up a fake leg and told me the doctor was sorry they'd had to amputate.

The nurse had given him hell when I burst into tears.

When I tore my ACL this time, Chip was on better behavior. He called the surgeon personally to make sure he was using the graft that was considered the gold standard for athletes these days. He cared. I knew that. It's just that it felt like pity most of the time.

"You okay?" he asked.

"I'm fine. Just kind of surprised *Just Lose It* had to send a letter. I already understood my contract was terminated when I left the show." The first episode of the season.

"I guess some lawyers got involved. They are pains in the ass about that stuff. You should see them when we patent new medical equipment." He had never liked lawyers. Until he started dating one last year. She was great.

"Lil?"

"Yeah."

"One more thing. They included a legal reminder that you agreed to give them all rights to your appearance on the show."

"I guess I did that."

"They might uhhh . . . mention the accident."

I clenched my hand around the phone and closed my eyes. It was bad enough that Rod Macintosh, one of the trainers on the show, had seen fit to inform the producers that my accident was entirely my fault. I had to use my own insurance policy for the surgery. But the knowledge that my injury might be mentioned in the first show of the season made me physically sick.

I didn't want Chip to know that I was about to puke on my knee brace. "Good. It might help others avoid the same kind of accident. I am sure they are just doing it like a public service announcement."

"Maybe. Oh, hey, I gotta go, Lil. I'm in Rome right now and it's like dinnertime. The hospital is hosting a great big conference and I am giving the keynote speech. Crazy, isn't it?"

"Really cool, Chip. I'm proud of you."

"You always say that, Lil. You're the best."

No, I wasn't. My evil mind was wishing that for once he would do something embarrassing. Not catastrophic, of course. Just minor. Like give the speech with a big piece of spinach between his front teeth.

"Love you, Chip."

"I love you too, Lardo."

I used to hero-worship my brothers. In return they tormented me. Admittedly, I gave them a lot of free comic material. Especially during my awkward stage. My unibrow, my crooked left tooth, my off-pitch singing.

The odds in the family had been against me since I was twelve. Three against one. Mom, Ned, Chip.

It had been better once.

I pulled out the necklace that was hidden underneath my workout clothes. Dad gave me the gold chain with the tiny rose pendant on my tenth birthday. It was my good-luck charm now.

I had been a daddy's girl. No shame there.

After my brothers were born, Mom and Dad thought they were finished having children. Then I came along. Mom told me when he held me for the first time, my dad broke down and cried. Two healthy sons and a precious little girl.

Dad was my buddy. He taught me the fine nuances of good ice cream and introduced me to every episode of *Star Trek*. He helped me with my homework and encouraged me to take up soccer. Our best times, though, were in the garden. We spent hours there. With my own set of pint-size tools I helped him plant annuals around the border of "our" perennial garden and prune "our" roses. When we finished, we would pull up a lawn chair, drink lemonade, and admire our work.

I loved the fact that he named me after his favorite flowers. Lily Rose.

Everything changed one bitter April morning. On a day when even the sunshine felt cold. I was playing the first soccer game of the season. We were tied. Instead of leaving me to huddle under a blanket on the bench, my coach put me on the field. With one minute left in the game, I cut around the defense in a breakaway, moving up the sideline. I still remember the heady feeling as the spectators on the sideline roared. I was on a sure path for the net. It was going to be such a good story to tell my brothers. I could taste my victory. The goalie crouched before I took my shot.

The ball went sailing . . . right over the goalpost.

The whistle blew and I stared at the empty goal, trying so hard not to cry at my failure. At first, I didn't hear the commotion in the stands. It wasn't until I heard my mom's voice shouting *Call 911!* that I realized something was wrong.

We moved to L.A. after my father's funeral, to be close to Mom's family. Just Mom and me. My brothers were in college by then. L.A. was dry, and we didn't have a backyard. Without Dad, I didn't want to garden again anyway.

Pulling myself up from the coffin and my self-pity, I started to pace. My three-legged stride echoed in the room.

The wide-plank wood floor would make a great room for a yoga class or even Pilates, after it was swept. I would have to double-check the reinforcements underneath if I was going to let people use any weights in here. Not that there were any. The room was wide and the ceiling was at least two stories high. At the very back of the room was a large balcony. In the old days, some store manager must have put his office there so he could oversee everything. I would have to check it out to see if it could be used for smaller classes.

I tucked my necklace back inside my shirt and wondered what Dad would say if he were here right now.

He would tell me that things weren't so bad.

Build your strength and study the game.
Be patient with yourself.
There is always a way to make a garden grow.

An hour later, I stretched my arms and shuffled on three legs to the next position.

"Trying to fly, or creating a new dance move?" asked a familiar deep voice.

I held up one finger and continued counting.

Edge held several folding chairs in his arms, and he put them down by the coffin. "Feel free to sit when you are finished with your ritual."

"I'm counting the number of people I can fit across the length of the room." I finished making my trek to the opposite wall.

"You might want to double that width for some people. Have you seen my great-aunt Addie?"

He was right. I should get the overall measurement of the space and make a few adjustments. "I don't suppose you have a measuring tape? I seem to have forgotten mine."

"You own one?" he asked.

I limped over to the coffin where my planner lay open, and made a note. "Now that I think about it, no."

He shook his head and walked out the door mumbling something about California girls.

"Hey!" I yelled. "Are you leaving me stranded here just because I don't have a measuring tape?"

Edge returned and held up his hand. "Here. No man this side of the state line would be caught dead without a measuring tape."

We turned toward the coffin at the same time, and I grinned. "Guess he was from somewhere else."

"Probably Ohio."

"Damn Buckeyes."

Edge clutched the measuring tape to his chest. "You know our football rivalries?"

"Are you kidding? I have two older brothers who think sports belong on the front page. I lose to them in fantasy football every single year."

"Now those are the kind of men I would like to meet. They probably have five measuring tapes each."

"Probably. But I'll warn you, Ned always picks the Buckeyes over State and Michigan." I held out my palm and wiggled my fingers. "I'll take that."

"I changed my mind. I don't want to meet Ned." He kept the measuring tape and moved beside me, peering over my shoulder. "What do you need measured?"

I explained and he did it for me, reciting the numbers as I recorded them. When Edge finished, he said, "Now that you know the dimensions of the room, what are you going to do with that information?"

I still hadn't forgotten the discussion this morning. "I don't know if I want to tell you, seeing as you forgot to tell me that there was no gym. I felt like a fool when I asked Regina Bloodworth where all the equipment was."

"You probably felt better than she did. It was her idea to apply for the grant for a fitness trainer without a fitness center."

"And you thought that was a stupid idea."

He shrugged. "You have to admit, it's a bit like the cart before the horse."

"Thanks for comparing me to a horse."

"Actually, you were the cart."

I thought on that for a moment. "I suppose to most people your logic makes sense."

Edge tossed the measuring tape in the air, carelessly flipping it and catching it in the same hand. "Ya think?"

He had lost the baseball hat and his hair was messy. It should have made him look like a silly slob. Instead it made him look hot.

"Not so fast, Mr. Sarcasm." I inhaled the odor of mint I remembered so well from yesterday and tamped down my wayward sex drive. "For the record, they have done studies about weight loss and trainers."

"And?" He moved closer. The room was warming up the closer he came.

Fanning myself with my planner, I blabbered on. "The study shows that while the people who worked out in a gym with no trainer lost weight, they actually gained less muscle. And they had far less strength. A competent trainer knows how to recognize weak areas and strengthen the whole frame."

"Maybe. But those competent guys probably still had a real gym to work in." He was within inches of me. Close enough that I could see a tiny scar on the side of his head. It started next to his eye and disappeared where his temple met his hairline. Maybe he got beaned by a teddy bear with sharp claws. I clutched my fists to my side to keep from reaching out to trace it.

Edge had no such problem touching me. His free hand waved in front of my eyes and I flinched when he flicked something off my hair.

"What was that?"

"I think it was a piece of fuzz." His eyes took on a mischievous gleam and pointed at Santa's rear end and the pile of paper wads I had thrown at it. "You and Santa been doing anything you shouldn't?"

I ducked under his arm and moved away. "Funny."

"Not so far-fetched. I caught that guy kissing my mom underneath the mistletoe one night."

Men. He was just like my brothers with a sense of humor that bordered on tasteless and corny.

I went for the jugular. "By the way, Aubrey Vanderbeek says hello. She sounds like she wants to rekindle something you once had."

"We never had any *thing*. God knows she tried, though." His ran his hand over his eyes and grimaced. "I heard she's back in the county, working the Harrisburg end of the grant."

"Yup. You should look her up. She seems perfect for you."

He snorted and rubbed his shoulder. "Just thinking about the way she used to ignore the rules and tackle me in flag football makes me hurt."

"She beat you, huh?" I couldn't help baiting him. "Maybe you need to come to my fitness classes. I'll whip you into shape so you won't lose again."

"You misunderstand. She didn't win. I . . . don't . . . lose." He said the words slowly and deliberately.

"Wow. I would have never guessed you were competitive, Edge. You never lose?"

"Either I win or I learn. But I never lose."

I rolled my eyes. "And what kind of game do you play? A teddy-bear trash toss?"

He put his shoulders back and puffed out his chest. "I'll have you know that I am the arm-wrestling champion around town."

"In the senior bracket? You're what, forty?" I couldn't help strangling his ego.

"Thirty-one last September."

I sent him a pained expression. "Then you are experiencing the loss of muscle that happens as you get older. It turns to—" I looked down at his stomach. "Well . . . I shouldn't talk that way."

I was quite aware of the fact that he didn't have an ounce of fat. But with his big shirt on, and the beard that hid his face, a person might mistake him for a retired lumberjack who had imbibed too many pints.

He set the folding chairs on either side of the coffin. "Come on, Lily Bud. Let's see what you've got."

I did a double take when he used that nickname. It was one of many nicknames my dad called me. "What made you call me Lily Bud?"

"I don't know. Something about your size and the fact that you don't seem fully bloomed yet."

"Bloomed? I'm only a few years younger than you."

He flexed his fingers and made a show of preparing to arm wrestle me. "Come on, don't change the subject here. Are you going to take on this challenge or are you too scared that you'll ruin your killer reputation by losing to a fat guy like me?"

My eyes scanned his rock-hard body. No way was he fat. His ego might be, though.

I sat down and propped my elbow on the pine top of the coffin. "You have an unfair advantage. I won't be able to brace myself very well."

"How about you use both hands and I'll start halfway back."

"Deal!" I jumped on the offer before he changed his mind. I had lost arm-wrestling matches to my brothers many times. Neither one of them had ever suggested letting me have an advantage like the one Edge was offering.

"Don't hurt yourself, now," he said.

"Mind your own business."

He chuckled but then turned serious. "I'm not kidding, though. Watch your knee."

I angled my knee out and braced myself. Leaning close, I gripped his fist with both my hands. He was close. His breath was like a feather on my cheek. The flecks of green in his gray eyes were twinkling, and that suspicious crater in his cheek was wiggling. Why didn't he shave so I could figure out what he was hiding behind that scraggly beard?

"You can be the one to count down," he offered.

I shamelessly accepted any help I could get. "Four, three, two, one . . . Go!" I pushed down with all my weight and felt my body shake with effort. Nothing happened.

A quick glance at Edge made me double my effort. He stared at me through bored hooded eyelids. "Did you start yet?"

"Oomph . . ." I dug one elbow into wood in an attempt to gain more leverage against him. He had the temerity to put his free hand over his mouth and yawn.

My arms shook harder. I raised myself to gain power.

When I wasn't sure I could stand it anymore, Edge calmly pushed until he was at a ninety-degree angle and our wrists were centered. He kept going, as if he were making no effort at all. He was going to win.

An old trick came to mind. It always got me disqualified with my brothers. Hopefully, Edge was as ticklish as Chip.

Pulling one hand out of his grasp, I reached out to Edge's armpit. He jerked back when I touched him. "Hey, not fair!"

"Were there rules?" I asked, reaching across the coffin again.

"In that case—" He dodged my hand and did the same to me.

Heat shot to my breasts at the nearness of his hand in the crook of my shoulder, but I managed not to flinch.

"Not ticklish," I said. I grasped his palm with both hands and pushed his elbow back down.

"Not ticklish? What kind of robot are you?"

"A killer robot." I pushed harder.

"Then how about this?" Before I knew what he was doing, his lips captured mine.

His mouth was warm and his scruffy beard felt surprisingly soft against my cheek. It produced a whole new erogenous zone I never knew existed. Fingers of fire spread across my body and I forgot about winning. The kiss ended too soon and I found myself staring at Edge's shirt.

I looked down to see the back of my hand splayed across the coffin. Edge had won.

The corner of his mouth turned up in a lazy smile. "Do you want to try again?"

I grabbed my crutch from the floor and stood on shaky legs. I skirted around him and picked up my bag, stuffing my planner inside. "Are you giving me a ride or not?"

"Unless you want to take the sleigh over there?"

My mind was too numb to come up with a quip.

Edge walked around me and reached for the door as if nothing had just happened. Except there was a satisfied smile on his face.

"At least you know I'm not getting any older."

"What?" I was having trouble keeping up.

"No fat. Admit it." He ran a hand over his chest in an exaggerated motion. "And no muscle loss."

I walked past him with a huff. I would get my rematch.

During the ride home, the radio blared, effectively eliminating any conversation we might have had about our wrestling match. While I felt off balance from our unexpected kiss, he was behaving like the whole thing was a joke. Fitting. He bobbed his head and sang a Rolling Stones song almost as badly as I might have.

Edge Callahan was a man-child. On the outside, strong, muscular, bearded. But inside he was like a ten-year-old. A kid who had just discovered an electric guitar but still slept with a teddy bear. Heavy metal meets Christopher Robin.

We arrived back at the Callahans' just in time. Edge was about to attempt a Prince song that might have broken a blood vessel in his vocal chords. I let him help me down and into the house, doing my best to ignore his satisfied smile.

When he left, I watched him walk across the street and disappear into the ranch house where he lived. Maybe it was best just to forget everything about today. What happened earlier was revenge for my cheating. And a spontaneous reaction from Edge. It came from the energy of our competitive spirits. It had nothing to do with any attraction we might feel for each other. Or at least the attraction that I felt for him.

Edge and I were as different as night and day. He was an immature goof-off who apparently couldn't even summon the energy to shave in the morning. I was a serious, goal-oriented professional.

He practically lived with his mommy, for goodness' sake. Well, technically I did, too.

I stared at the redbrick ranch house across the road. Louise told me this morning it had been Ivy's once. It was quite nice from the outside. Convenient. Edge could have privacy, and come back for Mom's home cooking whenever he wanted. The ranch was probably littered with underwear, open cans of soda, and half-eaten bags of potato chips. Edge probably brought over his laundry once a week for his mommy to wash. Pitiful.

I browsed creative fitness workouts on my computer for the next few hours, researching everything I could about successful fitness programs with limited budgets. I searched for inexpensive equipment as well. And then . . . well, an exit plan, just in case this job was over before it began.

Unfortunately, I couldn't use my own money to purchase equipment. My bank account was slim, thanks to my poor business sense. When I landed the job on *Just Lose It*, I made the cardinal mistake in Financial Planning 101. I spent money I didn't have.

My brothers were lavish with my mother. Ned had bought her a new Mercedes that she drove horribly. Chip had bought her a ten-year membership in a golf club. For once I wanted to be as generous as my brothers. Thinking I was going to enjoy a fine paycheck, I splurged and flew both of us to Seoul to visit family. She had a wonderful time. I enjoyed it, too, even though I grew tired of nodding and pretending I knew what everyone was saying.

The second mistake I made was my big plan of producing my own brand of protein powder. My appearance on *Just Lose It* was going to act as a springboard for selling it on my blog. Twenty cases of the protein powder were stacked in my mother's garage. They would expire in eight months.

I tried not to think about my massive failures in the financial realm. Or the other ones.

Instead I focused on a single number.

Two hundred and thirty-three. The leftover funds the Triple C's had in reserve.

With that amount I could buy some very basic exercise equipment.

As for the rest of my problems, well, there was a slogan on a yellow T-shirt that would guide me.

Dinner that night was tacos. The boys debated whether Mentos exploded best in Pepsi or Coke. Tracy and Louise talked about staffing at the senior day care. Olivia asked me all sorts of questions about Los Angeles. I ignored the way Edge's eyes flashed every time I looked his way.

"You have to know a lot of actors," Olivia said, putting her elbows on the table.

"A few." Actually, I did. I had helped train several minor television actors.

"What about a movie star? Melissa McCarthy? She looked great at the Oscars."

I shook my head.

"Leonardo DiCaprio?"

"No."

The funny thing was that at first I had been starstruck by my clients, too. But once I realized that they were real people with real food cravings and muscle-strength deficiencies, I focused on getting them in shape, talked them out of binge eating, and worked on changing their bad habits.

"Can't you tell us about anyone?" Olivia asked, leaning on her elbows.

"I helped Tina Delfio get fit before she went on *Dancing Divas* last year." The job had helped me get noticed by the producer of *Just Lose It*.

"Tina was an ice-skater, right? She trained outside of Detroit," said Tracy as she forced Justin to add more lettuce than cheese to his taco. "My friend's cousin was once her ice-dancing partner."

Olivia held her tortilla in the air. "Tina was at the same Olympics that Jackie—"

"Shhhh!" Sarah spit out, glancing sharply at Edge.

Edge passed the salsa with no emotion. His behavior appeared normal. But a tight muscle in his jaw gave him away. "We all went to the University of Vermont for a couple of years," he said easily.

Louise took the bowl from Edge and adopted a cheery voice. "Salsa, Lily?"

Olivia didn't notice the shifting mood. "Too bad about Tina's injury. She was a good figure skater. We all thought she would compete in the next Olympics and—" She paused and bit her lip.

Edge stared at his plate. "That's the way things go. Injuries happen. It's a way of life for athletes. I am sure Tina understood it just like anyone else."

He looked up and our eyes met. He was right. But it didn't take away the bitter sting that burst a long-held dream.

I wanted to ask him if he had played a sport. "What—"

All of a sudden Edge pushed back in his chair until he was on the back two legs and picked up a fork and a spoon, playing a beat on the table. "Guess what song this is, boys."

"Edgar," said Louise.

Justin and Jason imitated him, much to their mother's disgust. Everyone began speaking at once and the moment was lost. Not before I could tuck it away for later.

After dinner, I did my twenty minutes of therapy exercises and thought about my strange day. I wondered about the odd, emotionless way Edge talked about injury . . . I had only known him for a day, but something told me stone-like cynicism was not normal for Edge Callahan.

What was his real story?

Putting my curiosity on a shelf for now, I grabbed my crutches and oversize U-Fit Gym T-shirt and headed to the bathroom, leaving my brace on the bed. If I was sharing the bathroom with teenage girls, I was going to need to duck into the shower whenever the coast was clear.

Downstairs was quiet. I propped my crutch against the wall outside the bathroom, having learned too often that a wet bathroom floor and crutches didn't mix. This morning someone had cleared off all the makeup, cleansers, and tampons from the counter and left a clean towel in their place.

The shower felt like heaven after a long day. I ducked my head under the streaming hot water and let the weariness melt away. Afterward, I braced against the sink and toweled myself off. I donned the T-shirt, which covered me to midthigh, and combed my thick dark hair.

Feeling a million times better, I opened the bathroom door and looked around for my crutch. But it was gone.

Two young voices made strange noises that sounded like bombs from the recreation room at the end of the hall.

"You're under attack!!"

"I can still beat you, even if I'm wounded."

I hopped toward the sound.

Jason, I think, was attempting to walk across the room using my crutch while Justin shot foam arrows at him from the couch. When he saw me, he aimed my way. It hit me in the hip.

"Ouch!" The arrow was more painful than it looked. Footsteps pounded down the stairs.

Edge grabbed the next arrow midair and picked up the pint-size warrior, carrying him sideways as if he were a book. He set the boy on the couch and put another broad hand on top of the arrow launcher. Restraining both boys, he lowered his brow and spoke severely. "If I ever catch you stealing Lily's crutch again, I am going to put you in the back of Uncle Pete's garbage truck. Do you understand?"

They nodded.

He grabbed the remaining arrows. "And don't let me ever see you aiming these at a guest again. Or anyone. Ever."

They nodded.

Then he pointed his finger to the side door, where I could see a bright light from the apartment above the garage. "Your mom wants you home now. Bedtime!"

Without a word, they ran to the door, grabbed their coats, stepped halfway into their boots, and ran out the door to their apartment above the garage. Edge watched them until they reached their door.

"I'm really sorry, Lily. They have an overinflated imagination and anything is a weapon." He picked the crutch off the floor and turned back to me. "I will—" He paused.

I must have looked like a schoolgirl at a sleepover with my wet hair, T-shirt, and bare feet. The difference being that if I really were under sixteen, Edge's look would have been illegal in most states. He started at the top of my head, paused at my braless chest, and continued to my legs. He stopped at my knee, and all seduction stopped. He wasn't staring at my ugly, swollen right knee. He was staring at the faded scars on my other knee.

If I could have stretched my T-shirt down, I would have. Because standing in front of Edge, both knees giving away a history I didn't want to explain, made me feel naked.

"Twice?"

I knew exactly what he was talking about. "Soccer tryouts." For a walk-on position at USC.

"Tough break."

I felt the need to explain it was all right. "It made me switch majors and focus on kinesiology. So, I guess it was for the best."

"Good for you."

We were both lying. There was nothing good about not making a goal.

I took the crutch from him. "Well, I'm off to bed now. Thanks for coming to my rescue."

Edge raised his eyes and nodded at me. His mouth curled in a gentle smile. "Good night, Lily . . ."

I pivoted and crutch-walked back to *his* bedroom with as much dignity as I could muster. The boys had lost their battle, but I was still fighting my own. I couldn't understand how to combat the crazy way I felt when faced with the secret weapon that hid beneath a golden beard. Dimples.

LESSON FIVE

Educate Yourself

On Friday afternoon, Elizabeth Lively picked me up from the Callahans' in her Honda Accord for the big meeting with Truhart's Fit4You participants. On the way, she filled me in on the history of the area. "It was once a logging town with a booming industry. Unfortunately, when the logging industry moved west, so did three quarters of the population."

That explained the deserted buildings in town.

"What keeps the town going nowadays?"

"Mostly tourism," she said. I tried to imagine people flocking to the barren and bleak landscape and my face must have given me away. "Oh, I know, you're thinking why would anyone vacation in Truhart, right?"

I felt bad. "I've only been here a couple of days, and I've hardly seen the town."

"Don't worry. I'm not offended. Unfortunately, you came at the worst time of the year. We have winter, summer, and autumn around here. Spring, you'll see, is more like the muddy season. But summer is amazing. A dozen lakes and several rivers make water sports and fishing prime activities. Most of the cottages fill up with our summer residents from downstate. Truhart even manages to lure a few out-of-staters, like me."

"Where are you from?"

"Ohio." She turned onto the country road. "My grandmother used to live farther up on Crooked Road. I moved into her house and stirred things up. Long story."

"You don't need to tell me," I said.

"You'll find out eventually. I'm a little compulsive about cleaning and making things perfect. Coming to Truhart was one of the best things I ever did for myself."

"Best things?" I couldn't imagine what kind of redemption a place like Truhart could offer a perfectionist.

"Stay here long enough and you will understand. My first few weeks were an absolute mess. I was almost tackled by the deputy sheriff. I fell into a bog. And I pretty much started a mini war."

"And you stayed?"

"What can I say? I fell in love." She smiled. "Oh my God. I sound like a bad Hallmark movie. You must think I'm crazy." She changed the subject. "Tell me what you are going to say to everyone today."

I explained my ideas for getting Truhart into shape. By the time we finished we were approaching Main Street. The sun was going down and the lights from several establishments, including the diner, cast a glow on the snow at the side of the road.

"I love your enthusiasm, Lily. I can tell already that we picked the right woman."

I shook my head. "You picked the only woman for the job. Come on, admit it."

She laughed. "Well, we didn't have a lot of applicants. But yours was amazing. The ladies went crazy when they heard you had been on *Just Lose It*."

"You know, my accident happened before they taped the second episode."

"Doesn't matter. To everyone here you are a rock star."

I clenched my jaw. Someone should tell them I was playing an air guitar.

The new "gym" was already half full when Elizabeth and I walked in. When Regina saw me, she took my elbow and led me around the room. She introduced me to more people than I could ever remember. I scanned bodies, assessing their fitness levels, but it was hard given the way they were dressed for the weather. As coats were shed over the backs of the various folding chairs people brought, it became clear to me that there was work to do.

Over a hundred people gathered in the room. That was a far better turnout than I expected. Truhart was a town of 1300 residents. Ten percent participation was promising. In fact, by the time we were about to start, there were so many people crammed into the room that someone had to prop open a door to let the cool evening air in.

Regina started the meeting. "Good evening, everyone. Thanks for coming out. As you know, we received a grant from Fit4You to help our town get fit and healthy." She rambled on about the grant for so long that a few people started looking at their phones. Finally she held her arm out to me. "And so here is our new fitness trainer, Lily Shue. She comes with all sorts of wonderful recommendations. She knows a lot of stars in Hollywood and she was even on *Just Lose It* before coming to Truhart." My stomach contracted. "Lily comes to us from California, so please give her a warm Michigan welcome."

I joined Regina at the front of the room, impossibly trying to obscure my crutch. I could practically feel the heat of the stares on my knee.

Raising my chin, I imagined I was my brother Chip, and summoned my best public voice. "Thank you all for that great welcome!" Instead of sounding like a peppy motivator, my voice was like a strangled rabbit. I cleared my throat and tried again.

"It's great to be here in this beautiful town." Several people giggled. I wasn't trying to be sarcastic. Perhaps I didn't need to lather it on quite so much. "Well, I hear it will be beautiful when the weather changes." Louise Callahan sat next to Addie Adler and her eyebrow went way up. I took the warning and cut to another subject.

Taking a deep breath, I told everyone of my professional background. Not the one that had to do with TV shows or B-list Hollywood stars. The serious one. The one that came with a degree in kinesiology from the University of Southern California. I discussed my background in diet and nutrition. Then I listed a few specific accomplishments. The work I did with underserved populations. The after-school program in South L.A. Even the urban-garden work I had loved.

At that point a hand went up. An older woman asked, "But what stars did you work with?"

"Yeah!" several other people chimed in.

"Well, that is a bit confidential. But—"

A thin man with a big head of white hair leaned in. "Come on. We won't tell."

"I heard it was Leonardo," a woman nearby said.

I was losing control. "I always promise my clients that I won't talk about them in public. I hope you understand." Three people in the back of the room stood up to leave, and I panicked. "Of course, Leo was great to work with. A real gentleman."

And there it was. A shameless lie. Nobody knew that, though. Except Louise and the big bearded guy leaning against the back wall. Edge's grin was as wide as his shoulders.

I used the extra attention to my advantage and passed out some of the paperwork. "So if you are ready to get started on the road to fitness and health, we can begin."

Fortunately the subject of stars was dropped when I outlined my plan. I explained to them the three steps to working out. First, an assessment of their goals and health. "Dr. Manning at the Harrison County Hospital has agreed to partner with us and work with everyone who needs medical supervision during this process. If needed, we'll modify your workout.

"I am placing sign-up sheets for the fitness groups on the, uh, coffin here." Someone snorted at the irony. I held up the first sheet. "This is for the walkers. You can walk daily or weekly, depending on your schedule and the weather."

"That means never," someone grumbled.

I ignored him and held up the second paper. "This is for the creative fitness classes." I had no idea exactly how I was going to handle that with my knee, but I had notes all over the desk in Edge's bedroom.

"I am going to ask every participant to fill out a form." I passed the papers around the room. "If you participate, I must receive one. It includes a health history questionnaire along with your weight and height. Please be honest."

"Sure we will, honey." A large man winked at me.

"What is this paper for?" asked Marva, holding up a form.

"That is for our healthy nutrition challenge."

A tall bald man raised his hand. "Great idea. I can help with that." Regina explained "Mac is the cook at Cookee's Diner."

My heart sank as I thought of greasy burgers and French fries. At the very least I might be able to persuade him to offer healthy items on his menu.

"I am available at any time to work with you on finding healthy options for you and your family. I will be holding my first seminar Thursday."

I put the signs at my feet and shifted my weight off my bad knee.

"Just tell me I don't have to cut out beer," someone barked in the back of the room.

"You better not," said a grizzled man with sideburns, wearing a Grateful Dead T-shirt. "I still expect everyone to come out to Lori's for the NCAA finals tomorrow night. And the Tigers' home opener in a couple weeks."

Now was as good a time as any to start talking about good eating habits. I stepped forward. "The issue of food and drink is an important one. No one wants an overly strict diet that is going to make them miserable. Right? I don't plan on forcing you all to eat celery sticks and carrots all day."

That drew a big cheer. I was galvanized by the enthusiasm. "But it is also important to understand that to make a positive change, you need to alter the way you think about food."

The cheer morphed into a groan.

"It doesn't have to be major. But you do have to make some substitutions." My mind was going blank. I thought of the first thing that came to my head. "For example, I know it is really tempting to stop around the corner for ice cream after work or dinner."

Several heads turned, searching for something in the back of the room.

"Think about avoiding that kind of pitfall by substituting sweets with something else."

Elizabeth Lively stared at me with overly wide eyes and put a finger across her throat. I had heard she had a sweet tooth, but she shouldn't be so sensitive.

"We all like sugar. But it is like an addiction. Once our bodies have a little, they crave more and more until we crash. And study after study has shown the harmful effects of too much sugar in our system. Besides the obesity problem, diabetes is on the rise. Among other things, sugar lowers your immunity. If you want to be successful, you have to cut it out. Tell yourself *no* when you find yourself heading to the . . . the Dairy Cow, is it?"

Marva O'Shea nodded, with both hands over her mouth as if she were in pain. Perhaps she was just realizing that making a change to her diet was not going to be easy.

"I promise I can work with you to find something you like and something you will crave that is better for you than candy and ice cream."

The crowd was quiet now.

But there was a strange tension in the air I couldn't identify. I spotted Edge. He was no longer holding up the back wall with casual amusement. He was standing stiffly, his hands stuffed in the pockets of his coat.

Mr. Teddy Bear looked like Mr. Grizzly Bear right now.

I held the papers back up. "Don't be afraid to make changes in your life. You will be amazed at the way you feel when you challenge yourself to do this. You deserve this. Your body deserves it!"

I struggled for a final note, a rabble-rousing phrase to end my speech. Something that would make the walls shake and the crowd race to the front of the room to get their signature on a sign-up sheet.

Marva pointed at Addie Adler. "Show them your T-shirt, Addie."

She hopped up from her chair and faced the crowd. "The Triple C's had them made," she said proudly.

I stepped forward. "Addie is wearing a T-shirt that says everything you need to motivate yourself. If you sign up today you can all get a free T-shirt and start your journey to be the best you can be."

Several people stood up, ready to be first in line. I held up my hand. I wasn't finished.

"Remember these words and repeat them every morning and evening." I put my arm around Addie Adler. "Help me, Addie."

She pointed to each line on her shirt. "Aim High! Work Hard! Don't Quit!"

"Can I hear everyone say it?" I was on a roll. "Come on. Stand up, everyone."

In a giant wave of people, the room stood up. My heart soared.

"Aim High!"

"Work Hard!"

"Don't Quit!"

My heart beat so hard I could feel it in my throat when I said the last words. I couldn't stop smiling when I stepped backwards and watched the room come to life as the people of Truhart lined up to put their names on a poster board and claim their T-shirt.

This was going to work. Forget *Just Lose It* and my stale protein packets in Mom's garage. If only my brothers could see me now. I had just galvanized a town. Success was in my grasp.

I searched for Edge Callahan, hoping to get a thumbs-up of approval.

But he was nowhere to be seen.

Marva, Regina, Addie, and Elizabeth handed out T-shirts to everyone who put their name on the posters. I greeted people and listened as they told me about their struggles with weight. I encouraged several people to visit Dr. Manning before starting the program. I wrote down the names of volunteers who wanted to lead walking groups. We had a young mothers group, a grandparents group, and even a bridge club. I forgot all about my aching knee and my old grudges. This was what I was born to do. I couldn't wait to start.

Addie handed me a T-Shirt. "That's everyone. We're going to the fish fry now." I bit my lip. There would be time for more food talk later.

Marva and Elizabeth broke down the cardboard boxes that had held the T-shirts and stacked them against the door. "That went well, Lily," Elizabeth said.

"Thanks. I wasn't sure people liked when I talked about making diet changes. But I think everyone was willing to consider it."

"Almost everyone," Marva said. She and Elizabeth exchanged looks.

"Sometimes people need time to adjust." I shouldered my athletic bag. "Did you see Edge? I was hoping he would give me a ride back to the Callahans'."

"Yeah, um, he left. I'm giving you a ride home," Elizabeth said, looking away from Marva.

"I was surprised more people didn't sign up for walking tomorrow," I said.

Elizabeth put a hand on my arm. "Sometimes people make plans and can't change them."

Marva came to stand beside me. "The temperature is supposed to be over forty-five degrees tomorrow."

I nodded, wondering at the significance. "That's good, I guess."

"Edge scoops when it gets warm."

"Scoops?" An earlier conversation I had heard about scooping and freezers came to mind.

Elizabeth nodded to Marva. "See. I told you she didn't know."

"Know what?"

Marva picked up a stack of boxes and leaned against the door. "You tell her."

"Tell me what?" And then it hit me. Freezers. Kiddos. Scoops. And Edge's strange reaction every time I mentioned ice cream. I knew what was coming before Elizabeth said it.

"Edge owns the Dairy Cow. He's scooping ice cream for the Spring Thaw Grand Opening."

The Dairy Cow must have been doing good business, because I didn't see Edge the rest of the weekend. Sarah drove me to the gym to meet my first walkers on Saturday. And Elizabeth drove me home.

After doing my exercises Sunday afternoon, I wandered upstairs. The boys were huddled on the couch, playing a video game while Ivy watched. Tracy sat at the dining room table working on her laptop, and I wandered in on my way to get a glass of water.

Tracy raised her head when she saw me. "You look completely bored."

"Sorry. I didn't mean to interrupt your work. I'm just not sure what to do with myself."

"You can come sit down and tell me how you are doing."

I sat down and adjusted my brace under the table.

"Boys, turn the volume down," Tracy called into the living room. She wasn't fazed when they complained.

I couldn't imagine having two children at this point in my life. Or raising them on my own. Louise had mentioned an ex-husband who was out of the picture. Thank goodness Tracy had family nearby.

Whenever I thought about having children, I felt overwhelmed. I could never be half as good a parent as Dad. Or even Mom, who showed her love in weird ways. She wasn't the sentimental sort. Love to Mom was cooking lots of food. Teasing me. Nagging me. Mom was un-emotional, even when I went in for surgery. Both times.

Her joking words before they wheeled me into the operating room were, *Make sure they get the right leg.*

When I cried after the second surgery, Mom left the curtained room and let me sob to a nurse, who gave me ice chips and patted my shoulder.

Now I looked at Tracy and I wondered how she did it. She went to school in the evenings and worked at the adult day care during the day. And in between all that, she wiped noses, broke up fights, and put two little boys to bed.

"Are you studying?" I asked.

"Yes. I have a test next week and I swear I don't even know where the digestive tract connects to the stomach."

"I remember that unit."

"With two boys, you'd think I'd already know all about the digestive tract. But the place where the food goes in and out are only a small portion of the system. The body is an amazing, complicated thing."

I lifted my leg onto the chair next to me. "Well, feel free to pick my brain when you study ligament tears."

She sat back. "Oh, we already know plenty about that in our house. Both Edge and Peter tore theirs."

"That explains why you had an ice machine." I thought about Edge's grim expression when he saw my other knee.

"Yup. You name it, we have the equipment. Braces, crutches, ice machines, wheelchairs, blood-pressure cuffs. What do you think gave me the idea to be a nurse? I helped Mom patch injuries and nurse illnesses so often I figured I should get paid for it."

I totally related to a career built on personal experience.

"So, how did the ACL tears and other injuries happen?" I wanted to find out more about Edge.

Tracy leaned forward. "For Peter it was football. He never met a sport he didn't like. But for Edge it was always skiing. The first time my grandfather took him to Boyne Mountain, he went down the bunny hill once and decided he was ready for a black diamond."

"Wow." If I remembered correctly, that was the most difficult rating in ski talk.

"Edge was born to ski. Before he was ten he was winning junior downhill ski races throughout the state. By the time he was seventeen he was competing in the junior nationals in Colorado."

I couldn't imagine laid-back Edge competing in a serious competition. "What happened?" Before she could say anything, I caught myself. "Sorry. You don't have to tell me. It isn't any of my business."

"It's no secret, Lily. Everyone in the skiing community knows what happened." She looked in the living room and lowered her voice. "It feels like it was a long time ago, but I guess it was just that the boys weren't born yet. Edge was training for the Olympics. He was favored to make the final cut. He had an accident."

I felt sick thinking about it. "ACL?"

She shook her head. "Oh no. That happened when he was twenty. No. The accident happened when he flipped over a rough patch at the edge of the course. It took his helmet right off. It was his third concussion."

The thin scar on his temple must be a remnant of the accident. "Was it bad?"

"Far worse than the first two. It was a TBI. Traumatic brain injury. He had to lie in a quiet room for months. No light. No music. No TV. Everything was painful for him. When he finally recovered, the doctor gave him an ultimatum. Keep skiing and risk permanent brain injury. Or stop. It almost killed him. He lost his favorite sport, a lot of his friends, and his fian—well, let's just say some of his relationships fell apart, too."

Something sharp hit me below the solar plexus. I tried to picture Edge, tall and strong as he was now, forced to lie in bed for months. It made me reassess everything I had thought about him. With his oversize flannel shirts and silly sense of humor, he acted like life was one big joke. But it had been dead serious for him not too long ago. Edge had been a world-class athlete. A man with a goal and dream. I remembered the feel of his muscles under my fingertips when he lifted me into the truck. Somewhere hidden under all those layers of clothing was still an athlete's body. Even odder was the thought that buried beneath all the joking was an athlete's drive.

"So, he owns an ice cream parlor now?"

Tracy threw her head back and laughed, earning her the attention of her boys. "What's so funny, Mommy?"

"Just my twisted humor, boys."

They pinched their noses with their fingers and repeated the word *kooties* over and over.

Tracy rolled her eyes at her boys. "I'm sorry. I didn't mean to laugh at your question. It's just that I saw the irony for the first time. Edge left the snow and ice for another kind of ice."

I laced my fingers on the table in front of me. "Did anyone tell you I kind of trashed the Dairy Cow at the meeting?"

"Oh, I heard. Not from Edge. From Mom."

"Your mom probably hates me now."

"Oh gosh, if Mom got mad over little things like that, she would never have friends. She was fine with it. She agrees people might need to make fewer visits to the ice cream parlor and more to the salad bar."

"I don't think Edge is too happy with me. I haven't seen him since the meeting."

"It wouldn't hurt to see him get involved in this whole fitness challenge. He keeps busy coaching kids over at Boyne during the winter. And he substitutes for the gym teacher at the elementary school. He made a lot of money on endorsements and he invested well. It would be hypocritical of him not to care about physical fitness."

I was surprised. I assumed he only drove garbage trucks and scooped ice cream. Thinking of Edge around kids, though, seemed to fit. He had a way with his nephews. They laughed at everything he did, but they also snapped to attention when he gave orders.

I left Tracy to her studying and made my way downstairs to watch the NCAA finals by myself in the Callahans' recreation room. During the entire game, my brother texted me how great his team was. When his team won, he sent a picture of himself wearing a CHAMPION hat from courtside while the team cut the net!

I kept hoping that Edge would wander in so I could talk about what happened at the meeting. But he never appeared.

LESSON SIX

Start Slowly

Monday morning, I was greeted in the driveway by a late model Chevrolet pickup truck. Edge stood by the door, wearing a navy barn jacket that could have come from the fall issue of Esquire. I tried not to let him see how happy I was that he was still willing to talk to me.

"Where is the teddy truck?"

"Uncle Pete's back is better. This is mine."

I wasn't much of a car person. But even I could tell that the red truck with shiny chrome was high-end.

"You look surprised."

"As a matter of fact, yes." Not only because he was talking to me, but also because he didn't own a run-down beater with fuzzy dice hanging off the rearview mirror.

He held open the door. "Are you pleased?"

"Immensely." Not only could I get in by myself, but I might be able to apologize now.

Once out of the driveway, Edge gunned all eight cylinders. I clutched the seat to keep from falling toward his lap on a curve.

"Edge, I want to talk about what happened the other day—"

Without warning, music blasted from the impressive stereo system. Honestly, did the man ever drive in silence? This time the strains of Jimi Hendrix playing "Voodoo Child" shook the truck.

"Edge? Can we talk?" I shouted.

He bobbed his head up and down, and I was semi-sure one of the bobs was a yes to my question, so I kept talking.

"I'm sorry for mentioning the Dairy Cow the other night."

He stared straight ahead, his bearded chin still keeping beat.

"It was just the first thing that came to my mind."

We had reached the county road. As if I hadn't just apologized, he raised a finger in the air. "Wait for this part of the song. You're gonna love it."

I put my elbow against the window. "I know, I know, the guitar solo."

His head turned sharply. "Hey, you like Jimi?"

"Of course! Delta blues and rock and roll." My throat was getting sore from shouting.

We stopped at a four-way stoplight, apparently the only traffic device in Truhart. The guitar riff was almost over.

Edge stared at me with his mouth open as Jimi wailed on the wah pedal.

"Don't look at me that way. I *do* like music." Just not at this decibel.

He turned down the speaker with the button on his steering wheel. "But you know Jimi."

I smiled. It was always nice to impress men with my knowledge of music. "I know rock and roll."

Besides having brothers who blasted their stereos when Mom and Dad were gone, I had played bass guitar in a teen garage band. We were awful. But we had a lot of fun. I quit the summer before my junior year to concentrate on soccer. I rubbed my other knee, remembering how that went down.

The look he gave me could have steamed up the inside of the truck. "There is absolutely nothing sexier than a girl who likes rock and roll."

"Certainly not a guy who plays air drum on the steering wheel."

He laughed. It was a good sign.

"So am I back in your good graces?" I asked.

He put his foot on the accelerator. "Knowing about Jimi helps your redemption."

For the rest of the trip, Edge and I shared our favorite songs and laughed about the lyrics we still didn't understand. By the time we arrived at the gym, I felt a million pounds lighter. I opened the car door by myself and stepped out with no help.

Edge waited by the door, probably ready to catch me if I fell, and handed me my crutch and my gym bag.

"Have a great day, Lily." He looked down at me with a twinkle in his eye, and I couldn't help wishing for another arm-wrestling competition.

"Thanks for the ride." I put the key in the lock and opened the door to the gym.

"No problem," he said, as I stepped through the doorway.

I was about to turn around and tell him to have a great day, too, when I was attacked by a shower of black and white latex.

"What the—?" Dozens of balloons fell from the ceiling, blocking my vision and my path. They bounced over each other and across the floor of the gym. I swatted them away with my crutch and wondered who had done such a thing.

I picked up one of the balloons and looked at the picture printed on the front. It was a cow with ice cream cones under its udders. Big bold letters across the top said DAIRY COW.

I turned around to see Edge leaning against his truck. His lips were curled in a huge grin and he waved. "Happy April Fools' Day, Lily!"

When Edge picked me up in the afternoon, instead of getting angry, I made him take me to the grocery store.

"Are you punishing me for this morning?"

"Yes, I'm getting even," I told him. "It took me fifteen minutes to pop all those the balloons." And even then, I was still finding stray balloons in the corners of the gym.

I made Edge push the cart up and down the aisles of the Family Fare while I grabbed what I needed for the nutrition class. I had asked my mother to mail me my NutriBullet blender and a box of my protein packets. My plan was to show everyone how tasty a morning breakfast smoothie could be, as well as create a few meal substitutions that would help lose the inches.

"Just don't make me go down the hippie aisle again," Edge moaned while I wandered the fruit and vegetable department. The Family Fare had a very small organic food section. Edge had acted like a child being forced to eat spinach when I dragged him down that aisle.

"Lots of people shop the organic section." I placed a bunch of bananas in the cart.

"Only if they want to eat grass seeds and mulch."

"You can say what you want, but it beats chicken nuggets and cheeze puffs."

"My grandma eats that stuff and she is doing fine."

I didn't comment on the "fine" part, but I did point out, "In Ivy's day, organic food WAS food. It was unprocessed and straight from the farm."

He stuck his tongue out when I added broccoli to the cart.

"Can you reach that zucchini, there? The one that doesn't have spots on it," I said.

"Grocery shopping with you could be a fitness challenge all its own." Edge stretched his long arm to the far corner of the bin.

"Poor, weak Edgar. This morning I should have asked the guy with all the muscles to help me instead."

He handed me the zucchini and narrowed his eyes. "Who?"

"I can't remember his name. He was in the walking group. He looked like the guy who played Captain America." Actually, he was almost seventy years old. Edge didn't need to know that.

Edge opened his coat. "My shirt is practically ripping from these muscles. See?"

I didn't have to look. I had already felt those muscles just fine. I knew the contour and the firmness. It made my heart skip in circles just thinking about it. It almost made me wish for the teddy bear truck so he could help me in and out again.

I pursed my lips and clucked. "Are you sure your winter weight didn't creep up on you recently?"

He grabbed my hand and placed it inside his coat on his bicep. I ran my hand up and down his arm, pretending I felt nothing. "Hmmm, I'm trying to find the bicep."

He stepped closer. I tore my eyes away from his impressive muscles and tilted my head to look up at him. I studied his face, looking for signs of a weak chin or bad lips that might be the reason for his facial hair. There had to be a flaw.

"Feel them yet?" he asked. He held up his other arm for me to touch. His nostrils flared when I ran my hands up along his shoulders.

Just then, Marva O'Shea came around the corner. She spotted us and shoved a box of cereal in front of her face. "Oops. Sorry, you two. I didn't mean to interrupt."

"No. No. It's nothing."

"Lily was just checking out my size."

Marva lowered the Cheerios slowly.

"I was comparing Edge to the big guy in the walking group this morning . . ."

Marva stared at my hands. "Oh my."

I glanced down and realized I still held the zucchini in my fist.

"His muscles. On his arms!" I said, dropping the zucchini in the cart like a hot potato.

Marva cupped a hand around her mouth and whispered, "Just remember, this is the Family Fare, you two. Family Fare. Not Adult Fare. Get it?"

Edge's shoulders were shaking. "I take it back, I'm having a great time. I definitely owe you. I'll clean up any leftover balloons myself."

When Marva had completely disappeared, Edge picked up the zucchini and examined the size. "Not even close."

For the rest of our shopping trip, Edge made corny jokes about his size. I kept a straight face and told him he had the mind of an adolescent boy. Which of course made him try harder.

By the time we checked out, Edge had moved on to reading the tabloids next to the cashier. He held up the magazine. "Hey, Lily, did you hear this story about a man who woke up with a large—"

I was just about to tell him what to do with the magazine when I was saved by his phone ringing. "Hey, Mom, what's up?"

He placed the tabloid on the conveyer belt and I shoved it back on the rack. I did the same with the candy bar and the bubblegum he put in front of me, as well.

By the time we left the store he was finished with the call. "Mom has to stay late and needs me to pick up Grandma at the day care."

I was still thinking of ways to block his attractiveness from my temporarily wigged-out psycho-sexual drive, when we pulled into the parking lot of a sweet-looking one-story building with a wrap-around porch. A sign with a picture of a giant daisy read LAKEVIEW ADULT DAY CARE.

Edge unhooked my seat belt without asking. "Come on, let's go in."

I pressed back against the seat. "Maybe I should stay here."

"Why?" He stared at me as if I had just told him that I didn't want to visit Santa Claus.

I shrugged and said, "I can sit here and work on my notes while you get Ivy."

I had always had an aversion to nursing homes. Even when I did my mandatory volunteering in college. So many people sitting around with nothing to do but sleep and watch television was depressing.

Edge jumped out and circled around to my door. "Come on."

"Nooo. I really—"

"Are you afraid of a bunch of old people?"

"No. Of course not." I let him help me out of the truck and added, "I think old people are great."

"You do, huh?' he asked as I followed him up the front sidewalk to the porch.

He opened the door and waved me in ahead of him. "Yes. I mean, they are really sweet and nice and—"

"Get the hell out of here and never come back!" A tiny, ancient woman wearing a purple hat with paper flowers on the brim stood just inside the doorway. She pointed her finger at me and continued screaming at the top of her lungs. "Go on!"

"Polly! Come back and finish decorating our bonnets," called a woman from a room that read ARTS AND CRAFTS over the doorway.

Desperately, I looked to Edge for assistance. He stepped around me and smiled. "Good afternoon, Mrs. Fleetwood. Are you making a spring bonnet?"

In a millisecond, her face changed from fierce watchdog to puppy dog. Her dark brown eyes crinkled at the corners and she smiled.

"Do you like my hat?" She put her palms together under her chin and posed.

"I love it! But you missed a spot. See?" He pointed to a bare spot on the hat. She frowned. Putting his arm around her shoulder and guiding her into the other room, he said, "Go on and take the hat over to Bridget and she'll help you finish it."

"Well, okay. If you think I should." Unbelievable. If doctors could bottle Edge's formula for charm it would sell better than Xanax.

I stood against the wall and tried not to move or attract any un-wanted attention. Several people stood at a large desk. A man sat in a chair by the doorway and stared at me. Hopefully Ivy was ready to go.

Edge walked past the desk and waved at a woman in pink scrubs who was talking on the phone. "Hey, Kataya. What's up?"

She waved back and continued talking. He signaled me to follow him into a larger room around the corner. With lead in my feet and crutch, I shuffled across the hallway and paused at the doorway. The living room contained a large television on the wall, several couches and chairs, and plenty of room in between for walkers and wheelchairs to navigate.

"Come on," Edge said, beckoning me farther into the room. He kept his voice low. "It's the middle of the afternoon, so a few campers are still napping."

I followed at a snail's pace, hoping Ivy would appear quickly. I tried not to crinkle my nose. Several air fresheners were strategically placed around the room. Two men slept on the couches, their mouths hanging open, glasses askew. One even snored. Two ladies were politely watching what appeared to be an old movie on VHS. Humphrey Bogart was explaining to a small man with dark hair why he was wrong for the girl.

One of the ladies saw Edge and clapped her hands.

He bent down and gave her a hug. "Hello, Mrs. Overton. How's my favorite first grade teacher doing?" Then he stepped back and tilted his head. "What a pretty sweater you have on today."

She ran her hands up and down the nubby cardigan and preened under Edge's attention.

Two other ladies who had been in the arts and crafts room heard the commotion of our arrival and came in. They showed off their finished bonnets and clamored for Edge's praise.

Edge pointed my way. "This is Lily, everyone."

I leaned against a wall and waved.

"Anything happening in the world, Mr. Green?" he asked a man in a chair.

"Nothing today," came the reply from the man, a folded newspaper in his lap. He lifted the paper back to his face but kept an eye on Edge over the top.

Instead of assessing the people in the room for fitness, I was overwhelmed with a sense of futility at their inevitable decline. It was amazing that Edge remained so positive.

The sleepers woke, and instead of being angry about the noise, their faces lit up when they saw Edge. I stepped away from the archway, intrigued by the transformation of energy in the room.

I didn't notice Ivy sitting by the front window until I heard a familiar voice. "Mine."

She had been watching Edge, but after her single-word statement she wheeled her chair around and turned back to the window. Her hands rested on a crocheted throw blanket in her lap and she studied the county road outside.

A car passed and Ivy waved her finger in the air. "Not."

She did it again. "Not."

I couldn't figure out what she was focused on. The road? The cars? Another life?

Edge made his way to Ivy. "Hi, Grandma. How was your day?"

She pointed to a silver sedan passing outside the window and said, "Mine."

"No, Grandma. That's not your car. Sarah is driving it to school these days. Remember?"

She slouched down in her chair, the only person Edge couldn't seem to perk up today.

Edge pointed at me. "Look, Grandma. I brought Lily with me to pick you up today. What do you think of that?"

Slowly she turned her head toward me. "Now?"

"Yup. We're going to take you home now."

She cast him a glance that told him he wasn't getting it. Edge lost his smile for a brief moment. I wondered what Ivy was like before her stroke. And her husband? If they had lived across the street, Edge must have been close to his grandparents.

Louise entered and handed Ivy's coat to Edge. "Hi, honey. Thanks for taking Grandma home. I have two tours scheduled for later and I'm going to be late tonight. We can switch cars to make it easier for you."

"No problem."

"Tracy says she has dinner covered." She returned to the hallway.

"Ready, Grandma?"

Ivy backed her wheelchair up and let Edge help with her coat. He was gentle as he navigated her arms through each sleeve. Then he adjusted the blanket in her lap.

"Ready?"

Edge said his goodbyes. Smiles faded. The room deflated almost as quickly as the balloons I had popped this morning. I was struck with the strange desire to get more balloons and let them loose in the day care.

I followed, waving awkwardly. Just as we reached the door, the ancient man who had been sitting in the front hallway grabbed my arm, knocking me off balance.

Edge steadied me, keeping his other hand on Ivy's wheelchair. "Hi, Mr. Frasier. I didn't see you earlier. Don't you want to join everyone in the other room?"

Instead of responding, the man squeezed my arm with frail strength, keeping me in place. He smelled faintly sour. His clothes had stains from the last few meals he had eaten. And his hair had the flakiness that came from not being washed.

"We're out the door for the day, Mr. Frasier. Ivy is going home," Edge said in a cheerful voice, trying to remove his hand without looking rude.

The man ignored Edge and stared at me with wide, unblinking blue eyes. "Don't forget."

"I'm sorry?" I looked to Edge for some explanation. But he shook his head and helped shift Mr. Frasier out of the way so he could hit the handicap button I hadn't seen. The door opened automatically.

"Don't forget about me."

His fearful plea terrified me. Should we go find an aide to help him?

"See you later, Mr. Frasier," said Edge as if nothing unusual had happened. We moved to the porch and down the ramp toward the parking lot. I looked back. The older man stood in the window by the door. I waved. He scowled and did nothing.

While Edge loaded Ivy's wheelchair into the automatic lift on the minivan, I climbed in the passenger seat. I kept thinking about Mr. Frasier's words as Edge secured Ivy and the wheelchair.

Edge climbed into the driver's seat. "You okay?" he asked, studying my face.

"Did Mr. Frasier confuse me with someone else?"

He turned the radio on low and shifted out of the parking lot. "Don't worry about him. He says that almost every day. He sits by the doorway and hardly ever moves."

"Why?"

He shrugged. "Used to be in the VA home downstate in Ypsilanti. But his younger brother is here and wanted to keep him close."

I considered that. "So no one actually forgot about him or anything."

"No. But his brother is getting up there. Says he isn't sure how much longer he can keep him."

"But he can go back to the VA home if needed, right?"

"Have you been to a VA home, Lily?"

I shook my head.

He searched for his favorite station on the radio. "Neither has anyone else. Forgotten. Every last one of them."

LESSON SEVEN

Address Real World Issues

On Tuesday, Marva O'Shea arrived at the first fitness class wearing leg warmers and a headband.

"You look like you've been sweating to the oldies," laughed a young redhead.

Marva adjusted her spandex shirt, which kept riding up her stomach. "I'll have you know I used to do the Jane Fonda workout every single week. I was skinny in the old days."

"You and Santa over there," a lady said, pointing to the fireplace. Several young women laughed and Marva turned red.

"And what's wrong with Richard Simmons, June?" asked Corinne, blocking Marva's embarrassed face.

A man with a sleeveless shirt that exposed more hair than was on his head groaned. "Is this a girls' class? If so, I'm outta here."

Before anyone broke into a fight, I interjected myself. "The one thing about working out is that there is something for everyone of every age. A lot of people love music classes. Zumba is really popular. Others like the practice of yoga. And men often prefer weight lifting and strength training."

"Yeah. I wanna get a six-pack," said a man in an oversize Detroit Red Wings jersey.

"Me too," said the man in the sleeveless shirt. "We can swing by the Family Fare for some Budweisers after this."

I gave them a moment to laugh at their joke, then started the portable speaker I borrowed from Regina. Fortunately, Elizabeth

Lively had some experience with yoga, and she caught on quickly with the other moves. She stood up front while I shouted instructions. The music shifted from light to energetic, and eventually to slow and soft for a cooldown. The floor was hard, and the abilities in the room varied. I wouldn't let everyone do a plank pose or a down dog until I was confident they wouldn't hurt themselves. Unfortunately, anytime someone spread their arms or lost their balance, which was often, the person beside them was smacked or kicked. I changed tactics and called out as many static exercises as possible so no one would be black-and-blue the next day.

After we ended with some cooldown stretches, I announced, "Next time you come, I have a list of items I want you to bring."

"How about boxing gloves?" said Corinne, rubbing the side of her head. She had been hit by Marva at least a dozen times.

I read the list. "Any old soccer- or volleyballs you might have at home and aren't going to use. An old blanket, towel, or even a rubber bath mat—"

I had been having trouble figuring out how to improvise exercise bands. But when I saw Addie Adler adjusting her garters after knee lifts, a lightbulb went off above my head. "Panty hose or tights. Umm . . . wash them first."

A man balked. "I am not going to let my buddies see me wearing no panty hose."

"I promise I won't make you wear them. If you feel better with another option, you can bring the rubber inner tube from an old tire or a rubber appliance belt instead."

When I finished my last item, Elizabeth raised her eyebrows. "Two fifteen-ounce cans of tomatoes? Lily, are you sure you aren't confusing us with the nutrition class?"

"We can always turn it into one if we bring some beans and onions, too," added Corinne.

I set them straight. "The cans of tomatoes are going to become your hand weights."

"I'm hungry!" one of the men in back announced.

Marva pointed to the corkboard by the front door, where free advertisements were posted. "When the Dairy Cow opens, there's a free miniature golf deal with the purchase of a Truhart Temptation Sundae."

A half dozen people wandered over to the board.

"Just remember, your goal is a healthier you. You just did something good for your body. Don't let the craving for sugar ruin your motivation. Even one scoop of ice cream will set you back."

When the last person left, I marched on my three legs over to the board and yanked off the flyer for the Dairy Cow. I couldn't believe Edge would post this in the gym. He knew what we were trying to do and yet he purposely placed the flyer right in the middle of the board for all to see. My gaze wandered to the other advertisements. A neon orange flyer for the fish fry on Friday was pinned next to a flyer for the pancake breakfast at St. Francis church.

I pulled all the flyers off the corkboard and tore them up. My mission that was becoming more crucial every day.

On Thursday, I held the first nutrition seminar. I showed everyone the modified food pyramid that was really a plate now. The guide that was completely different from the one I had grown up with. It took some convincing to make the class understand how experts had changed their minds about what we eat. I pulled from the grocery bag the food Edge and I had bought and set the items on the coffin, the only table I had at my disposal. Then I described the healthy substitutions that could be made for potato chips and white bread.

"What the heck is that stuff again?" a short man with a long white beard asked, pointing to the box at the end.

"Quinoa." I said.

"Is it Hawaiian or something?"

I shook my head. "Actually, it originated in South America."

"I would rather have a Taco Bell."

I was getting used to the humor in Truhart. "Keep in mind that it is a very healthy substitution for rice and bread. It contains essential amino acids and even has some level of calcium, phosphorus, and iron. Even better, it is high in protein. You can use it in your salad, as a rice substitute, and even on top of hot soup."

"I like oyster crackers in my soup."

I kept my smile planted on my face even though I wanted to scream. I thought the nutrition classes would be the easiest for me. My limited mobility wouldn't be a factor. And it didn't take too much change to make a difference in a person's weight. But it was clear that changing people's food choices was going to be more difficult than I had previously thought.

"Is that all we can eat?" Flo stared at the food I had placed on the table.

"Yeah, did you even go down the cereal aisle?" said one young mom. "That's what my kids eat for breakfast and a snack."

Another woman with five kids spoke up. "This is all fine and nice, but there's no gourmet chef at home. We eat out a lot. None of these ingredients are on the menu at Lori's or the Gas 'N' Go Café."

I quieted the room before it became a giant whine-fest. "You can still make good choices. Take the bun off the burger, order a baked potato instead of fries."

"Maybe I'll just stick with beer," Joe O'Shea, Marva's husband, joked.

I had been meaning to talk about alcohol. "Try to limit your alcohol to one drink. And if possible, don't eat or drink alcohol after seven p.m."

"Pacific Standard Time?" Joe asked, nudging his friends.

"I can't get excited over this stuff," Flo said, pointing to a bag of apples.

I sighed. "Okay, this may not look like your groceries this week, or even next week. But who is willing to make some simple changes for one or two meals? Pick the meal you care least about and make it healthy."

Heads nodded slowly.

"Breakfast changers, raise your hands." A half dozen hands went up. I handed them some of the fruit I had bought.

"Eat an egg and a slice of cantaloupe. Skip the juice. Limit the creamer in your coffee. For those who are interested in trying a breakfast smoothie, I will send a recipe."

"I'm not drinking a green milkshake," Flo said.

I handed her a bag of lettuce. "Then consider a salad for lunch. Put quinoa or grilled chicken or a boiled egg on it with as many vegetables as you want. Even pumpkin seeds are good in a salad. Top it with a light dressing or a balsamic and oil mixture."

"I'll be hungry within an hour," one of the men said.

"That is why protein is so important. It will keep your hunger at bay," I promised.

I pointed to a picture of a flank steak. "For dinner, think lean meats and vegetables. Potatoes are all right, but no fries, and hold the sour cream."

"Can I have two potatoes with butter?"

I ignored his question. "Finally, eight glasses of water a day, folks. Water is a perfect weapon for fighting off the hunger monster that battles inside you. Try it for a week and see how much better you feel. I promise you will have more energy and you will stop craving sweets after just a few days."

I was going to email my recipes for smoothies, soups, and main courses that would help everyone who took on the challenge.

Elizabeth Lively waited until the last person left before planting herself in front of me. "Are you doing all right?"

I sat down on a folding chair. "Honestly, I am exhausted and it's barely noon."

She patted my shoulder. "Hang in there. Just give it time. Baby steps. Think of it as a marathon, not a race."

If only I could. But that felt like a cop-out. I wanted to attack with strong, clear tactics. Not wait around for people to "think" about making changes.

"Let's go to Cookee's. You can talk to Mac about healthy eating. You'll make his day."

I could only imagine how that was going to play out. But Elizabeth was excited and I was hungry.

I pulled a poster out of my bag. "Can we put a poster up if we go?"

She reached for it. "I'll carry it!"

The cold wind hit us as we left the community center. Yesterday's snow was starting to melt. Elizabeth walked slowly so I could focus on keeping my crutch from skating on icy patches. We passed the bookstore and a Laundromat. A bakery was closed and had a FOR SALE sign in the window. At least there would be no freshly baked breads to tempt my clients. I gazed across the field and saw the ice cream parlor. The weather had grown colder since Monday morning. But the melting snow meant "scooping days" were sure to be back soon.

I vowed to redouble my efforts when the weather heated up.

The tinny sound of a bell on the door rang as we entered the restaurant.

Several customers in the lunch crowd called out when they saw us. I had to grin at the ambience. The diner belonged in a 1950s television show. At the counter were vinyl-covered stools that spun around, and booths lined the front where a long window looked out over Main Street. The Hamilton Beach milkshake machine made even me think about a tall cold one.

Even more retro looking was the cook behind the counter.

Elizabeth introduced me to Mac. He was a large man with a white apron and no hair. "I met you at the meeting."

I was prepared for more jokes about healthy food and was surprised when we had an engaging conversation about the healthy options Mac had added to the menu since last fall. My flagging spirits rose as I listened to him. If he was cooking vegetarian and vegan dishes, someone in town was eating them.

Elizabeth held up the poster and called across the diner. "Can we put this up somewhere, Corinne?"

"She owns the place," Mac explained to me. Mac turned his head sideways to read it. "Truly Fit for Truhart—Fitness Classes, Nutrition Counseling, Walking Groups."

Corinne joined us. Her thin lips turned into a big smile. "Oh, Lily, that poster looks great."

She pointed where we could put the poster on the front window. "Just put it over there with the rest of the posters. Feel free to take down any of those old notices. I always forget to do that."

While Elizabeth talked to Corinne, I took the poster and moved to the cork board. A large sign read PETE'S TREATS GRAND OPENING— APRIL 8 AT THE DAIRY COW.

Before anyone noticed, I slapped my poster on top of it. My immature retaliation for his posters at the gym.

Feeling only slightly guilty, I returned to where Elizabeth was sitting.

Corinne appeared at our elbows with a menu. She handed one to me and asked Elizabeth, "Usual for you, honey?"

Elizabeth's cheeks turned bright red. "You know, Corinne, I think I'll change things up for now. What's the soup today?"

"Clam chowder and, on special, Mac's s split pea. No ham. Just spinach and all the other things he tosses in."

"That sounds perfect," Elizabeth said, squirming in her seat. She ran a hand around the scarf at her neck. "With a glass of water, too."

"I'll have the same," I said.

"Suit yourself," Corinne said with a crooked smile at Elizabeth.

Corinne held her hand out for the menu and I asked, "Do you mind if I take a quick look at the menu?"

"What do you want to do that for?" Corinne asked.

"I want to make a list of some of the healthier items on the menu. It might help as we discuss nutrition."

Corinne's eyes gleamed. "Oh, Mac will love that. You have a lot of work cut out for you, Lily. We still serve Froot Loops and milk-shakes for breakfast, lunch, and dinner around here." She slapped Elizabeth's back. Elizabeth ran a hand across her face.

The bell above the door announced another customer. Elizabeth seemed grateful for the distraction. I looked over my shoulder and my gaze was met by a laughing set of gray eyes.

"Hey look, Grandma, Aunt Addie. It's Lily and Elizabeth."

Edge pushed Ivy's wheelchair our way and was followed by Aunt Addie. People greeted him on his way past each booth as if he were a celebrity.

When they paused next to us, Addie reached down and gave me a great big hug. For a moment I couldn't breathe. Not just because she was holding me so tight, but because my mouth and nose were smothered somewhere in her chest . . . or maybe it was her stomach. They all seemed to go together on Addie.

"How wonderful to see you two together," Edge said with a twinkle in his eye. "You have so much in common with your taste in food and all . . ."

Elizabeth waved him away. "Ignore him, Lily. He's always got a joke."

Again, that funny red rash swept up her face.

Edge slapped Elizabeth on the back and said, "Mom is at some meeting in Gaylord, so I stopped in to Lakeview and picked up Grandma. Aunt Addie decided to join us. If we get too loud for you ladies, just tell Corinne to cut us off. Coffee does that to me some-times."

Addie patted Ivy's arm. "I always have lots to catch up on with my big sister."

Ivy hadn't taken her eyes from me since she walked in the diner. "Good . . . now."

"Grandma hates the food at Lakeview and I promised her I'd spring her whenever Mom was away."

They moved to the booth behind us, where they could wheel Ivy up to the table without blocking the aisle. Over Elizabeth's shoulder I could see Edge clearly. He kept the conversation up with an exaggerated tone and grand gestures with his hands. Addie laughed incessantly. And Ivy giggled a time or two.

The whole thing was rather charming until they ordered. "Two bacon double cheeseburgers with large fries and onion rings for Aunt Addie and me, Corinne. And a clam chowder, macaroni and double the cheese for Grandma. Oh . . . and a chocolate milkshake for each of us. Large."

Addie turned and her eyes fluttered my way. "Maybe I shouldn't have the burger, after all."

"What? You love that! Come on. It's almost the weekend," said Edge.

"Well . . . I guess this will be my way to celebrate the last hurrah before I get down to the business of eating healthy."

The daylight was fading when Edge picked me up from the community center later. Nirvana was raging with "Smells Like Teen Spirit" and Edge was keeping the beat with spastic head banging, as usual.

We passed a snowplow clearing the slush to the other side of the road. The day had grown warm. That meant that soon the walkers wouldn't have to worry about winter boots and ski pants.

"Edge, turn it down."

"What?"

"Turn down the music just a bit."

He lowered the volume.

"Do you ever have a serious conversation?"

"Why would I do that?"

I took a deep, calming breath. I was ready to get Truhart eating better. Starting now.

"I want to talk to you about what happened at the diner."

"I'm sorry," he said without taking his eyes off the road. "I know I shouldn't make you keep secrets from my mother. She has this thing about Grandma interacting with the other day care campers. But Grandma hates the food at Lakeview, and truth be told, she isn't much of a social person. I just like to get her out sometimes. Besides, it was with Addie. She used to love being around her little sister."

"That isn't what I want to talk about."

"It's not?"

"No. I want to talk about what you ordered for lunch."

"What I—" He scratched his head. "My hamburger was really good. You should have ordered one."

"No, I'm talking about the food you ordered for your great-aunt and grandmother."

"Ha. Aunt Addie finished before I was halfway done."

"And that was a good thing?"

"Wait a minute . . ." He sent me a sidelong glance. "Are we talking about the whole nutrition thing?"

"Yes."

His brows drew together. "Oh, come on. They're old. They haven't got that much time to enjoy the good things in life."

"So are you trying to hurry them to the other side?"

"That's ridiculous."

"It sure looked like you were rushing them there, the way you were encouraging them to eat. You should be more conscientious with Addie and Ivy. Every bite of junk they take is like subtracting minutes from their lives."

We slowed down as we came upon a road crew filling potholes. Edge's lips clamped shut and he steered around several men who were shoveling up steaming piles of asphalt from the back of a truck. He concentrated so hard on getting around the blockage that I could tell he was mad.

"I am not trying to criticize you. I know you love them very much and you wouldn't want to hurt them. But it isn't in their best interest to eat food that is high in sodium and fat and low in nutrients their bodies need."

We were around the road crew and back on the open road. Edge's foot was heavy on the accelerator.

"Your great-aunt is quite heavy, as I am sure you already know. At her age all that weight takes its toll on her joints, not to mention her arteries and heart. And your grandmother is sedentary in that wheelchair. The worry for her is that her digestive system needs fiber and food rich in probiotics to keep things running smoothly. These are real issues for people their age."

We turned down the lake road. The evening sun was low on the horizon. The light inside the pickup truck flickered as the sun peeked through the trees. Edge's face looked like a strobe light was bombarding it. I waited for his expression to change at each bright flash. But it remained the same. Rigid.

"Don't be angry. I just wanted to point things out."

Edge waited until we had pulled into the Callahans' driveway. He shifted into park and turned to face me. "You know something? When the Triple C's hired you as a fitness trainer, I thought it wasn't a bad idea in theory. There are lots of people in this town who want to get in shape and live a healthier lifestyle. Great for them. But here is the problem I had with the idea. Not everyone wants to eat rabbit food and train for the Ironman—"

"I hardly think that a little exercise is the same as training for the Ironman."

He cut the engine and pulled his keys from the ignition. "You missed my point." He jumped out of the car and walked around to open my door.

I leaned back in the seat, refusing to budge until this was resolved. "Don't stop there. Explain what you mean."

"What I mean is just what I said. Not everyone wants to follow your workout and fitness routine. Don't guilt the rest of the town."

"I'm not guilting anyone. Just stating my concerns," I said.

"Thanks, but no thanks. I am comfortable with my lifestyle. Grandma is comfortable with her lifestyle." His eyes were dark in the dim light. He held out his hand to help me out, but I could do this alone. I pulled my crutch out of the car and stepped down.

"Thanks, but no thanks." I threw his own words back at him. They floated like a giant wedge in the air between us.

Edge's frustration came out as a growl. He watched me with a stony face as I stepped down from the truck. When I was on the ground and steady on my three feet, I shuffled past him.

As I reached the door I turned to him. I wasn't finished. "Just because you aren't training for the Olympics doesn't mean you have to give up on fitness."

Edge's face turned to stone. "You heard about that? Which sister told you—wait, never mind. I don't care."

He reached around me to open the door to the house before I could get to it. It bothered me that I still needed his help. "Just because my knee is in this brace doesn't mean I'm a weakling."

"I'm just using the manners my mama taught me. But if you want me to stop, then, hey." He closed the door in my face.

I grabbed the knob and yanked the door open. When I stepped inside I turned around, surprised to see that he wasn't there. He was already down the driveway, stomping back to his truck.

Of all the people I had met so far, Edge was the last one I ever thought I would alienate. Drivers stopped on the road to wave to him. Diners greeted him in Cookee's as if he were a local celebrity. Even the seniors at Lakeview acted twenty years younger when they saw him. I was probably the first person in years who had pissed him off.

Leave it to me to anger the most popular man in town.

LESSON EIGHT

Make It Fun

Sunday morning, Ivy frowned at her plate of cold eggs while I finished the last of my coffee. When I had tipped the pot upside down to get out the very last drop, Louise asked if I wanted her to make more. I declined, not telling her that I hadn't slept well. Not since Edge and I had our disagreement. He had missed the family dinner for the last three nights. I was sure he was furious at me. I debated apologizing. But why? Everything I'd said was true. He was acting like a child.

Louise read the newspaper at the end of the table. It was one of the first times I had seen her relaxing. The digital clock in the kitchen read 9:26. Two minutes later than the last time I checked.

Without looking up, Louise said, "You waiting for something to happen, Lily? If you are wondering when the girls will get up, I gave up on Sunday mornings a long time ago. Thank goodness for Saturday afternoon church services. "

I remember the days when I wanted nothing more than to sleep forever. But there was always something to do. A soccer game to go to. An extra practice for the week. A test to study for in college. I rarely slept past eight o'clock, even when I was a teenager.

"And Edge?" When I hadn't been staring at the clock, I had been staring out the window looking for signs of Edge.

She raised an eyebrow at me over the top of the newspaper. "Cranky as anything when I try to wake him up before he's ready."

"Oh." I looked down at my coffee, shrugging off any interest.

"But he is usually up by eight on the weekends."

My eyes strayed to the picture window. I made a lame excuse for asking about Edge. "I need to figure out my schedule for the week. I am not sure Edge will be able to drive me for the early classes."

Ivy said, "I can. Do."

"Mom, you can't drive. We've already talked about that dozens of times," Louise said, finally looking up from the paper.

"Can!"

Louise reached across and gently touched her mother's hand. "Ma. Your reflexes aren't what they used to be. Driving a car would be way too dangerous. Remember that's what Dr. Manning said."

Ivy slapped her fork on her eggs. Louise stood up and took the plate from her. "You do a good job driving the wheelchair, though. A really good job."

Ivy grunted and backed away from the table, knocking into one of the dogs at her feet. He yipped and jumped out of the way.

"Are you sure you don't want more to eat?" Louise asked from the kitchen.

I got up from the table and limped into the kitchen with my coffee mug. "I'm sorry I'm such a bother."

"Honey, I have two teenage daughters who, when they aren't sleeping, are fighting. A disabled mother who thinks she can drive herself around town, and two grandsons who won't stop with the potty talk. Having someone sane to talk to in this house is an absolute godsend."

"You have Edge."

"And Tracy. But both of them are busy. And even though they are close, they still have to live their own lives."

I leaned down to stack the dishwasher.

Louise swatted me out of the way. "Stop it. You'll fall over."

"I'm moving better and better each day."

"You are, honey." She gave me a hug. "You are doing a great job."

I wasn't expecting the hug. I cleared my throat. Why was I so emotional? I hadn't taken painkillers since I came to Truhart. It must be the long week catching up with me.

"Just go on over there." She nodded toward the house across the road. "You two need to talk about whatever is bothering you."

"How did you—" Was it that obvious? Every hour without clearing up our disagreement was driving me crazy. Edge had been the first person to help me since I arrived in town. I should apologize. This new division between us was awful.

"Go on, Lily. The ice on the driveway has melted. And it's almost forty degrees this morning. Downright tropical for April in Northern Michigan!"

I put my finger in the air and giggled. "Forty degrees! I'll have my mom send my bikini soon."

She tilted her head. "You have a nice laugh, Lily. I hope I see you do it more often while you are here."

I didn't understand why Louise thought my laugh was so great. I had a raspy, deep voice that transformed into a hoarse kind of laugh. But when I giggled, the sound was light and airy. Kind of funny if you had never heard it before.

I used to laugh all the time.

My father called me "gigglegirl" when I was younger. My brothers preferred the alternate name, "jigglegirl," because my tummy shook whenever I erupted into hysterical fits of unstoppable laughter.

My abs were tight now. And my laugh was a little rusty. I tucked it away and decided to go in search of Edge. He might refuse to talk to me. Or he might take another bite out of me for interfering. But I had to find out. At the very least I would know where I stood with him.

I walked carefully down the sloped pavement and across the street. Louise was right. Forty degrees felt balmy after the last few days of frigid temperatures. My North Face fleece was all I needed. From the base of the driveway I had my first clear view of the ranch house and the lake that was partially blocked by evergreens. I had learned from Louise that the lake was named Reply Lake. A sister lake to the one that sat at the end of Main Street.

The redbrick ranch trimmed with white lattice work was quite charming. Empty window boxes promised flowers in summer. Lumps that were either boxwood or azaleas covered in burlap bordered the front door. To my right, the driveway dipped down to an attached two-car garage. Edge's pickup truck was parked next to a pile of two-by-fours and crates. The garage was open and a buzz of machinery erupted from within.

Edge was definitely awake.

I headed toward the noise and stopped just inside the garage. Edge guided a long piece of wood across the blade, splitting it down the middle. With his attention focused on the wood, I stopped to enjoy the view. He was wearing clear goggles over his eyes and a backward baseball cap. His long-sleeved T-shirt was torn at the hem and looked like something he might have worn in high school. For once Edge looked serious. He let go of the handle of the table saw and cut the motor. Then he lifted the piece of wood and ran a hand up and down it, as if he wasn't sure if he had accomplished his task to his satisfaction. It must have been acceptable because he set it against the wall and pulled another piece of wood from nearby and started whistling.

"What are you making?"

"Wha—oh, hey!" he said, lifting his safety glasses. He placed the wood against the wall and turned to me. "Do you need a ride somewhere?"

"No. No. I'm just coming to talk. I mean I wanted to . . . Your mom told me it would be all right to stop in."

He slapped his palms together to remove the sawdust. "Be careful where you step."

The floor of the garage was covered in sawdust and tiny pieces of wood. "What are you building?"

"Everything."

I strained my neck to see inside the open door that led into the house. "Inside?"

"Yep. Feel free to take a look. It's a bit of a mess." We had just said more than a dozen words to each other and he didn't sound mad. It was a good sign.

With new optimism, I walked to the door and peered in. The room had been gutted down to the studs. New drywall still showed seams and the floor was covered in plywood. There was no molding on the windows or doors. Even so, the main room was inviting, with a large window and an open floor plan to the kitchen.

"You live here?"

"Where did you think I lived? At the Dairy Cow?" The sarcasm was back.

I shrunk against the door frame as he walked by with the wood he had just cut.

"I guess I didn't realize you were renovating." I had imagined him living among dirty laundry and empty carryout containers. The new image of Edge working, instead of lying around on the couch watching sports, was unsettling.

"This is what I do when I'm not stuffing my grandmother and the rest of the town full of sweets. Oh, and for the record, I bought this house from my grandmother free and clear. I'm not trying to poison her so I can inherit the place."

I closed my eyes and wished I had used different words the other day. "I know you're still a little mad at me right now."

He placed the wood against the window and pulled a pencil from behind his ear. I had offered him an olive branch and he still ignored me. He was not only still hurt, but surprisingly stubborn.

He made a mark on the wood and I decided to change tactics. "This renovation is going to be really nice."

I meant it. Unlike the outside, with its traditional brick and paned windows, the inside was more modern, with a wide-open view to the lake. The room had a brick fireplace at one end and sliding glass doors led out to a deck still covered in snow. The large living area opened directly into a kitchen that was as light as the living area because the long wall of large windows continued. Newly installed maple cabinets and a double-door refrigerator sat against the opposite wall. A large island was covered in plywood.

Edge saw my curiosity. "The granite counter isn't ready yet."

Maybe it was best to keep the conversation neutral. I asked more about the remodel, genuinely interested. "What was this like before you moved in?"

He shrugged. "Dark paneling, and lots of small rooms. I opened it up."

"Has Ivy seen what you've done with her house so far?"

"I brought her by last week. She loves it."

He walked back into the garage and adjusted the table saw. I followed, hoping for an opening in the conversation. "I think we should ta—"

The table saw started and my words were drowned out.

I waited until he finished. "I didn't mean to be ru—"

The table saw started again.

He did that on purpose.

I moved until I was standing right in front of him. He couldn't miss me this time because I stood between him and the wall where he was going to need another piece of wood.

Edge stopped the saw and pulled his safety glasses up on top of his head. "Do you mind?"

"I will move after you let me speak."

He shifted on one hip and looked up at the garage ceiling. "If you stand there I have to give you safety glasses."

"Do you have another pair? I want to discuss what—"

"Do you talk this much in your fitness classes?"

"I wouldn't have to talk so much if you would just shut up and listen."

He shut off the saw and stepped back. "Fine. Talk. You have my full attention."

I took my weight off my crutch and stood up straight. "I want to tell you that I completely understand how you think my comments about your meal were inappropriate. I shouldn't tell you or anyone else what to do on your own time. But being a fitness coach means that my role here crosses over into the personal. There will be times when I will remind someone how to eat or coax them to get moving and work out. If that makes me a nag, then so be it."

"Did you plan that long-winded speech?" He picked up the wood he had just cut and headed into the house.

I followed him. "Don't you understand?"

He turned abruptly and we were inches apart. "I get it, Coach. But you also need to understand that sometimes life's little pleasures are worth enjoying. We aren't children who need a slap on the hand every time we reach for the cookie jar."

"But what do I do if that cookie jar is offered to one of my clients with the full intention of sabotaging their diet?"

Edge stared at me. He was so close I could see the indentation from the safety goggles in his hair. I clenched my fist rather than reach up to smooth his curls. This strange attraction wasn't fair. The heat of his breath mingled with the scent of the sawdust. I breathed deeply. Enjoying my own guilty pleasure.

His eyes wandered down to my lips and back. "Can I ask you something?"

Edge's abrupt question made me blink. "Okay."

"Do you ever have fun?"

"Of course I have fun!"

"When? When was the last time you had a good time?"

I looked away. "That's a stupid question."

"Just answer it, then."

I liked it the other day when we arm wrestled. No way was I going to bring that up. "I—I have fun."

"What do you do for fun?"

"Just a few months ago I went with my brother to a Lakers game."

"A few months ago? That's the last time you had fun?"

I planted my crutch in front of me so that it stood between us like a sword in the concrete. "For your information, I just laughed inside with your mother."

"You did?"

"I did. She said I made a good joke."

He put a hand on my crutch and pulled it out from between us. "Tell me."

"I—I told her that if the weather was so nice I would get—" I paused. For some reason I didn't want to say it.

"Get what?" He reached his big hand around to the small of my back and pulled me close. "Come on, Lily. Don't lose me. Remember what a punch line is?"

"Of course I know what a punch—" Oh. He was teasing me. "I just said that I would have to have my mom send my bikini."

His face lowered toward mine. "Bikini? Mmm, that *is* fun."

"I just meant that it was warm today. Well, I mean for Michigan it was warm, but not for L.A. It was a jo—"

I never finished my sentence because Edge's lips were pressed against my own. They were irritatingly light and his beard was surprisingly soft. I waited for him to press harder. To part my lips and give me more. But he paused and went no further. Why was he stopping?

I opened my eyes. Edge was looking straight back at me. I could see a fleck of green in his gray eyes. He pulled back and murmured, "Do you want to have real fun, Lily?"

I leaned into him. "Yes." I jumped back. "No! I mean no!"

His face broke into a big grin. "Just as I thought."

"You are twisting this whole conversation."

"I'm just talking about life, Lily Shue. Life and fun. The same thing I was talking about the other day."

Fun? Ridiculous. I made workouts fun for my clients. I played music and encouraged them to move. I enjoyed showing them how to eat healthy. They learned to live a better life. My reward was my fun.

I pulled my crutch out of his hands and shuffled out the door with as much stomping as a woman could do with only one good stomping leg. I could hear Edge laughing as I crossed the street and headed back to the safety of his boyhood room.

LESSON NINE

Support Others

The gym was empty and I was making notes in my journal when I heard the front door open. A familiar-looking young man walked inside. He had dark wavy hair and the awkward shadow of a mustache that comes with adolescence. He was quite overweight.

"Hi," he said, stuffing his hands in the pockets of his baggy jeans.

"Hi! Come on in." Hopefully I didn't sound too eager.

He stepped farther into the gym, looking nervously toward the window as if he was afraid to be seen. I realized where I had seen him before. That first day. He had been the target of the snowballs outside the diner. The one I had tried to save with a teddy bear.

"Miss Shue, I'm Rocky Stone."

"Rocky?" I tried not to smile at his full name.

"Well, my real name is Robert Bock Stone. Everyone just calls me Rocky. Sometimes Big Rock and Mountain. I act like I think the names are funny. But . . ." He paused. I regretted my reaction to his name. More than anyone, I understood the pain of nicknames. Even when they came from people who loved you.

"Nice to meet you, Rocky."

His eyes darted back to the window.

"Let's stand over here," I said, guiding him away toward the back of the room.

When we were away from the window, he pulled his hands out of his pockets and fiddled with a lock of hair that hung low on his face. "I guess you're wondering why I'm here."

I smiled, trying to pretend I had no clue why he was here.

"I really want to join your program. But I don't want the kids at school to think I'm going to fat camp."

"I understand." It's hard to be a teenager, no matter what size you are. "Are there others at school who might be interested in getting fit?"

"No one I know." His voice broke and his eyes grew moist. In the space of a moment I could see all the pain he had been carrying for years. He wiped his eyes. My own grew moist, remembering the gut-wrenching stage of adolescence, when all I wanted was to be like everyone else.

"Rocky, are you teased a lot?"

He nodded. "But I don't know how to do this without them making fun of me worse."

We sat down by the coffin and had a heart-to-heart conversation. After he told me all about his weight gain, I tried to give him reason for optimism. I nudged him with my toe. "You realize how lucky you are, don't you?"

He shook his head. "Why would I be lucky?"

"Teenage boys have it much easier than most people who want to lose weight. Their bodies respond well to exercise and a change in eating habits. It's much harder to be a woman, or even worse, a middle-aged woman when the metabolism slows down."

"You don't look like your metabo—you know, slowed down yet." That was a reality check for me. I guess to him I was a middle-aged lady.

Keeping my face straight, I said, "I have to work really hard. But it's worth it."

We spent the next half hour talking about simple things he could change in the next week. Walking after school. Changing out the after-school snacks for fruit. He promised to come back and share his experience. And I gave him my phone number to text me whenever he needed. It was our secret for now.

After he left I reached back in time to remember the way I felt when I was a chunky adolescent. Funny how that self-image could stick with a person their whole life. Even now that I was physically fit and a size six, I still sometimes felt like that insecure, chubby little girl, especially when I was with my family. It would have been so much easier had there been a sister or friend going through the same struggles. Or a grownup who could help me navigate the difficult road.

I made a note to find a program for teenagers that would allow Rocky to receive the support that he needed. I put three stars next to it so I wouldn't forget.

Later in the afternoon, I had just said goodbye to my last weight-loss participant, when Corinne walked in.

I looked down at my clipboard and then back at her. "You aren't on my weight-loss list, Corinne." She was much too thin to participate in the program. I was happy she was in the gym classes and part of the walking group. It would help keep her strength up as she aged.

"No. I'm not here for myself. I just want to make sure Marva is doing all right."

"Marva? She weighed in earlier. She's doing just fine."

Corinne nodded. "She's been struggling with her weight for the past five years. And I always felt guilty about it."

"Guilty? You know, not everyone has the same metabolism. Don't feel bad."

Corinne lowered her voice. "I kind of feel like it's my fault she gained so much weight, though."

"Your fault?" She moved toward the coffin and sat down. I took a place next to her and stretched my brace in front of me. I had been in Truhart long enough that I was becoming comfortable with everyone. Except Edge, of course. He still drove me to the gym with loud music and teasing. But I kept my distance when he tried to help me down from the truck. I guess it was a cease-fire of sorts.

"I was sick about eight years ago. Breast cancer." She paused. "I'm sorry. I don't like to think about it."

I didn't realize she had struggled. She never put the information on her medical forms. Thankfully, she hadn't done any weight lifting. But now that I knew, I would make sure to work with her on nutrition and antioxidants.

"I was alone when I was diagnosed. My boys weren't living here at the time. And my brother was busy with his own family. And my husband, well, he's been out of the picture since the boys were small. No loss there."

Corinne had the sweetest granddaughter, Jenny, who liked to come and watch the creative gym after school. She had Down syndrome and told me all about how she was a cheerleader.

"Before I was diagnosed with breast cancer, Marva had been active in a bowling league and a softball league in the summer. She even attended an aerobics class in the basement of St. Mike's church over in Gaylord. She was big boned, but not heavy."

My first assessment of Marva was that she was strong despite her size. I could see her as an athlete.

"From the moment I first called her, crying with the news, Marva dropped everything. It wasn't an easy time. Double mastectomy. Radiation. Chemotherapy . . . two rounds."

I couldn't begin to imagine how scary that must have been. Especially as a single woman with no family around.

"Marva moved in with me. Her husband, Joe, couldn't have been sweeter about it. He would come over and eat dinner with us, or at least with her. My appetite was gone." She took a deep breath and I waited until she was ready to continue.

"We fight all the time, in case you haven't noticed. My daughter-in-law calls it *blovering*, for bickering and loving."

I put my hand on hers. "That's kind of beautiful."

"My point is that, when Marva stopped everything for me, she gained weight. She hasn't gone back to exercising or eating right since then. Says it hurts her knee to move and she can't get back to her old routine."

"She's doing well now. Did she tell you?"

"No. She's kind of sensitive about it when I ask."

"I can't give you details." Client privacy was extremely important to me. "But she is working hard. You know that. You walk together."

"I'm worried she'll lose interest and go right back to how she was before."

We spent the next few minutes talking about ways to motivate friends. I encouraged her to continue to compliment Marva on a job well done, and find ways to enjoy healthy things together. Hiking or walking before or after work. And sharing tasty and nutritional recipes.

When we finished, Corinne hopped off the casket. "Thanks for listening, Lily. I feel better knowing you'll keep an eye out for Marva. The only body I want to see in this thing is Bridget dressed as a corpse and covered in ketchup on Halloween." The irony of sitting on a coffin and discussing health for life wasn't lost on either of us.

LESSON TEN

Identify Weaknesses

The walkers were late.

I sat on the coffin that had been dragged to the front window of the community center so that people could sit down to take off wet boots before the fitness class. No sign of anything but a truck with a load of gravel and a man walking a mangy-looking dog.

They should have been back awhile ago. They named themselves the Walkie Talkies last week. It was fitting. They were so chatty, their mouths moved faster than their feet.

It had been more than three weeks since I first set foot, and crutch, in Truhart. By now I had hoped the program would be running smoothly. Unfortunately, the road had been as rough as the potholes on Main Street.

Only six people attended the nutrition class yesterday. Even more depressing was the thought that I had lost my bullied adolescent friend, Rocky. He missed our appointment to talk after school on Monday. And when I texted him he said he didn't need help after all. I pleaded with him to come by after school so we could discuss his feelings. But he never responded.

That night I watched the Red Wings play the L.A. Kings by myself in the Callahans' recreation room. The Kings lost and my favorite player was out with a concussion.

On top of all that, yesterday my mother called and complained about the L.A. heat wave and how the midday sun made walking the dogs difficult. It sounded like heaven to me. I was so homesick that when she asked, I lied and told her how beautiful Northern Michigan was in April.

Now I stared out the window and wondered if spring was really a season in this part of the world. What had Elizabeth called it? The muddy season?

I checked my watch for the umpteenth time. Still no walkers.

I imagined all sorts of possibilities. Someone might have slipped on the icy shoulder of the road and cracked their head open. Or a car could have failed to see them and plowed into the crowd. The other day, one of my walkers had felt the call of nature halfway through the route. She stopped at a complete stranger's house and asked to use their bathroom. Anything could have happened to her. Fortunately, she was fine. Almost. With a bright red face, she confessed when she returned that she had clogged the toilet. The homeowner was not happy and threatened to call the city council on us. I called Grady Fitzpatrick, the handyman at the Amble Inn, to pay a call on the house with his plunger.

Staring at the empty street and thinking about the declining interest in the Fit4You grant was too much for me. I pulled on my coat and boots and went in search of my walkers. Elizabeth had driven me to the doctor in Gaylord on Tuesday. He cleared me for walking without a crutch except in situations where I might get jostled or lose my footing. My new freedom was heady.

Moving slowly, I kept my eye on the street and watched for hidden pockets of ice. I clutched my coat around me and retraced the route the group had taken. I turned left at the end of Main Street and headed toward a crowd on the other side of the old tennis courts. I clutched my white parka in the cool breeze and followed the trail of boot prints in the slush around the tennis courts and the open field behind the community center. There was nothing in the area that would cause a distraction. Just a hardware store. A beauty salon.

And the Dairy Cow.

I stumbled toward the pink building with the ridiculous sign of a cow's rear end. A sinking feeling settled in my chest as I drew closer.

Edge Callahan stood by the door shouting, "Free treats today!" He held a basket and handed bags tied with white ribbon to each of the walkers as they passed.

I couldn't believe he would sabotage the town like this.

Everything except Edge blurred in front of me as he became the target of my frustration, which had been building all week.

The crowd in front of Edge must have seen my dragon breath coming, because I was marginally aware of a path parting in front of me.

When I was less than five feet from Edge, he had the audacity to wave a bag in front of me with a friendly smile. "Want one? Pete's Treats is celebrating the Tigers' home opener with the rest of the town."

I grabbed the bag and gave him the kind of evil eye that would hex him had I been given the power.

Edge lowered his brows and held out his hand. "Are you okay, Lily? There's a restroom inside if you need it."

"I can't believe you are doing this."

"Being generous?"

I lowered my voice. "You know what I mean."

"It's normal marketing. Uncle Pete is starting up a new business and he's opening a counter at the Dairy Cow—"

"And you just waited for my walkers to come by?"

"The promotion has been going on all day. Anyone who stops in gets a bag." Edge smiled and passed a bag over my head to June Krueger. "Pete's Treats. Your kids will love them."

I pulled his hand down and then, realizing that I had an audience, I turned and raised my voice, "Thanks for helping me show everyone what happens when we let temptation sabotage our resolve."

Edge leaned down and whispered in my ear. "You sound like a preacher." His hot breath swept down my neck and made me even angrier.

I elbowed him in the chest. "Ha. Ha. See how easy it is to get derailed from a challenge, folks?"

"I like to think of it as a reward for all your hard work today," Edge said, passing another bag to one of my young moms.

"You aren't thinking of anyone but yourself right now," I murmured out the side of my mouth.

"Actually, this is for Pete." There was that hot breath again. And the faint touch of those whiskers on the edge of my ear.

I yanked my head away. "This elusive Uncle Pete I've never met? Somehow I doubt this was his idea."

Edge held up the basket. "I've got more for anyone who wants to take some home."

I moved around Edge and climbed the front porch, away from his hot lips. I smiled at Addie Adler, who was picking out the chocolates and popping them in her mouth. "Just a few. You don't want to add more calories than you worked off."

She frowned and twisted the top of the bag to keep from eating more.

"Good job, Aunt Addie," Edge said. "Save some for later."

This time, I returned the earlier favor and let my mouth linger near Edge's neck. "You have no shame, Edge Callahan." I didn't need arm strength for this game. And I intended to win.

Edge turned until our faces were inches apart. His voice was low. "You have enough shame and guilt to go around, Lily Shue."

"Looks like you two need to get a room somewhere," a man at the back of the crowd said.

Edge's eyes traveled from my leggings to my ponytail, and his nostrils flared. "Lily here is reminding me that there's always time for dessert."

Several people cheered and gathered around Edge for another bag.

I stepped down and put my arm out, preventing anyone from taking more candy. "Edge is joking. Again. One bag is plenty." I put my hand on the top of the basket. "Every time you are offered sweets, you have to ask yourself if it is worth it."

A tall woman near me pointed a finger to her mouth. "I'm asking but no one is answering except my sweet tooth."

"Take a deep breath and remember that it gets easier every time you say no."

Edge had the indecency to laugh. "You sound like a public service announcement on drugs."

"That makes you a dealer, then." I said it with as much sugar as the bag in his hand.

"Should I call the sheriff?"

"That's funny." I wasn't trying to keep quiet now. "Go ahead. I would love to file a formal complaint."

With complete ease, he put his arm around my waist and pulled me close. "But I'm not the one standing here on a perfectly legitimate business's property, preaching to a crowd."

I stepped away. My cheeks were hurting from fake smiling. "Just one more loop around town, everyone. But let's end it before you get to this corner. I'll see you all next week."

In one large, uneasy clump, the walkers moved back toward the lake and the last loop. I watched them, ready to pounce if Edge came anywhere near with his basket of sweets. He was the only person in town who was deliberately sabotaging me.

I thought about the apartment I was originally supposed to live in—the one that had been leveled by the flood and fire—and decided to ask about it when I got the chance.

I made it all the way back to the community center before I realized that I was still clutching the bag of candy.

Ugh! I tossed the bag in the trash and imagined all the ways I could get even with Edge. Cayenne pepper in all his ice cream containers. Zucchini in his candy bags. And the Bee Gees on his playlists.

I was ready to close the gym for the day when a figure hovered outside the door. At first I thought it was Edge, and I prepared to tell him that Elizabeth was giving me a ride. Permanently. But when the door opened and a dark head appeared, I realized it was my young friend Rocky.

I almost hugged him, I was so happy to see him. "Come on in, Rocky."

He wandered in with slumped shoulders and his hands in the pockets of his sagging jeans. I knew that posture. I had been feeling the same way ever since my encounter with Edge.

"How are you doing?" I asked gently.

A rush of words tripped over themselves to get out. "I did all you told me to do. Changed my breakfast and ate healthier snacks. But my sister overheard me telling my mom about my new diet and she told her friends. Then they told everyone. Kids were all throwing apples and carrots at me in the cafeteria. They laughed at me as if I was a freak. And then when I got on the scale, I didn't even lose a pound. Nothing. After all that, it didn't work . . ." He stopped abruptly and ran a hand across his eyes. "Sorry. I'm just . . ."

I put my arm around his shoulders. "Sit down and let's talk."

He looked toward the folding chairs and the window and deflated even more. He was nervous to be seen again.

"Come sit against the wall with me." We moved to the back of the room and sat down with our legs in front of us. It was awkward for me to do with my knee brace, but Rocky helped me.

I thought my day had been bad. But when Rocky told me every last horrible detail of his own day, I wanted to cry. The extent to which kids could be mean to other kids always blew my mind. I wanted to march over to the school and give them all a piece of my mind. The principal needed to know about the bullying that was happening. I would call him first thing Monday morning.

"Are there other kids who are getting the same treatment?"

"Some. Mostly they're girls. And sometimes they aren't even fat. The special needs girls get it a lot. But then they started a cheerleading team." Rocky shook his head. "The kids would really tease me if I were in a fat club."

At some point Rocky was going to have to get over what other kids thought. It sounded like they had decided to tease him no matter what he did. My mind searched for possibilities. Rocky needed an excuse to hang out at the gym. One that would minimize the teasing and help him reach his goals.

"Rocky, how about a job?" I don't know why I hadn't thought of it before.

"Huh?"

I pointed to my knee. "As you can see, I'm not the best at moving around. I need help cleaning the gym and getting flyers around town. And I need occasional rides," I said, thinking about a certain red pickup truck I no longer wanted to ride in. "You drive, right?"

"Yeah, that's my mom's car out front." He gestured out the front window to an older-model sedan.

"Do you think you would feel comfortable working for me?"

"I don't know. The kids might figure it out and tease me more." His face fell and I put my hand on his knee.

"Please consider it. I really do have trouble keeping up on my bad knee." In truth I was doing better every day. He didn't need to know that. I made it sound like he would be doing me a huge favor.

The back of my mind kept screaming at me, *What are you thinking?* My paycheck from the grant was slim. I had already spent my own money on groceries for the fitness class, and now I would be giving up more of my salary. On the other hand, maybe if Rocky was exposed to more support and adults who were going through the same pain, he wouldn't care so much about the kids at school.

I vowed to start a program for teens as soon as possible. I would also find a way to contact Rocky's family and get them on board with supporting his efforts.

"I can't pay you more than minimum wage, but it would sure be a help for me. I almost fell on my face moving equipment the other day." Never mind there was no equipment. I was already lying, might as well make it good.

"You mean you would pay me?"

A gust of cool air caught our attention.

Edge stood inside the door. I ignored him. But Rocky's eyes lit up.

"Hi, Edge!"

"Rocky! How goes it?" Edge avoided looking at me. Did he really think I wanted to ride home with him after his corn-syrup-and-sugar-dealing ways?

Rocky stood up and wiped his cheek. "Just stopping by to help Miss Shue. She says she needs a—a—" He looked at me, unsure what he would be called.

"An assistant."

"A job! Good for you!" If Edge made any comment to Rocky about being able to spend more money on candy and ice cream, I would clobber him with one of the tomato cans we were using for weights. Fortunately, he stayed silent.

I rejected Edge's hand and let Rocky help me up. "You don't need to pick me up today. I've made other arrangements."

Edge's brows drew together. "Other arrangements?"

"Yes. Rocky is going to take me home. Right, Rocky?"

"Sure. Is it okay if I go call my mom and tell her I'll be a few minutes late, Miss Shue?"

While he talked to his mother, telling her all about his job, I turned to Edge. "Obviously, I don't need your assistance anymore. I'll take care of my own rides until I move into the apartment."

"The apartment?"

"My leg is better. I'm going to check out the space next door as soon as I can."

"Mom is sure going to be upset."

"I'll have Rocky bring me around to visit her."

He adjusted his hat. His mouth curled in a tight smile. "I'm dumped as your driver and you're moving out? You're hurting my feelings."

"You have no feelings. Just jokes."

"Ouch." He clutched his chest, but the humor wasn't reaching his eyes. "What is it that hurts so bad then? Indigestion?"

"This will help you feel better." I pulled the bag of candy out of the trash and shoved it in his hands.

He stared down at it. Losing his smile. "For the record, Lily, I have a business to run. And people like my business. So don't blame me for promoting my product to Truhart and any tourists we might get around here. That's part of what makes Truhart appeal to tourists."

"Putt-putt golf and ice cream?"

He held up the bag. "And now Pete's Treats."

"I haven't met a single tourist yet." I lowered my voice so Rocky wouldn't hear our argument.

"Memorial Day is around the corner. You will."

"You think that candy and the chance to hit a golf ball into a clown's mouth will bring tourists?"

His gray eyes turned cloudy. "In case you haven't noticed, Truhart doesn't have movie stars and sunshine three hundred and sixty-five days of the year. We don't have theme parks, and shopping malls, and resorts. We don't even have a gym, as you found out." His voice was soft, but full of something that made me realize just how much Edge cared about this town. There was passion in his tone. "What we also don't have is an industry. Logging peaked almost a century ago."

I had wanted to see Edge serious for once. I changed my mind. It was like staring into the sun.

I looked down at the bag in his hands and swallowed. Now I knew something that stirred Edge. Something that mattered greatly.

But I had things I cared about, too.

"You have your goals and I have mine."

"Don't judge me for trying to help my hometown, Lily. You, more than anyone, should know what it's like to try for a comeback."

"You save the town, and I'll save its people." I sounded waspish and sanctimonious, even to my own ears.

"We don't have to be on opposing teams, Lily."

"I plan on winning, just the same."

LESSON ELEVEN

Everyone Has Bad Days

On Friday night Elizabeth and her fiancé invited me to Lori's Restaurant for dinner.

I hadn't been out with friends in ages. And I was tired of hiding in my room at the Callahans'. Louise needed time with her family. And maybe if I wasn't around tonight, Edge might visit the house. We had been avoiding each other once again.

Besides, tonight was a night when I had a particular reason to keep busy. Tonight was the season opener of *Just Lose It*. I didn't trust myself to stay away from the television. Getting out was a nice distraction.

Elizabeth pulled up at the Callahans' at six thirty, and when I walked out, a tall, dark, and handsome man held open the back door of her Honda. I was surprised to be greeted by the deputy sheriff, J.D. Hardy, whom I met at the Fit4You meeting. J.D. shook my hand and reintroduced himself. He was equally handsome out of uniform, in jeans and a chambray shirt.

When I climbed in, he asked, "Are you comfortable in the backseat of this tiny go-cart?"

Elizabeth turned around from the passenger seat. "Enough about my car, J.D. Just because you drive a monster truck with flashing lights doesn't make you any better than the rest of us compact-car drivers."

"At least I don't get stuck in a snow drift a dozen times a year," he said with a crooked smile my way before closing my door.

When J.D. sat behind the wheel, Elizabeth said, "That was only four times. And why are you driving my car if you hate it so much?"

"Because I don't want to see you get stuck a fifth time." He grinned as he backed down the driveway.

Elizabeth sent me an apologetic look over her shoulder. "Sorry, Lily. J.D. has had a lot of fun teasing me about my car this winter. What he doesn't know is that I get stuck on purpose. Then he gets to play hero and come to my rescue." She scooted closer to him.

He put his hand on the back of her headrest. "You're out of luck. There's no snow in the foreseeable future. In fact, it looks like we might have an early spring."

"Isn't this spring now?" I asked.

Elizabeth laughed. "Spring is late May around here. And it lasts about two weeks. Then we go straight to summer."

"You mean it still might snow?"

"Not might. It will. A few years ago, it snowed in the second week of May," J.D. said.

I pictured my walkers stumbling through snow drifts. It would be messy and difficult. On the bright side, trudging through foot-deep snow would be a good workout for them.

"Maybe I could have the walkers put on their cross-country skis and pull me in the sleigh." Ha. Too bad Edge didn't hear me. I wasn't above humor after all.

Lori's was crowded. The parking lot overflowed to the road and J.D. dropped us close to the door before parking on a side street. The scent of French fries and burgers smacked me in the face before we even entered. If the air had calories, I would have had to fast for days.

Inside, the heat and buzz of the crowd and the music in the background filled the air, almost overpowering the smell of greasy food. Elizabeth and I stood next to a very politically incorrect cigar-store Indian statue and waited for a waitress to clear a table. People around us greeted her with as much enthusiasm as they greeted Edge. I smiled as she caught up with a family of five at a booth and waved toward the bar, where an older couple from my fitness class was eating dinner. When they saw me they leaned forward over the counter. I wondered if they were in pain until I realized they were trying to cover up the basket of fries they were sharing.

The bartender placed a bottle of ketchup in front of them. When he looked up, I felt like I had just drowned in a shot of whisky. I swallowed past the fire in my throat and took a deep breath.

Seriously?

How many jobs did Edge have? A garbage truck driver. An ice cream scooper. And now a bartender?

He wore a green Spartans baseball cap and a gray T-shirt with the Detroit Tigers' D emblazoned across the chest.

He tipped his hat toward me.

I clenched my fist and acted like he was invisible. Now I had an idea where he had been the past few nights. He had been playing bartender to the home crowd while I had been hiding in his bedroom.

Someone down the bar called out something, and Edge grabbed two mugs from the shelf behind him, expertly filling them before sliding them down the bar. He knew what he was doing. The layer of foam was just right and nothing spilled. Show-off!

"Lily? Our table is ready." Elizabeth's voice startled me. She turned her eyes to see what I had been staring at. "Edge helps out Bootie on busy nights."

J.D. waited for us by a table near a flat-screen television. There were four large flat-screens strategically placed around the restaurant. My heart raced and my palms grew sweaty. I didn't know there would be so many screens at this restaurant. Taking a deep breath, I reminded myself that sports were the only thing people in bars ever watched. Not television shows about weight loss.

With its knotty-pine walls and the long bar, Lori's could have been a classic dive bar. The kind men loved to slip out of the house and visit on winter nights. However, the hand of a woman had touched the restaurant, giving it a G-rated feeling. Fresh looking, pink-checked gingham curtains hung at the windows and sprigs of flowers in tiny vases dotted the center of the tables. My guess was that "Lori" was to blame for the feminine influence.

As soon as we were seated, a familiar-looking grizzled man appeared at our table.

Elizabeth introduced him to me. "Bootie, this is Lily Shue, our new fitness trainer."

Bootie shook my hand. "I was at your first meeting. Welcome to Truhart! I'll send a round of Single Ladies Ale, which my wife, Lori, loves."

"Uh . . . I'll just have a Heineken," J.D. said with a frown.

Bootie slapped him on the back. "Set the date soon if you don't want her to drink it." He wagged an eyebrow at Elizabeth, who fingered her engagement ring. Then he leaned down and told me, "Lori can't wait to get out of the house for one of your classes, Lily. She's anxious to get back in shape and lose her baby weight. She's home with our little girl right now."

"Tell her I'm looking forward to meeting her. It's hard to find time for yourself when you are taking care of a newborn." I had a lot of clients who struggled to schedule time each week. I reminded them that everyone benefited when moms and dads were strong and had more energy.

Bootie leaned down and placed a hand on his large stomach. "I kind of need a little work myself. The baby is crawling everywhere and I'm starting to have a hard time keeping up with her."

"Get a babysitter and come together, Bootie. Lily can help you both," said Elizabeth. When he left, she touched my shoulder. "Just a few weeks in Truhart and already you are in demand. Good job, Lily . . . Oh no, don't look now, but guess who just walked in?"

I turned around to see Aubrey Vanderbeek. The one who *had* gym equipment and plenty of money to build her program. She was standing next to a short little woman with fuzzy dark hair and an unusual yellow honeycomb coat, and a man who could have been Aubrey's twin except for the ponytail and the lack of breasts. His square face and the broad ridge above his eyebrows had the same Cro-Magnon look of toughness. Aubrey spotted us across the room and headed our way.

"Is it too late to hide?" Elizabeth asked. It was nice to know I wasn't the only one whose gut instinct was to dodge behind a menu when Aubrey walked in.

"Just smile, E. I'll cover for you," said J.D.

Aubrey stopped at our table. The smell of strong perfume mingled with the aroma of fried food, making my stomach cartwheel.

"Out for some healthy Truhart food, everyone?" She laughed at her own irony.

"We can't resist two-for-one night at Lori's," replied J.D. "Are you taking advantage of the deal too?"

"Good God, no. We're just stopping in before heading out to the Grande Lucerne. Our reservations aren't for another hour, so we thought we would enjoy a drink." Aubrey leaned down and winked at me. "Mine will be just a Perrier."

"Really? Can't handle your booze?" Elizabeth asked, fluttering her eyelashes.

"I can't have all that beer going to my gut like some people." She eyed the Single Ladies bottle in front of me. I resisted the urge to cover the label with both hands. Then her eyes drifted to my knee brace. "You still have that on?"

Aubrey was in charge of the grant on the west end of the county, so she should stay on her side.

I patted my knee. "Doctor's orders."

She whispered something in the man's ear and he laughed. I wanted to yank her ponytail.

Elizabeth took over where Aubrey's manners had failed. "Lily, this is Andrew Vanderbeek and Reeba Sweeney."

Reeba was small and wide. And when she shook my hand I realized where the scent of perfume had come from. Her grip was surprisingly firm. Almost painful. No doubt she had strength and stamina. But she would need to lose weight if she wanted to avoid injury to her joints. Andrew shook my hand absently. As if I wasn't interesting enough to remember. He might be strong, but his personality was weak.

Aubrey's eyes grew wide and she cupped her mouth with her hands. "Edge Callahan, where have you been hiding?"

She walked across the restaurant, ignoring the people who were forced to dive out of her wake. She leaned over the bar for a kiss and practically hauled him over the top in her enthusiasm. He was saved from such a fate only by his sheer size.

Beside me, J.D. practically gagged. I felt the same way he sounded.

I remembered Edge telling me that Aubrey had tried to start a "thing" with him, but I hadn't believed it. Now I understood what he meant. To anyone else, Edge might look like he was enjoying the conversation no one else heard. To me he looked like he wanted to stick his head under the tap. He kept running his hand over the back of his neck while Aubrey did all the talking.

When she finally moved away to join Andrew and Reeba, who had found a table, Edge ran a hand across his face where she had kissed him. I picked up my beer and took a big sip to hide my smile.

Edge glanced my way and our eyes met. I raised the bottle in the air in a mock salute to old flames. Instead of being embarrassed, he put his elbow on the bar and raised his hand, subtly offering a re-match of arm wrestling. Touché.

I turned in my chair and gave him my back.

"Oh look, it's pouring on all the fans." Elizabeth pointed to the television on the opposite wall. Sheets of rain descended on the out-field at Comerica Park. The camera panned the crowd as Tiger fans in soggy ski hats and winter jackets ran for cover, trying to avoid the downpour. "Hopefully it's just a passing shower," said Joe O'Shea, who stopped at the table to greet us.

After a moment he pointed to the menu and curled his lip. "No smoothies or quinoa on the menu, Lily. What are you going to eat?"

I didn't bother correcting the way he pronounced quinoa, *keenya,* instead of keenwa. "I'm sure I can find something healthy on this menu, Joe."

He crossed his arms in front of him. "Go ahead. Give it a try."

Joe wasn't the only one who complained about eating healthy at restaurants. Marva was waiting several tables down looking at her salad sorrowfully. In fact, more than a few people around us were grinning at me with skepticism. This was a good time to prove him wrong.

I understood his skepticism. It was one thing to live in a bubble and control everything that went into your mouth. But real life was full of all sorts of temptations and very limited choices. If I was going to get Truhart eat healthier, I needed to help people make deci-sions outside of their own kitchens and grocery carts.

I picked up the menu and scanned it. "I could take the bun off the hamburger and just eat the meat with the lettuce, pickle, and onion."

The man behind me snorted. "Oh, *that* will taste good. Not!"

"Or I could order a grilled chicken sandwich on wheat toast. That's a healthy option."

"Hey, Bootie," Joe called across the room. "Do you serve wheat toast here?"

Bootie made a face. The waitress saw us checking out the menu and stopped at the table, her pencil hovering over her notepad.

I scanned the menu again and slapped it down when I had my an-swer. "The chili, without the fries. Add a side salad and I'll enjoy this beer with no guilt."

Joe shrugged and turned toward the table behind us. "Too bad. I already ordered the chili fries."

Elizabeth laughed and pointed to his table. "Actually, Marva is eating your chili fries, Joe."

"What?" He moved across the room far faster than he had during today's walk. The two of them exchanged words. Then Joe sat down and they both dug into the smothered fries.

As I turned back around, I caught Edge staring at me from behind the bar. This time it was his turn to mock me. He held up a mug and returned my salute. I wanted to throw a French fry at him. But he would probably do nothing more than catch it in his mouth. Instead I put my elbow on the table and offered to arm wrestle. I don't know why I did it. It only made me remember the way he had kissed me in order to win.

Elizabeth and J.D. had finished ordering. She was cocking her head my way, trying to understand what I was doing with my arm. I made a quick recovery and ran my hand through my hair.

She misinterpreted my gesture. "Don't let them get you down, Lily. Everyone is a just letting loose tonight. The game always gets everyone rowdy. But now that it is rained out, they need something else to entertain them."

I almost choked on my beer when she said that word. *Entertain.* The game was rained out. I hadn't thought about that possibility.

I held my breath and scanned the televisions around the room. One was still on the Tiger game as two sportscasters discussed the upcoming season. Two were showing a hockey game between the Edmonton Oilers and the Chicago Blackhawks.

I twisted my head to see the fourth TV on the wall behind me. Bootie was standing under it with the remote control in his hands. The ends of my fingers prickled as I willed him to find another baseball game. Anything else but the GATE network. But luck hadn't been on my side all year.

He flipped through various news shows and stopped.

My body went rigid when I recognized the scene on the screen. I had never had the opportunity to see the tape when I was on the *Just Lose It* set. It was a shock to see through the eyes of the camera what I had experienced firsthand.

The television screen showed me standing with the other three trainers beside our clients as the camera scanned the elite studio gym. I remembered the moment well. I had been so excited to be there on that first full day of shooting that I had barely slept the night before.

The camera crew had already interviewed me. With the bright lights illuminating my wide smile, I proudly told them all about my background in kinesiology and nutrition. I described my experience at the Pacific X Gym. I shared my successes and my goals.

The cameras had been there when I first met my client, Farrah, who was one of the contestants trying to win the prize for who lost the most weight. I had been involved with preproduction meetings with the other trainers. Including the arrogant Rod Macintosh, who had already been on the show three seasons and was considered the veteran trainer with the most knowledge. The man had called me cute when he first shook my hand. My stomach burned now, as I watched him smile and cross his arms for the opening theme sequence.

I searched the wall for a plug to pull or a cable box to smash. What else could I do? Wrestle the remote from Bootie's hands? Cover the television set with a napkin? Smash a chair through the screen? All I knew was that I had to keep the whole restaurant and town from watching me make a fool of myself.

Before I could do anything, Marva O'Shea yelled, "Hey, that's Lily! It's *Just Lose It!*"

Heads turned my way.

Across the room, someone pulled the remote from a nearby shelf and changed the channel on another television to the GATE network.

"Please don't—" I started.

But Aubrey Vanderbeek drowned out my pleas by shouting over the crowd. "Turn it up! We wouldn't want to miss the celebrity in our midst now, would we?"

The opening sequence cut away to a commercial. Thank God. I took a deep breath. "Maybe the rain has stopped. Check it out, Bootie." He flipped channels on the television near our table, while the other TVs returned to the hockey game.

I took another deep breath. I shouldn't feel so terrified. When my injury happened, the crew had been filming Rod. They would probably segue right into the next segment with nothing more than a mention of my replacement.

Elizabeth leaned across the table. "This is exciting stuff. Seeing you on television, our own Truhart fitness trainer."

"The game is exciting, too. We should watch it!"

She waved my suggestion away with the flick of her wrist. "Look at you. You're so humble."

Oh Lord, if she only knew. Bootie switched back to the show. I picked up my beer and drank the whole thing as they showed a clip of the participants being weighed. The screen split for a video montage of the first day in which participants used the equipment for the first time. The bikes. The ellipticals. The weights.

The beer that I had just inhaled was doing somersaults in my stomach. I covered a burp.

Then the screen shifted to an interview with Rod Macintosh. He stood with his arms crossed in a he-man stance that made him look larger than his five foot nine. As he talked, Aubrey shouted, "Hey! Shut up. I can't hear what he is saying, everyone."

I couldn't pull my eyes away from the screen. The camera angle shifted over Rod's shoulder and my palms grew sweaty. I clutched the end of the table.

To my horror, a blurry Farrah and I stepped on identical treadmills. The camera refocused and our images were clear. My treadmill increased at a faster rate, while she settled into a walk. How had they filmed this? I thought they were doing the Rod interview.

The scene replayed in my mind. The way my index finger pressed down on the treadmill's control panel. The feel of the smooth surface and the exact spot where I adjusted the setting to a lower speed. Or so I thought.

I saw myself turn back to Farrah. The slow-motion replay was cruel.

I looked around the restaurant at the people of Truhart who were about to witness the second worst moment of my life. My gaze rested on Edge, who was looking at me, not the screen.

Someone nearby said, "It's so cool she's right here in Truhart to help us now."

Not cool. Not cool! I wanted to scream. I stood up and looked for an escape. I couldn't bear to witness what the network had evidently decided was a good ratings ploy.

I was out the door before it happened.

But not soon enough.

The sound of the bar erupting in a collective groan followed me into the cool night air.

No need to see the calamity, I knew what they were showing. Me. Catching my foot on the edge of the treadmill. Falling toward my client, tripping up her stride as well. She almost missed me as she went down. But she didn't.

I broke her fall.

She landed on top of me in an embarrassing moment for both of us. The only thing the television didn't capture was the sound of my knee. The tiny pop echoed inside me like a cannon for a long time after that. Even now.

Pop . . . pop . . . pop.

A breeze from the trees nearby blew across my face, turning the hot moisture on my cheeks to ice. Standing in the chill in nothing but a thin cotton shirt, I should have been cold. But all I felt was heat. An unbearable surge of fear and mortification that wouldn't stop.

This was what Chip had tried to warn me about in his phone call. My contract said that all images of me from that first day of filming were the property of the network. When he mentioned it, I hadn't given the incident another thought. I assumed that my replacement, the overeager Jaimie from the Pacific X Gym, had been quickly substituted, with little comment, to fill my slot. She was cute and looked like Reese Witherspoon in *Legally Blonde*. The camera would fall in love with her for sure.

It had never occurred to me that somewhere a lens or an angle had caught my accident. I shut my eyes and squeezed tight, trying to forget the moment the camera had zoomed over Rod's shoulder.

A door opened, leaking the raucous noise of the restaurant into the parking lot.

I opened my eyes and peered through the window of the restaurant, relieved to see an advertisement on TV of a man and a woman frolicking across a bed.

"Saved by an erectile dysfunction commercial."

Edge.

I couldn't face him, even in the dim light. Not because I didn't want him to see my tears, but because I didn't want to see his pity.

"They ought to put a warning on those things," he said.

I was confused. "Treadmills?"

"No, Viagra."

Inside, people were back to their chili fries and conversations. Unaffected by my career-ending smashup. I, on the other hand, felt newly devastated.

I pretended to wipe away a stray piece of hair and managed to brush off the tears on one cheek.

"Not funny, huh?"

"No-o." I pretended to look at my shoes and went for the other cheek. Silly. Who the hell was I fooling?

I tried to cover my sniffle and gave up. "Can you believe I did that?"

"Left the bar? It is a lot nicer out here. We'll hit sixty degrees before you know it."

The gentle way he avoided the elephant in the parking lot only made me feel worse. "I feel like such a fool."

"For standing outside in nothing but a T-shirt? No need to feel embarrassed."

"You know what I mean." My raspy voice was even more raspy than usual. I swallowed and tried again. "I fell off a flippin' treadmill."

"Is that what happened? I thought you were attempting to cushion her fall."

I couldn't stand the way he was trying to be so kind. I turned around and faced him. "What kind of trainer does something that stupid?"

His answer was gentle. "I don't think trainers have a corner on stupidity . . . or falling."

"Seriously, stop being nice."

"Think of it this way. At least you weren't going eighty miles an hour on icy snow." His tone was meant to be self-deprecating. But it sounded more bitter to me.

"God, Edge." I stepped toward him, until light from the window hit his face. His eyes looked black.

"Just saying . . ." The corner of his mouth curled up, but his eyes were sad. Weary. I was, too.

He reached for me and pulled me close. I buried myself in his arms. The sounds of the people inside and the April night were replaced by a beating heart and slow, even breathing.

"I had no idea they were filming it. I never would have shown my face here tonight if I knew there was a chance people would—oh no." I croaked. "Aubrey saw it, too."

Edge's hand found my chin and he cupped it until I was looking him squarely in the eye. "Nothing changes because they saw your accident. Nothing. You are still the same lady who is going to help this town get healthy."

I grabbed the wrist that held my chin. "No, Edge. It's all different. No one will ever take me seriously around here again."

He turned me around to face the windows. "What do you want from them?"

That was an odd question. I didn't understand. "Nothing. I don't want anything *from* them. I just want to help them."

"Then how are you hurt because they saw something bad happen to you?"

"They won't respect me. They'll think I'm . . ." I collapsed against him. "Oh. I know where this is going."

"Yeah, yeah, you can pay my therapist fee tomorrow. For now, just answer the question. What do you want? Do you want to help them or do you want respect from them?"

"Do I have to choose?"

"You tell me. Only one of those two things is in your control."

I leaned against him with a sigh. He was right. I had no control over respect. Even though I wanted it in the worst way. Not just here in Truhart, or the county. I wanted Chip and Ned and my mom to finally see me as a success. I wanted to make something of myself. Be the kind of person my dad would be proud of. The little girl who still lived inside me felt like no one was ever going to feel that way again.

I closed my eyes and let myself remember how I reacted that other time. After the worst moment of my life . . . The day that was far worse than falling off a treadmill on national television.

After Dad's heart attack, when Mom and I came home in the late evening to an empty house and the knowledge that our lives had just been shattered, I grabbed my soccer ball and ran outside. In the frigid night, I kicked the ball over and over against the garage, trying desperately to make that imaginary goal I had missed. My heartbroken, childlike mind thought I could make time return me to the moment things went wrong. For hours, I kicked that ball until Mom made me come inside.

I fingered my necklace. Tonight, that same feeling of futility washed over me. More than ever I wished I had scored that damn goal. I hated to think that the last thing Dad saw was my failure.

I didn't pretend this time. I wiped my tears and took the napkin Edge handed me.

When I finished my pity party, Edge asked, "So, you want to come back inside with me?"

I shook my head. "I can't face them."

"Okay. We can play tonsil hockey in my truck instead." His hand slid down to my breast and I pulled out of his arms.

"Oh my God! You make a joke of everything."

He laughed and trailed behind me as I marched back inside Lori's to face the madding crowd.

LESSON TWELVE

Push Yourself,
Even When It Hurts

No one said a word to me as I walked back inside the restaurant. No one had to say anything. The muffled hush that descended on the room was enough. With burning cheeks, I made my way back to the table where J.D. and Elizabeth had just started digging into their meal.

Edge followed behind me, as if nothing had just happened. He held out my chair and I sat.

"Hey, how's the chicken wings tonight, J.D.?" Edge asked. "I tried them with sriracha last time and I tasted them for days afterwards. It was like having leftovers."

"Gross," Elizabeth said, sending me a bright look. I could tell she was concerned.

Elizabeth's fiancé played the game of diversion almost as well as Edge. "The way you treat sriracha as if it's soup, I'm not surprised."

I sent them a grateful smile and then a booming voice interrupted us. "Man, that was tough to watch, Lily. I've never, and I mean *never*, seen someone wipe out on a treadmill the way you did."

Aubrey planted her hands on the table and I shrunk down on the chair. Before she could sit next to me, Edge plopped down on the vacant seat.

Aubrey wasn't put off. She wagged her thumb at the television screen behind her that had shifted back to Comerica Park. They were removing the tarp from the infield.

"Seriously, Lily. I'm not sure I will ever get on a treadmill again after witnessing that catastrophe. But hey, don't be embarrassed by what Rod Macintosh said afterward."

"What did he say?" I asked in a tiny voice.

Across from me Elizabeth stuffed chili cheese fries in her mouth at an alarming rate.

"Oh, you didn't hear?" Aubrey's eyes glowed and her lip curled. Then she faked decency. "Maybe I shouldn't—"

Edge reached across the table and grabbed a wing and the bottle of sriracha. "Hey, Aubrey, whatever happened to that problem with cold sores you used to ha—"

Aubrey ignored him. "Rod was all about the fact that some trainers have less experience than others. And the safety-first thing, of course."

My cheeks felt as hot as the sauce Edge was currently using to drown the chicken wing J.D. had offered him.

Rod had been an ass since I met him. He had flirted with all the females and even some of the males. Twice he had asked if I wanted to *work out* with him. Everyone knew what that code word really meant. Rumor was the man approached sex like he lifted weights. One of the girls on set had described it as heavy breathing, lots of grunting, and a tendency to watch his biceps while thrusting. Even without the TMI comments, I would have refused him. He made my skin crawl.

The thought of Rod commenting about me on national television was nauseating. I looked at the chicken breast on the plate in front of me and pushed it away.

Edge waved the chicken wing in front of Aubrey's nose. She put a hand on Edge's shoulder. "Aren't you supposed to be behind the bar?"

He untied his bar apron. "Done for the night."

She leaned across his body and smashed her breasts against his shoulder. "Hopefully this whole thing won't affect—"

Edge freed his arm, grabbed her waist, and squeezed.

She jumped. "Edge!"

"Yup! Still the same Aubrey," he announced. He took a bite of the wing and set it down.

"I've got more muscle than I used to."

"You do?" He cocked his head and spanned her waist with his hand. "Where?"

She grabbed his wrist and planted his palm on her glutes. The sickening smile she sent him made me want to yank his hand away.

"Well . . . maybe there is a little more—" Edge played dumb better than anyone I had ever met.

"And here!" She lifted his free hand to an area right above her breasts.

Edge's face was straight. But I had a close-up view of his perfectly formed ears. They were turning as red as the sauce on his wing. "This is a family restaurant now, Aubrey. Bootie isn't into that kind of behavior in the place these days."

Elizabeth put a finger to her throat as if she were gagging and J.D. covered his laugh with a cough.

Edge tried to remove his hands. Aubrey wouldn't let him. Still unfazed, Edge said, "Eh. Not bad. They're almost as firm as Lily's. You trainers must work really hard to develop that kind of muscle tone."

I lowered my head into my hands. Was this really happening?

Aubrey's brother, Andrew, suddenly appeared at her elbow. "Take your hands off my sister!"

"I wasn't—"

He pushed Aubrey out of Edge's hands. "You've had a thing for her for years, but you're too late."

Edge raised his brow. "A thing? Like a bad memory, you mean?"

Aubrey didn't seem to care that her brother had leaped to the wrong conclusion. She held her arms across her chest as if Edge had just attacked her.

"You're nothing but a washed-up loser with a rinky-dink putt-putt golf course to keep you busy," said Andrew.

"Now you're hurting my feelings. I might not let you play next time you bring your mommy."

The little woman, Reeba Sweeney, who was sitting with Aubrey and Andrew, arrived at the table. "I told you we should have had drinks at the Grande Lucerne. Truhart is full of crazies."

Andrew's nostrils widened when he sneered, making him look slightly bovine. He narrowed his eyes. "This town can't even hire a trainer who knows how to use a treadmill. They're not only crazy, they're dumb."

Abruptly, Edge pushed his chair out and stood up. He was taller than Andrew and close enough that he forced Andrew to arch his neck.

"Funny you should be talking about dumb, Drew. I seem to remember a time when you cleaned your daddy's car with an S.O.S pad."

Andrew's face turned purple and he pushed against J.D.'s chest. "I was just eighteen, you scum."

Edge touched his chin. "Oh, I forgot, too young to read the box." They stood toe to toe and nose to eyebrow. Even though Edge was taller, the challenge was obvious.

Elizabeth moaned. "Not again. Bootie just fixed the place up so it looks nice after the last fight."

Speaking of . . . Bootie arrived with a bowl of nachos. He shoved himself between both men. "Free nachos to whoever wins an arm-wrestling match." He winked at Edge. So this was how it was around here on Fridays? I had thought Edge was joking when he first mentioned arm wrestling to me.

Andrew looked down his nose at Bootie. "Arm wrestling? Gross. That means I'd have to touch him. We're leaving now."

Bootie offered the nachos to Edge. "Winner by default."

"I could totally beat you if I wanted," Andrew said, a bead of sweat forming at his hairline.

"Name a date and time," Edge said, casually grabbing the plate of nachos and sitting down. "I'll give you time to work out with your fitness instructor since I can see batwings under your arms, Drew."

Andrew Vanderbeek couldn't help peeking at his sagging under-arm fat. "There's nothing—"

"If you flap you might fly."

"You want to arm wrestle now? I'll totally do you now."

Edge took a bite of the nachos and shrugged, as if the idea were mildly interesting but not quite enough to hold his attention. "Okay."

"I'm gonna shatter his wrist when I slam it," Andrew said to his big sister and Reeba with the brown halo around her head.

Aubrey adjusted the girls in her bra. "Now, now. Be a good sport and don't hurt Edge. He needs his hands to scoop."

Word of the challenge passed from table to table. Andrew swept his hair to the side of his head as a small crowd formed around us. "Maybe your girlfriend should give you a few pointers."

Edge put his arm around me, practically pulling me into his lap. "Maybe she could. But that would be an unfair advantage."

Andrew sneered. "Didn't you see *Just Lose It* just now? She's a disaster. I'm surprised she hasn't already fallen off her chair and broken her leg."

Edge's arm slid off my shoulder and his fist dropped on the table. I jumped. So did the table next to us.

Aubrey looked unsettled for the first time. "Come on, Andrew. We'll be late for our dinner." She grabbed her brother's arm and tried to get him to leave.

"No. I'm gonna wrestle his sorry ass right here, right now." He pulled a chair up and nudged Elizabeth out of the way.

Edge looked down his nose at Andrew. Even sitting, Edge towered over him. "I think we have a booster chair in the back room, Vanderbeek. You sure you don't want Aubrey to get it for you?"

Andrew placed his elbow on the table and held up his hand. "Come on, Callahan. Stop being a funny man. Or are you scared?"

Edge looked directly into Vanderbeek's eyes and placed his own elbow on the table with casual disinterest. "Fine."

The noise level in the rest of the room had risen during the interchange as the crowd speculated on who would win. Some of the spectators stood on chairs. I heard bets being made at the bar. Flo Jarvis was holding a piece of paper and taking cash.

Edge pulled my chair, with me still in it, away from the table and next to him where I wouldn't get in the way. "Sit right here, Lily. You might learn a thing or two from my technique."

The only thing I was learning so far was that beer combined with nachos created temporary IQ loss.

Bootie shoved the baskets of fries and chicken away and stood over both men. He clutched their fists and raised his voice to the crowd gathered around us. "Hey! Quiet. I'm not going to start 'em until you settle down."

When nothing happened, he put his fingers to his lips and let out a high-pitched whistle. "Shut up!"

That did the trick. "Now, here are the rules. Keep your butts in your chairs. No illegal topping. I don't want to see anyone's arm broken this time, Edge."

"Aww. You're taking all the fun out of it, Bootie," said Edge. Andrew stared at his arm and gulped. Bootie sent me an imperceptible wink.

"And here is the final rule. No one, I mean it, no one in this room tells my wife what's going on. Do you hear me? I promised Lori this would become a family restaurant. If she knew we were hosting another wrestling tournament she would be on a bus back home to her mother. So, none of this gets talked about outside the restaurant."

"Sure, Bootie. What happens at Lori's stays at Lori's," one of the mechanics from Auto Doc garage said.

Bootie put his hand back on the two fists. "Are you boys ready?"

Andrew focused on the two fists and sat up straighter. "Yes."

Edge slouched down. "I guess so. But someone tell me what happens in the game. I don't want to miss the inning."

"Here," someone across the room shouted. They turned one of the television screens toward our table. "You can watch it while you wrestle."

Edge sent him a thumbs-up. "Great idea. Thanks, Vance."

I couldn't believe the spectacle the match had turned into. The room had turned from a loud, cheesy-fries Friday-night hangout, to a center-ring match at the local arena. If this was what a little arm-wrestling match did to Truhart, what was a real game like?

"On your mark. Get set." Bootie dropped his hands. "Go!"

The wrestling match began.

Neither fist traveled far for the first minute or two. Andrew scrunched up his reddening face and his lips stuck to the top of his teeth. His hand shook and the faint shadow of a dark stain appeared in his armpit.

Edge, on the other hand, looked as if he couldn't care less. He stared at the game on the television. When someone struck out he said, "Man, they should have traded that guy when they had the chance."

With a smile on his face, Bootie reprimanded Edge for talking.

To the rest of the room, Edge looked like he didn't care, but I had a closer view. The muscles in his arm were tense and his beard twitched above his jaw. When Andrew's fist took a little ground, Edge's eyes flashed beneath his lowered lashes. He did nothing to regain the lost ground. It was if he was waiting for the moment.

For my own part, I sat on my hands and forced myself not to kick Andrew, or help Edge. I stared at the two hands, practically willing Edge's hand to move. I would have tickled Andrew if I thought I could get away with it. But thinking about touching Andrew made my skin crawl.

Shouts of protest erupted from the crowd as Andrew's arm took another inch of territory. But Edge didn't care. He continued to stare at the television. With each passing moment, it looked as if Andrew was going to win.

When Andrew's arm pushed Edge's fist even farther toward the table, I could stand it no longer. "Come on, Edge."

My voice seemed to wake Edge up. "What's that, Lily?"

"Don't let him win," I hissed.

He turned his head my way. "You really care what happens in a silly arm-wrestling match?"

I looked into his beautiful gray eyes. "Yeah. I care."

"Why?"

"Because I want you to win."

Andrew was getting annoyed with our side conversation. He tried to say something, but he was out of breath from exerting himself. Bootie pretended he didn't hear us.

Aubrey Vanderbeek curled her lip in premature triumph. "Maybe you should pay attention to your arm instead of your little gimpy trainer, Callahan."

"Do you like it when people call you that?" Edge asked me. He spoke to me as if no one else were in the room. We could have been having a candlelight dinner for two, it felt so intimate.

I shook my head and never took my eyes off him. "No."

"Neither do I." He gazed at his arm and appeared to take an interest in the match for the first time since it started. Slowly his arm shifted in the other direction. While Andrew sputtered and huffed, Edge gained leverage until Andrew's wrist was an inch from the table.

The crowd was out of control. Even J.D. Hardy, who had watched, emotionless, from the very start of the interchange, was cheering for Edge now. Andrew reached out and grasped the table with his other hand. It wobbled as he struggled for leverage.

"Now, Andrew, that's illegal," Bootie said quickly. But he was drowned out by the sound of the crowd. It didn't matter anyway. Even holding the table wasn't helping Andrew Vanderbeek.

Edge was millimeters from winning when the table suddenly shifted under us. All the food that Bootie had piled in the corner slid towards Andrew. Andrew and Edge's fists separated just as the table did a nose dive. Cheesy fries and nachos flew and Andrew's chair toppled backwards. He landed on the floor with a pile of nachos in his lap.

A shocked silence was followed by peals of laughter. Andrew scooted away from the food and flicked the salsa off his crotch. Eventually his sister helped him off the floor.

"You did that on purpose. You cheaters!" Andrew yelled.

"I told you not to hold the table, Vanderbeek. Some of them are wobbly," Bootie said, signaling to a waitress to clean up the mess. "This one must have been one of the tables Dylan Schraeder tossed at you last summer, J.D."

J.D. tilted his chin. "Must be."

Andrew stood, brushing off his pants, missing a French fry in his fly. Edge pointed and Bootie thought that was hilarious.

Aubrey took Andrew's shoulder. He cradled his hand. "We should have never stopped by this place. Too close to Truhart."

The tiny lady with the honeycomb coat pushed her way through the crowd and headed toward the door. "I tried to tell you that before we got here. Come on, your dad is waiting for us."

Aubrey led the way, almost knocking over several patrons as she made her way to the door. Without looking back she said, "This place is falling apart like the rest of the town. Come on, Mommy, we'll pick up another shirt for Andrew on the way out."

My mouth dropped open as it dawned on me that this tiny lady was their mother. Elizabeth grinned at my expression and put an arm around my shoulder. "Reeba Sweeney's husband, Roger Vanderbeek, is rather tall."

"Seriously, Edge. You totally could have beaten that prick in the first second," a young man wearing a Red Wings baseball hat said.

Edge helped the waitress clean up the fries on the floor and lifted the table back in place, making sure to screw it properly into the pedestal. When it was stable, he took the fresh napkins and condiments from the waitress and passed them around our table.

"We'll get you some replacements for those chicken wings and cheesy fries," Bootie said, intercepting a basket of cheese-smothered nachos that was meant for another table and placing it in front of us.

"Want some sriracha, J.D.?" asked Edge.

J.D. offered the basket to Edge. "Have a seat and join us."

Edge sat down. "Don't mind if I do." He drizzled the sauce all over his nachos. When he was finished he picked up a piece that stayed attached to a huge melted wedge of cheese. He stretched it above his head until the cheese string broke. Then he held it up to me. "Want some, Lily?"

I opened my mouth to tell him that it was going to go straight to his gut, when I froze.

He lifted his eyebrows. "Do you?"

I blinked, unable to answer. The music was playing, people were talking, and no one seemed to care about my calamitous and very public accident. My mind was registering a very important fact. Edge Callahan had just single-handedly taken all the attention off my mortifying crash. I don't know how he did it. Or even if he did it on purpose. But the twinkle in his eye made me wonder.

Deciding that I wasn't interested in the nachos, Edge turned his attention back to his food. I watched as he devoured, in one bite, a piece that was bigger than his fist. It really should be gross. A turnoff for any proper woman who had been raised with table manners. But it wasn't. It was bold. And masculine. And incredibly . . . crazy, the way it made my senses reel.

My heart had just shifted into his cheese-covered hands. He licked his fingers and I was a goner.

LESSON THIRTEEN

Find a Partner

Arcade Fire played softly from the speaker and the headlights lit up the road in front of us as Edge drove me back home at the end of the night. I stared at his profile in the dim interior of the truck, and waited for my heart to calm down. Strange to think that a remote control had changed everything . . . Dinner with new friends. A baseball game on television. Then a rain shower in Detroit.

Edge's run-in with Aubrey and Andrew Vanderbeek had magically derailed my downfall.

"What are you looking at?"

The answer was too trite to put into a word. Instead I asked him the question that had been on my mind for the past two hours. "Did you do all that on purpose?"

He made a face. "Usually I eat that much when a game is on. I am not very good at—what do you health nuts call it? Purposeful eating?"

"You know what I mean."

He still played dumb. It was a trick he pulled often. Pretending he didn't understand a direct question. He was very good at it. But I was catching on.

I twisted toward him until the seat belt caught me. "You caused a scene inside Lori's to take everyone's mind off what happened on *Just Lose It.*"

"What are you going on about?" He reached for the radio. "You want to hear some Led Zeppelin?"

I grabbed his wrist and he acted like I had taken away his puppy dog. "Whaa—"

"I know that trick, Edge. Change the subject with music. You do it a lot."

"Me? I don't know any tricks. I really just like music." He reached again for the radio and I poked his armpit to tickle him the same way I did when we arm wrestled.

He squirmed. "Hey, that's not fair."

"Who said anything about fairness?" The truck hit a pothole and Edge slowed. Reply Lake was on my right. A vast blackness in the night. "You know, if you're going to beat me at arm wrestling, you're going to have to get over being ticklish."

"I'm not ticklish. Just sensitive."

"Right." I hovered my hand over his armpit and grinned. I was feeling loose and silly after two beers and a reprieve from disgrace.

Edge kept his eyes on the road. "You'd better be careful, Lily. Remember what happened last time you tickled me like that?"

Remember? Oh yeah. I remembered what happened last time all too well. Heat shot straight through me at the memory of his lips on mine and the feel of his rock-hard body.

I took a deep breath and deliberately ran the tip of my finger up his wrist. "Ticklish. Ha! What kind of big strong macho guy are you?"

I couldn't recall the last time I had teased a man this way. I had never been the flirty type. Some new woman was temporarily inhabiting my body and I was happy to let her do so.

My finger continued up his arm. I traced the outline of a vein on his wrist, and moved to the soft hair on his forearm. He sucked in his breath. He hadn't bothered to put on his coat, so it was easy and all too tempting for me. The palm of my hand brushed across his triceps. Pushing his sleeve up farther, my fingers circled his bicep. I licked my lips and wished I were brave enough to use my tongue.

Edge's hands clutched the wheel. He stared straight ahead and said nothing. Night shadows crossed his face and his expression was blank.

I faltered.

Maybe I had been wrong about his feelings for me. Maybe he wasn't interested in my advances. Compared to the women he had been with, I was probably boring and awkward. And there was my brace. I had just had surgery a little more than eight weeks ago. Was I seriously considering fooling around so soon? How was that going to work with my knee encased in metal and Velcro? I could take it off, but the logistics of sex might be a bit tricky. I dropped my hand and clutched it in my lap.

The headlights of the pickup truck bounced off a house in front of us. For a moment I was disoriented. Then I realized we were parked in front of the house that had been Ivy's. Edge's now. He pushed a button on the visor and the garage door opened.

The music died and the truck was silent. A vein in my neck throbbed madly against the collar of my coat. Edge cut the engine and exited the vehicle without a word. His shadow bounced off the hood. The beam of the headlights illuminated his face. His expression was stern as he marched to the passenger door and swung it open. Was he angry?

"I can walk across the road if you want . . ." My voice trailed off as he scooped me up like ice cream and carried me into the house.

Once inside, he kicked the door closed. He put me down and stood in front of me, arms at his sides.

Other than a light outside on the deck facing the lake, the room was dim. It took a moment for my eyes to adjust. A smell of sawdust and freshly cut wood filled the air.

A gust of wind outside and the sound of our breathing filled the room.

"Well?" His voice was hoarse.

"Do you want me to apologize?" I asked.

"For what? Making me horny?"

My heart started racing twice as fast as it had a moment ago.

I swallowed and waited for a cue from him.

"I'm warning you, Lily. If you tickle me again, I might react like I did the last time."

"Oh?" Confidence returned like a shot of adrenaline. I raised my hand until it was near his shoulder. He stared at it. I could feel his body heat in the air between us. With deliberate slowness, I moved my hand closer . . . and closer. Until it lingered between his arm and shoulder.

I let my fingers fall, and traced along the line of his upper arm. He shuddered.

It was nice to be in control. My turn to hold back now. I stayed as calm as he had during the wrestling match with Andrew. "Did you know that this area commonly called the armpit is technically the axilla?"

"Hmm." His voice was like a soft growl.

"This area contains the axillary vein and artery."

"You don't say." He stepped closer. His lower body was a hairs-breadth from mine. "Tell me more."

"Well, it also allows unimpeded access to your heart, since at the underarm the rib cage no longer provides protection to the chest cavity."

His head lowered. I could feel his breath hovering over my neck. "What else?"

"Most people just think of this as the sweat gland, but it produces pheromones that are crucial to how humans attract each other. Maybe even more than the genitals."

His hand rose to my hair and held it away from my neck. "Who knew BO could be sexy."

I stifled a giggle. "Hopefully it's more subtle than that."

"And why am I so ticklish?" His lips dropped to my neck and he gave me tiny butterfly kisses. I arched my neck to give him better access.

"Some scientists think we are ticklish in places that aren't usually touched by others. The soles of the feet. And here." I was still holding back. Barely touching him. Enjoying the building tension.

"You're making me hot with all your talk about medical stuff." The soft pressure of his lips was doing a whole other pheromone dance that made me want to scream. The neck is a powerfully sensitive erogenous zone. Edge seemed quite aware of it.

"So soft," he whispered against my tender skin. I giggled.

"That's funny?" he asked without lifting his mouth.

My tongue went in search of his ear. "No."

"I found it. You're ticklish there." He rubbed his beard back and forth and I threw back my head, unable to keep from laughing.

"No. I'm just . . ." *Happy*, I wanted to say.

"Everyone is ticklish. I'll find your spot if it kills me . . ." His beard felt like coarse velvet as it trailed down my neck.

At last, he lifted his lips and I finally inhaled. Except for my ragged breath, the room was silent.

We stood without touching now. Poised at the line. The tension in the air was like the beginning of a race. Runners waiting for the starting gun.

On your mark . . . Get set . . .

I pulled the trigger and reached out to tickle him.

He reacted like a sprinter off the block. He pulled me toward him and captured my lips. I buried my fingers in his thick hair. He tasted like fire and beer. A brew that made me crazy. Soft. Hard. Warm. Slick. More.

Our lips were busy, but my hands wanted in on the act. One by one I unbuttoned his shirt, letting my hand graze the carpet of his chest. While I admired the cashmere softness, his roughened hands went on their own adventure. We were like a couple of explorers who had been waiting for the chance to cross into new territory. Each unchartered region was thrilling and awakened the hunger for more.

He was hard and just as excited as I was. I almost forgot my knee as I curled my leg around his body in an attempt to get closer. Before I realized my mistake, Edge was there, lifting me in his arms and holding me close.

"I hate how awkward I am . . ." I said breathlessly.

"Not awkward. Just a little fragile, Lily Bud." He carried me across the room to the kitchen. I never thought for a moment that he would drop me.

When he set me down on the counter, I jumped at the unexpected chill. "You have granite now."

He cupped my glutes in his hands. "I must be doing something wrong if you want to talk about kitchen remodeling."

"I was just thinking about hard things. That's all."

"You were?" He deftly hooked a leg around a nearby stool and pulled it toward me. "Try this." He propped my leg up. My good knee wrapped around his waist safely now.

He stood between my legs and ground himself against me. I moaned.

"Still thinking about the countertop?"

I reached between us—my answer was obvious. He growled and moved against my hand. "I might be a little ticklish there, too, Lily."

"Really?"

"You might need to double-check."

It turns out his assessment was fairly accurate. After a moment, he grabbed my hand and made me stop.

"I'm only human," he grunted before going on his own search of my ticklish regions.

He raised my shirt over my head and removed my bra. His lips trailed down to my nipples and he found them with a gentle tug.

I shrieked.

"You *are* ticklish!"

"Not fair. I didn't use my teeth."

"Hmmm."

As Edge's mouth made me crazy, the rest of him committed me to an asylum. Chiseled muscle, light sprinkling of hair. I wanted more, though. I grasped his jeans.

"Are you protected?" he mumbled in my ear.

Reality washed over me like a cold shower. "Oh my God, I went off the pill when I had surgery." Not that I had needed it for a long time.

He licked the underside of my ear and chuckled. "Good thing I stopped by the pharmacy after our wrestling match the other day."

Boing! The heat returned and went straight to my core. I couldn't resist a jibe. "You were that sure?"

"I was hopeful . . . You were a pretty amazing wrestler."

"Thank God for your ticklish axilla," I teased.

He planted a kiss on my bare shoulder and said, "Don't go anywhere. I'll be right back."

Once he was gone I kicked off my shoes and attempted the awkward removal of my brace and my pants. I pulled the Velcro on my knee as quietly as possible, cringing at the harsh sound, like nails on a chalkboard. The brace dropped on the floor with a clunk. I shifted my weight back and forth as I shimmied the pants down. They were caught up in my knees just as Edge returned, holding up a condom.

"Here's to axillas," he said, holding up the packet.

He stopped when he saw my distress. "Let me help."

"No, I can do it," I squeaked as I almost toppled off the countertop. My panties were caught under me and I couldn't lean down far enough to get the stupid stretch pants past my knees.

I felt as helpless as I did the first day I met Edge. Only now, instead of a being unable to get into a truck, like a frail old lady, I was like a child unable to get my own clothes off.

"Some kind of trainer." My voice cracked with my frustration. "Can't even get my damn pants off before—"

"Hey." Edge's arms went around me, steadying me.

I buried my head in his chest. "I'm sorry. I'm just a klutz. Let's pretend this night never happened. Okay?"

He pulled away. "That was a rare joke from you, right?"

"This is just so stupid. *I'm* so stupid."

He cupped my cheek and gave me a tender kiss. "Yeah. You're being kind of stupid."

"Wha—?"

"You think I care that you aren't agile? Geez, Lily. Don't you know that removing a woman's clothes is like the biggest turn-on for a man? Ever."

Well, yeah. I knew that. But my experience was pretty limited. I'd had a grand total of two lovers in my life. One who had broken my immature heart at the age of twenty-one when he had stopped returning my calls after three months of being together. And one who I dated two years ago. We lost interest by mutual agreement. Since then I figured that I just wasn't the kind of woman who was suited to relationships and explosive sex.

I didn't know how to be sexy for him. We were both winging it.

Edge put his hands on my hips and made sure I wasn't going to topple over. Then he backed up to examine where I had left off. The light from the bedroom bounced off his face. His eyes sparkled with a wicked glint. With his beard and his hungry expression, he reminded me of a devil. A sexy one.

Slowly he peeled my pants down, running his palms over the sensitive area in the back of each knee. He followed each inch with a kiss that made goose bumps break out all over. He lingered at my ankles, taking the time to kiss each one.

Finally, he dropped my pants to the floor with relish. "Success."

The exciting tingle of cool night air caressed my exposed center. He lowered himself until he was kneeling between my legs and the coolness was replaced by the molten heat of his tongue.

I threw my head back and arched my spine, letting my elbows drop to the counter behind me. I forgot all about my embarrassing ineptness as I cried out.

"Hold on, baby, we might need to protect you from injury here."

Edge pulled back, a cheeky smile making him look more devilish. He stood up, holding my brace in one hand. He looped it back up my leg until it was in the correct position.

"I'm not walking anywhere," I whined. "Are you delaying this for fun?"

His chest rumbled and he grinned. "Just being safe. I have no idea how out of control you get under these circumstances."

Neither did I, actually. Once the Velcro was in place I opened my legs wider. He took the invitation and returned to what he had been doing.

I was beyond incoherent as he brought me close to a peak. Before I could catch my breath, he stood up and adjusted the condom.

I grasped him around his back and pulled him into me. We clung to each other and finished the journey we started. It was exhilarating and crazy, and scary the way my self-control shattered. It was the explosive sex I didn't think I was capable of. Edge took me on a dizzy ride that brought me far away from the room, the town . . . and from myself.

A moonbeam made its way through the skylight and traveled across my face. I studied its slow path and enjoyed the warmth of Edge next to me. Instead of a pull-out couch or a hammock, as I had somehow imagined, Edge's mattress was deluxe and his sheets were as fine as silk. My skin prickled in all the tracks Edge's beard had forged across my skin. Instead of feeling chafed, I felt like he had given me a new layer of nerves I hadn't known existed.

I shouldn't gloat. I had probably just broken one of the cardinal rules of fitness trainers. Not technically. Edge wasn't one of my clients. But in a way the whole county was my client. By sleeping with one of the town's favorite sons, I may have opened myself to some sort of ethical dilemma.

Unless—it was just a one-night fling.

I was so naïve I probably wouldn't recognize a fling if it reached out and bit me.

My brace lay across the bottom of the bed where I had taken it off before I went to sleep. The back of my head rested on Edge's arm.

The moonbeam had shifted to his face now. He threw a hand over his eyes. "Turn off the light," he grumbled.

Someone was testy. Louise had told me he was grouchy about waking up. Interesting. "Sorry, sleepyhead. I can't reach to turn off that particular light."

"Hmmm?" He stirred and I lifted my head in case he wanted his arm back. But he caught my shoulder and pulled me close. I curled into his side at the invitation.

He threw a hand across his eyes and whined, "That's like a headlight, it's so bright."

"Why did you add a skylight if you don't like being woken up by light, Mr. Grump?" I asked.

I thought he was falling asleep again. Then he spoke. "Wasn't it full the other night?"

"I can't remember. I think it's waning now . . . or maybe it's waxing?"

He turned on his side and kissed the top of my breast. "Hey, I'm in bed with a really smart lady. Waxing . . . Waning . . . First anatomy, now astronomy. Tell me more."

"Waxing means making its way to a full moon and waning means—" I stopped and glanced down at his grin. "Wait a minute. I saw a textbook on astronomy in your bedroom in the main house. You know exactly what the two mean."

"I guess I forgot," he said, forging a new journey across my body with the tip of his tongue.

I savored the massage. Then curiosity got the best of me. "You like to make yourself sound stupid on purpose sometimes. Why do you do that?"

"I guess low expectations means I never disappoint."

I closed my eyes. "I'm living proof of that."

He let out a low whistle and fell back against the pillow. "Does that mean you weren't disappointed?"

I rolled over, careful not to put pressure on my right leg, until I was on top of him. "Satisfied customer."

"As a businessman I love to hear that. Perhaps you would like to join my frequent shopper club?" He wrapped both hands around my lower back and let my right leg sink between his legs. I loved how he seemed to understand where my knee would be most comfortable.

I wanted to take him up on his frequent shopper offer, but my earlier worries weighed me down. "I have to tell you, I feel a little weird about all this."

"This?" he asked, thrusting his hips toward me. There was no doubt he was ready to improve customer satisfaction. But I wasn't going to be derailed so easily.

"No really. I'm screwing things up all over the place." I scrunched up my face at the bad choice of words. "You know what I mean. I am not doing too well. Attendance at my weekly fitness and nutrition classes has been dropping each week. Everyone in town will know about my disaster on the treadmill by tomorrow. I'm not sure being with you is . . . I wasn't planning on starting a relationship."

"I wasn't either. But life is like that. Before my grandma had her stroke, she used to say, *You can't plan on anything. Especially the weather.*"

"Are we talking about snow or sex now?"

He kissed my nose. "She meant, just take it as it comes. We can't predict the future. Live in the now. She was really good at that."

I bit my lip. I didn't tell him that wasn't my style. My notebooks were full of all sorts of ideas. Things I wanted to do. Ways I wanted to help get Truhart in shape. Thoughts I had for a gym. Thinking about the sorry state of my plans made me crazy.

Edge pulled my lips down to his, sending all my worries up into the night. I stared up at the beam that illuminated the wall behind us now. Like the moon, I wasn't sure if my troubles were waxing or waning.

LESSON FOURTEEN

Be Creative

Finding a chance to replay our amazing night had been virtually impossible over the weekend without alerting the whole Callahan family. Edge worked at the Dairy Cow all weekend. The girls wanted me to watch a chick flick with them Saturday night. On Sunday night, Louise and Ivy watched an old movie until late, sitting on the couch next to the window that overlooked the ranch. Edge had crept in after work and we fooled around. But the noise of his impressionable teenage sisters arguing about the cap on the toothpaste had stopped us both.

I reminded Edge that we were adults and shouldn't make a bad impression on his sisters.

"We are adults. Why don't you just come to my place and spend the night and to hell with my family," he said.

"We'll figure it out when the time is right, and I don't have to explain to your sisters," I told him before pushing him into the recreation room, where we watched the rest of the Wings hockey game.

If anyone suspected our liaison, they didn't say a word. Although I did notice Louise looking at me speculatively the morning after I slept at Edge's house.

"Are you getting a rash on your neck, Lily?" she had asked. I'd never been with a man who had a beard.

I patted my neck. "Sensitive skin. I used my emulsifying scrub this morning."

Edge showed up for the family dinner Saturday and Sunday. To my surprise, he cooked dinner both nights.

When Louise saw my jaw drop as he walked up the stairs carrying a pot of soup, she laughed. "I made sure all my kids knew how to cook before they were old enough to drive," she told me. "We're still working on Olivia."

Tracy added, "None of us are brave enough to eat Peter's cooking. And mine is basic. Edge is the only one with the real talent. Thank God he has his counter installed now."

I stared at the white chicken chili and tried not to think about what had been cooked on that counter. Edge must have read my mind because his smile made his beard as large as a throw rug.

Edge stopped by on Monday after my creative fitness class. Rocky couldn't drive me home, and Edge offered to come. While he waited for me to mark the last of my walkers' progress, he played on the equipment that Joe O'Shea had made for me from PVC pipes and wood planks. He jumped around like a kid on a playground. He tested the old soccer balls Rocky and I had filled with sand and threw them against the concrete block wall. He bounced on the boxes with the excitement of a first-grader. He slung the ropes we had anchored by hooks into the wall, back and forth with amazing ease.

When the last person left, he pointed at the cans and water bottles stacked against the wall. "Are you having a food drive soon?"

I picked up a can and lifted it like a barbell. "These are the weights we are using until the ladies can raise enough money for real weights."

Edge picked me up and set me on a platform box Joe O'Shea had helped make. We had lined them with a thin layer of padding from the local arts and crafts store and then covered them with duct tape and vinyl. I looped my arms around his neck and enjoyed the fact that I was slightly taller than him for once.

He ran his roughened thumb under my shirt and caressed my hip. "You have done wonders with the budget you have been given. Even with a ThighMaster."

"Flo found that at a garage sale." I took advantage of my newfound height and messed up Edge's wavy hair. "I just wish all this creativity would inspire a few more people to attend my gym classes."

"That bad?"

"Yeah. All the enthusiasm people felt for working out and getting fit has worn off. Attendance has dropped to almost half of what I had in the beginning."

"There were a lot of walkers today."

"Yeah, but it has become a bit of a social thing now. I'm trying to get them to increase their mileage. One or two miles seems to be fine, then people start peeling off for garage sales, double coupon day at the Family Fare, and coffee. I even had three people stop in for cookies at the church bake sale the other day."

He soothed a sore muscle in my back. "Give it time, Lily Bud. On the bright side, we could figure out a whole new use for this platform. You on top, legs wide, or me on top, you inverted—"

"Stop it!" I picked up my duffel bag with my notes and my own personal equipment in it and he grabbed them from me.

"After you," he said, waving his hand in the air. "I have to make a run to Lakeview. You don't mind coming with me, do you?"

I shook my head. Spending more time with Edge was always good with me.

I followed him to the truck, staring at his back and thinking naughty thoughts about the gym and ways we could use the equipment to our advantage. By the time he started the engine, I was breathing in short little huffs and trying to ignore the tingle in interesting parts of my body.

Edge must have been feeling the same way, because he kept clearing his throat. When we pulled into Lakeview, Edge yanked the truck into park and we crashed against each other like overeager teenagers who had just discovered the wonders of necking. The way my body acted on its own when I was around Edge was crazy. His truck had become my conditioned stimulus, like food was for Pavlov's dogs. Each time I saw it I went into heat.

Edge's hand was inside my coat, working its way under my shirt when some sixth sense caused me to open one eye.

Three faces peered out the day care window as if we were the nightly news.

"Uh, Edge—Edge! We have an audience."

He turned and waved at the onlookers. They waved back and dropped the curtain in place.

I collapsed against the seat. "Oh my God. You go in, I can't show my face."

"We just made their day," Edge said, closing his eyes and struggling for control.

"Maybe you should come back later. On your own."

"Come on," he coaxed me. He reached behind him. "Besides, you haven't had a chance to witness my amazing talent yet."

"What?"

He pulled a guitar case out of the back. "Me and Jimmy Page were like one person once. You'll love this."

I let him lead me by the hand into Lakeview and wondered if Edge was ever boring. Every day was different with him, whether he was handing out Pete's Treats under the udders of the Dairy Cow or running around playing hide-and-seek with his nephews. Each day was like unwrapping a piece of him and finding something new.

"Hey, everyone, Karaoke with Callahan–time!" he announced as we entered the front door.

A half dozen white-haired campers greeted him with smiles on their faces. "Can you play 'Camptown Races' again like you did last week, Edge?"

Camptown Races? I put my hand over my mouth to hide my amusement. Edge looked at me with a straight face. "It is a good song."

"Whatever you say . . . Jimmy."

He put his chin in the air and pretended irritation as he walked ahead of me to the meeting room and set his case on the floor. Behind me, one of the aides moved into the arts-and-crafts room and then down the hall, clapping her hands. "Edge is here. Come on, everyone. Time for Karaoke with Callahan!"

Seniors popped out from various corners of the facility. Some were pushed by aides, others shuffled along behind their walkers. It was like rush hour at the Golden Corral. I saw two able-bodied ladies almost trip each other as they entered.

"Take your time, ladies. There is room for all," Edge called out to them.

I made myself comfortable against the wall near the back corner and looked for Ivy. She sat by the window. Still watching the traffic as it passed.

While everyone in the room settled, Edge walked over to her and squatted down at her feet. "Hi, Grandma. Want to help me sing?"

She smiled and pointed at the guitar. "Crap."

He overdramatized disappointment. "Aww, don't you like my singing?"

She sputtered and slapped him on the shoulder. "Play mine."

"Your favorite? What is that again, 'On Top of Old Smoky'?"
Ivy grunted.

Edge kissed her and moved to the front of the room, placing the guitar strap over his head and shoulder. With goofy eyes that alternated winks at various ladies, he tuned the guitar. He was almost finished when he caught my eye. "Don't look so amused. I have a wonderful voice. Tell Lily, Grandma."

Ivy turned toward me and grumbled an unintelligible response. Even though she looked as stone-faced as ever, the way she darted her gaze around the room told me that she was delighted to show off her grandson. Or maybe that was my delight. He was such a shameless charmer.

Finally, everyone was in place. Without introducing himself, Edge began.

"Hello Muddah, hello Faddah,
Here I am at Lakeview Day Care . . ."

He made his surprisingly nice, deep voice speak in a very silly accent. It was delightful. When he substituted names and verses with people in the room, the campers giggled . . .

"Now I don't want this should scare ya,
But my aide here has malaria.
You remember Jay Galardi.
They're about to organize a searching party."

Jay Galardi was a heavyset man who was missing a leg from the knee down. He slapped his thigh and grinned as everyone in the room pointed at him.

If I wasn't head over heels for Edge after the other night, I was now. He was corny and made people laugh despite it. He flirted without being offensive. He charmed without trying. Sigh.

It was when he started to sing "Head, Shoulders, Knees and Toes" that a different feeling of excitement passed over me. The last time I was at Lakeview, the atmosphere had been depressing and sleepy. Except, of course, when Edge walked into the room and lit up someone's day by greeting them. It was different now. The entire group, including Ivy, were touching their heads, shoulders, and knees. Even if they couldn't reach their toes, they were making an effort to put their hands low and stretch.

As a fitness trainer, seeing the combination of Edge's energy and his music make people move was inspiring. If I could do that with the fitness center, getting Truhart on board with the Fit4You grant would be a breeze. What was his magic formula?

Then I saw Mr. Frasier. The man who begged me not to forget him. He stood just outside the doorway, watching with a grim line to his lips, as if he wanted to join but he wasn't sure he should. I shuffled along the wall until I was next to him.

"Hi, Mr. Frasier."

"Hello, pretty lady."

I tilted my head. "I'll bet you say that to all the girls."

His down-turned lips tipped into a crooked smile. "Only the pretty ones."

Edge had finished "Head, Shoulders, Knees and Toes." He raised his voice.

"Did I wear you all out, now?" Heads nodded around the room. Except for Ivy, who was back to gazing out the window.

Edge strummed a guitar introduction. "Let's slow it down until you get your breath. But just for a minute, 'cause I'm gonna make you pick up the speed of this song in a minute. This old song was written around the time of the Civil War, an oldie but a goodie that my grandparents used to sing."

While Edge sang a ballad I hadn't heard before, Mr. Frasier's toe tapped to the beat. I joined him and our feet moved in unison.

Edge saw us and his smile grew broader. "Hey, look who's having fun, everyone," he said when the verse ended. "Say hi to Lily, campers."

"Hi, Lily!" a chorus of cheerful voices called out.

I waved, feeling like a schoolgirl at a Justin Bieber concert.

"Mr. Frasier—Lily, there, is shy. She might need a little prodding. Can you give her a nudge and bring her into the room so she can join the rest of us?"

Mr. Frasier stood straighter and squared his chin, as if he was proud to have a job assigned to him. He grabbed my elbow and walked with me into the meeting room. A camper with a reddish tint to her gray hair scooted to the corner of the couch and patted the open area next to her. I pulled Mr. Frasier along. Together we sat down.

As if nothing out of the ordinary had happened, Edge kept singing his song. The beat grew faster, and we were forced to clap to a more frenzied pace. As happy as the tune was, I couldn't help feeling that the words were sad.

"I'm gonna learn to live in peace
With my friends around the world
With my friends around the world
With my friends around the world
I'm gonna learn to live in peace
With my friends around the world
We won't study war no more."

I peeked at Mr. Frasier. His eyes were glassy as he sang along.

Most of the people in the room were old enough to remember World War II and certainly a few of the men had participated in Korea and Vietnam. Very few still had spouses who were alive. They suffered from so many aches and pains that they were on a dozen medications. The day campers struggled to find meaning in the day, even if it was making paper flowers. A knot formed in the pit of my stomach when I realized my problems were nothing in the scheme of things. Why had I taken my embarrassing accident and my diminished career so seriously?

It was strange to think about these things while singing corny songs. But there it was. A realization that my pain was a speck in the whole wide world of pain. If they could sing silly songs that made them feel happy for one hour, then I could, too.

Edge shifted to "B-I-N-G-O" and I raised my voice and joined him.

That night, I was almost asleep when Edge knocked on the window of his bedroom. When I opened it, he was carrying a grocery bag and a blanket.

"What are you doing? Why don't you use the door?"

"This is more fun," he said. "I'm kidnapping you for voice lessons. Your rendition of 'Bingo' was shameful."

I leaned out and kissed him. "I never claimed to have a voice. But you feel free to try."

He wrapped me in the blanket and carried me across the street while I made halfhearted protests and kissed his neck. It all seemed so juvenile and lovely.

"What's in the grocery bag?" I asked when he dumped me on his bed.

"You'll see."

He lit a candle on the bedside table and turned off the overhead light.

"Mood lighting. Nice."

He flipped a switch, and smooth notes of soft jazz filled the room. He pulled a bottle of white wine from a wine cooler and poured two glasses.

"Is this a date?" I asked, surprised that he was going to so much trouble.

"A date with benefits . . ." he said in a low, sexy tone.

I was blown away by this new romantic side of Edge. He was such a jokester that I couldn't imagine him planning this moment. My heart melted like the hot wax of the candle.

"Let's get you more comfortable, shall we?" he asked, settling next to me. He took his time removing my nightshirt. The featherlight touch of his hands and the glow of the candle made me crazy with anticipation. I was breathing hard and ready for more when Edge pulled away.

"What?!" It was unfair of him to stop.

"I forgot, there's more." He retrieved the grocery bag and held it in front of me.

"You brought food? I'm still full—"

He dangled the bag from one finger. "This is dessert."

The ultimate romantic. I would tell him how great the gesture was when I wasn't hyperventilating from estrogen overdrive. This serious side of Edge was wonderful; however, I didn't need wine and candlelight and jazz. I was just about to explain it when he pulled the contents out of the bag.

Whipped cream.

Chocolate sauce.

"You brought ice cream from the Dairy Cow?"

He showed his teeth, but it was more feral than a smile. "No. No ice cream. Just the toppings. Any ideas what they should go on?"

I collapsed back on the bed. "Oh . . ."

He shook the can and dessert started.

"I think I need a shower."

Edge ran a finger across my breasts. "The cherries were a nice touch at the end, don't you think?"

I lifted my hands over my head and stretched. "Delicious."

"Next time I'll take you to a movie."

"Don't you dare. But next time I get to choose the menu."

"My mind is having trouble imagining this will be as fun with hummus and celery."

I turned on my side so we were facing each other. "So what are we doing?" I wanted to take the words back before I finished the sentence. Where had that come from?

It was a stupidly typical girl thing for me to say. The words had *cold shower* written all over them.

I put my sticky hands over my face. "Sorry. Forget I said anything."

"Why do you want me to forget?"

"I don't need you to take a multiple-choice test so I can feel good about our relationship."

He put a hand under my hip and pulled me until I was on top of him.

"Pretend I never said anything, all right?" I said. "In case you haven't noticed, I'm a little . . . serious. Not like you. I have a hard time unwinding."

"What was your life like in L.A.?" he asked, playing with my hair.

"I used to leave the gym at nine p.m. and go straight to bed so I could get up at six a.m. and start the day all over again."

"What about your days off?"

"I would visit my mother most of the time. She has a great big Korean family and many of them live in the L.A. area. When we get together we eat."

"Korean food. I've had it before. I like the barbecue. Unfortunately we don't have so many Korean restaurants in Northern Michigan."

I missed Mom's cooking, I had to admit. "It's one of the only types of food I really crave."

"Will you make it for me sometime?"

Sometime? That sounded like a commitment of some sort. It made me happy and nervous. I stalled. "I don't know if I could find the ingredients anywhere in Truhart."

"Not too many Asians around here. Sorry, Lily."

I nuzzled his chin and let my head rest on his shoulder. "Kimchi isn't exactly the most romantic food." It tended to make your breath awful. "When my mom would get out the kimchi jar, my dad would always grab a set of chopsticks and joke that he had better eat some, too, if they were going to sleep in the same bed."

"Well, I like kimchi. So you're safe." He found my mouth and when we came up for air he asked, "Your dad?"

"He's been gone for about fifteen years."

The strange lump in my heart that came in waves swept over me. I thought I had cried all I could cry that first year Dad passed away. But it never seemed to end. It popped up at the oddest times. Instead of pushing it away like I usually did, I let it rise to the surface. Soupy eyes and little confessions felt safe with Edge.

"Dad was pretty much my best friend when I was growing up."

It occurred to me that Dad would have appreciated Edge's goofy sense of humor. It was one of the things he had loved about my mom.

"He liked gardening. That was something we did together. So, I guess that counts as something I did for fun." Other than the gym, gardening was the one place I felt truly at home.

"You don't garden anymore?"

"When we moved to L.A. after Dad died, I dug up one of the lilies in his garden. It didn't survive the trip. I helped lead an urban garden last year." We had a grand harvest celebration and my mom and brothers came. The sky opened up and it poured before I could take them on a tour. We ended up huddled under the awning of a taco stand.

"Grandma used to garden. We still keep her roses and perennial garden going each summer. Maybe you can help us this year."

Being here in the summer, gardening with Edge, it was a commitment as far as I was concerned. I buried my face in his neck to keep from letting him see my delight. I licked an area around his ear that looked suspiciously like whipped cream and laughed.

"What do you look like without hair all over your face?" I asked after a moment.

"Like Chris Hemsworth," he said, fluttering his lashes. He was joking, but I could almost see a resemblance.

"Are you sure you aren't trying to cover up a major flaw?" I teased.

"Naw. I just don't want the women falling all over themselves to get to me."

I rubbed his face. "Your mom told me the other day that she has given up begging you to shave it."

"Yeah. She doesn't remember the old days when crowds of women threw lingerie at me."

"Funny how she never mentioned it." I turned on my back and stared at the ceiling, trying to keep my face straight. "Just sayin', I'm not sure dried chocolate sauce on a beard is the most attractive thing."

He felt his beard. "Second dessert for you?"

"I'll pass."

"Come on. Let's shower. I'll give you a soap massage. You'll like it . . ."

I did.

LESSON FIFTEEN

Allow for Setbacks

The first week of May was gorgeous by any standards. Even my warped L.A. sunshine-state standards. The mud-crusted snow had melted. Several days of temperatures hovering around sixty degrees had tinted the gray ground to green. If I looked closely I could see the hint of buds sprouting on the trees around the lake. Amazingly, everyone walked around town coatless, and some in short sleeves as if it were eighty degrees and July. Olivia even wore flip-flops and shorts one day.

On Monday, my spirits were as bright as the sunshine. The midday walkers returned around two p.m. and I made notes on each of their walk journals suggesting they add an extra quarter mile to their walk by Friday. When the last person left, I started to prepare the gym for a group of moms who wanted to work out while their kids were at soccer practice at the middle school.

I was just about finished writing out a workout plan for the moms, when two shadows fell across the doorway. Marie Joiner, who was in charge of the fitness grant, and Reeba Sweeney, Aubrey and Andrew Vanderbeek's mother.

Trying to sound more welcoming than I felt, I said, "Hi, ladies. Come on in."

They stepped into my makeshift gym and looked around the room as if they were afraid for their safety. Marie's face was strained as she clutched a clipboard in her hands. She looked like she would rather be anywhere else but in Truhart.

Reeba Sweeney was dressed in a red suit. Even with spiky high heels she was still short.

A strange silence filled the room, and I had the sense that Reeba was waiting for Marie to speak. Marie shifted back and forth so much I wondered if she was in pain.

"I can't offer you a chair, but you are welcome to take a seat," I said, waving toward the homemade boxes Joe O'Shea had made.

Reeba took one look at Marie and rolled her eyes. "See what I mean?"

Something wasn't right. The tips of my fingers prickled.

The side of Marie's mouth jerked back and forth as if she had a facial tick. "Lily, have you met Reeba Sweeney?"

"Uh, briefly." I held out my hand, but Reeba bypassed me and walked around Marie, inspecting the posters on the wall. My sign-up sheets were almost half full now.

Marie tried to cover up for Reeba's rudeness. "Lily . . . It's good to see you without your crutches." Her tone was too sugary. She smiled. Something was definitely wrong.

I played along anyway. "I've graduated to walking with just my brace," I said, imitating her cheery tone but sounding like a cricket.

"I have a meeting at four, Marie." Reeba Sweeney tapped her watch and glared impatiently.

Marie looked down at her clipboard and cleared her throat. "Lily, I've heard some things about the fitness program here in Truhart that have me concerned."

"I can't imagine what the—"

"According to several witnesses, you were an instigator in an unruly wrestling match at a local restaurant."

Now I understood. Andrew's mommy was getting even. "It was just an arm-wrestling match. Nothing was damaged."

Marie looked down at her clipboard. "It says here that a table was broken, a chair was overturned, and a participant broke his finger."

"A participant broke his—"

"Andrew is still in pain," Reeba said, picking up a ThighMaster in the corner.

I took a deep breath and tried not to tell her what wee little Andrew could do with his fat finger.

"I also have reports of groups of people who were supposed to be walking but ended up shopping at garage sales and going from door to door looking for candy, as if was Halloween."

"The Dairy Cow had a promotion—"

Reeba had finished her tour of the gym and was standing next to Marie now, arms crossed, chin out. "People saw you and Edge Callahan holding out bags of candy to a group of your walkers. Do you deny it?"

"I was holding the candy, but Edge Callahan was—"

"A boy has been hired to help you, correct?" Reeba asked.

"Rocky has been driving me, and he helped move some equipment the other day—"

"That's another problem, Lily. We aren't insured for other employees. And the balls, the platforms, they aren't regulation gym apparatus," Marie said apologetically.

Reeba's nose pinched. "I have also heard that you are using bath mats for yoga and nylon hose for stretching. What kind of gym is that?"

"We were being creative," I explained.

Reeba shook her head at Marie. "Can you imagine trying to explain to the rest of the grant committee how someone injured themselves using control-top panty hose? We'd be laughed out of the state."

"Reeba is on the DHHS committee that approved the grant, Lily."

I bit my tongue to keep from telling Reeba what I thought of her revenge. But Reeba was too important to anger now.

"We had no idea it would be administered this way. I've never seen such a two-bit operation," Reeba said.

I swallowed past the brick in my throat. "As you know, the budget was very limited and we couldn't afford a lot of equipment."

"You managed to buy T-shirts with your logo on it. Some people might call that self-promotion," said Reeba.

I didn't bother to explain where the T-shirts had come from. Addie Adler was already a joke around the county. I didn't want to hear what Reeba had to say about Addie's misdirected enthusiasm.

"I know this isn't the most orthodox fitness center. But people are starting to like this gym."

"That sign-up sheet really shows it," Reeba said with a smug smile.

"There are more people joining our walking group each week." It was a lie.

Marie sighed and looked down at her clipboard. "I have a bill here for a damaged toilet."

"One of my walkers had to use the restroom on the walk."

Marie flipped to another page on her clipboard. "What about this report of landscape damage?"

Landscape damage? I scoured my memory, wondering what she meant. "Are you talking about a broken tree limb? One of my walking moms was trying to put back a bird's nest that had fallen . . ." It sounded ridiculous even to my own ears. I let the excuse hang in the air without finishing the story.

Marie closed her eyes and let out a long sigh. When she opened them, she fixed me with her gaze. "Lily, I am sorry. This just isn't acceptable."

"I can remove the equipment that isn't professional grade." My legs were beginning to shake.

"That's not the problem."

"I will personally walk with each group and make sure that they don't stray—"

"That's not the answer," Reeba interrupted. "Even if we hadn't seen the video of you falling off the treadmill on *Just Lose It*, we would come to the conclusion that you aren't the right person for this job. Your leadership and judgment are sorely lacking."

Marie tried to soften it. "The grant committee feels we need to make a change."

My knee could no longer hold me. I stepped backward and collapsed onto the coffin behind me. "Please don't."

Marie held up a sheet of paper. "As of today, the fitness program for the east side of the county will merge with the west side of the county. We are closing this facility and sending everyone to Harrisburg."

"But that's too far. It's hard enough to get people to come to a local gym. If they have to drive a half hour, they will never work out."

Reeba put her hands on her hips. "Maybe with a decent gym we'll get more participants."

No, they wouldn't. The last thing the people of Truhart and the neighboring area wanted was to work out in Harrisburg. The grudge between the two towns was so strong there might as well be a mountain between them. Rocky had lost five pounds in the last two weeks. Using the excuse that he was my assistant wasn't going to work in Harrisburg. Would the walkers have to walk in Harrisburg? Their friends were here. They loved to walk together and gossip.

This was happening so fast, I didn't know how people would accept the change. "Can you give us some time? Maybe let me keep the gym open for a few hours a week. That way I can transition my participants to Harrisburg slowly. I can bring their records with me on the days I work in Harrisburg. Or I can even make duplicates."

Marie's face was red. "I'm sorry, I'm not making myself clear, Lily. We are relieving you of your job."

This couldn't be happening.

I blinked rapidly. Letting it sink in. Of course that's what she was talking about. The closing of my makeshift gym wasn't because of the equipment, or the mishaps that the walkers had faced. It was about me.

"The grant was approved for two fitness trainers. Wouldn't it be easier if I helped Aubrey get to know everyone here? I can assist her and introduce her to Truhart's participants."

"Oh, we already have your replacement," Reeba said with a smile. For the first time I noticed that she had pointy eyeteeth. Blood sucker.

"Who?"

"Andrew." The triumph on her face was obvious. "He minored in physical education."

Marie clutched the clipboard to her chest and looked at me with something akin to sympathy.

"But I thought you said he was in pain. He has a broken finger. How can he be a fitness trainer if he can't . . ." I stopped myself. Reeba was staring at my knee.

"Yes?" she said sweetly. "You were saying something about working with an injury?"

I pressed my lips together. There was nothing more to say.

I knew deep down I deserved this. I hadn't been able to control the situation from day one. I had let people do things their way. The T-shirts, the equipment, even helping Rocky. Instead of commanding the kind of change and leadership Truhart needed, I had caved.

"Just to be fair, your paycheck will extend to the end of the week,

Lily," Marie said. "We will also contribute half the cost of your return trip to L.A." Magnanimous of her. I could probably afford to go as far as Wichita now.

My eyes traveled over the room, wondering what the Triple C's were going to do with it if there was no gym anymore. I thought about life going on in Truhart without me. An empty bedroom in the Callahans' house. No one at the window at midnight.

I pictured Edge saying goodbye. Would he make our goodbye lighthearted? Joke that he was going to miss my singing or my awkward brace?

The fitness class would arrive soon. I didn't want anyone to witness the breakdown that I was about to have. Marie's eyes darted from Reeba to me. "I'll see you out and put this sign up on the door." She pulled a folded paper from the bottom of her clipboard.

I rose to my feet and felt like I had just put on an extra hundred pounds. I gathered my gym bag from the coffin and pulled out the paperwork and records of my participants. I left them stacked neatly on the wooden surface. Some people had notes and health histories from their doctors. I had carefully included my own notes as to their fitness plan and nutrition needs in each file.

"These are the records and paperwork for each participant on this side of the county. Please make sure to give them to Aubrey." My voice cracked. I zipped my bag shut and walked toward the door. I almost forgot. "Here is the key." I held out my hand. "Please give it back to the Triple C's when you see them."

Marie nodded and took it from me. She looked almost as sad as I felt. "Look, Lily, I am really sorry about this."

"No. I understand." Why was I comforting her? She was more spineless than me. I clamped my lips shut before I said anything else I would regret.

She extended her hand and I offered her my numb handshake.

Reeba didn't bother. "Aubrey and Andrew are waiting in the car."

Of course they were. Like hyenas, they were waiting for the killing so they could pounce on the dead meat.

Out on the sidewalk, I looked over Marie's shoulder at the sign she was placing on the window. CLOSED BY THE DEPARTMENT OF HEALTH AND HUMAN SERVICES. RESIDENTS OF HARRISON COUNTY PARTICIPATING IN THE FIT4YOU GRANT MUST USE THE HARRISBURG GYM.

Thankfully it said nothing about the fact that the fitness trainer had just been fired. I might be able to escape town before anyone realized the truth. Not that pride mattered. I had no more pride to preserve. What I couldn't handle was the disappointment.

I turned away from the community center and bumped into a wall. One with two hard knockers.

Aubrey.

Next to her stood a sneering Andrew, his hand encased in a sling.

Aubrey's two hawkish eyebrows rose to meet her hairline. "Tough break, Shue."

I averted my eyes and moved around them. She made a clucking sound that followed me.

I could lash out at Aubrey and Andrew. Say something nasty that might put a chink in their cold, hard skin. But that would make me look even more pathetic.

The sooner I left, the sooner I could return to my mother's couch and ramen. I would surround myself with massive amounts of tissues and let myself cry until next winter.

I ignored the sound of Reeba Sweeney's Lexus starting nearby. She pulled away from the curb and sent me a little wave out her back mirror as she whizzed by me. The tears that had threatened to fall throughout my conversation didn't come. Instead I was left with strange deadness inside that made my ears ring. For some reason this failure felt worse than any of my other recent defeats. It didn't make sense. A torn ACL, a lost job, a televised public shaming . . . This should have been the least of the bunch. But it felt like I had just lost the grand prize.

I headed away from town, walking toward the lake road. Not Reply Lake, but her sister, Echo Lake.

I needed to be alone.

What was going to happen to the gym I had grown so proud of? The rollers made from padded PVC pipes. The water bottles stacked against the wall. Like Santa Claus and the sleigh, would everything just gather dust until next year? Never mind the other thing I was going to miss. Not a *thing*. A man. The thought of saying goodbye to Edge was like rubbing salt in an open wound.

I was going to miss the way my heart skipped a beat when I heard the sound of rock and roll coming from a pickup truck.

A silly man with a beard, and a makeshift gym.

When had I turned into such a fool?

Somewhere between my life in L.A., with the state-of-the-art gym equipment, and my life here, I had completely lost my perspective. Not to mention my heart.

I passed the three-mile mark I had so recently mapped out on the lake road. It was the point where my fittest walkers turned around and headed back to the community center gym. I shifted my bag and felt a familiar ache in my knee. I welcomed it. It was a nice contrast to the feeling of detachment that had settled over the rest of me.

The beautiful spring day and the faint promise of summer was nothing but an ironic joke to me now. When the weather finally did turn in Truhart, I would be back in L.A. getting ready for the long, hot part of the year. Everyone would hide inside their air-conditioned homes and wait for the heat to break. Water would be rationed and lawns would turn brown. It was more unbearable than a Michigan winter.

The faint sound of an engine behind me prompted me to move over to the newly sprouted grass on the shoulder. The pickup truck slowed down next me. The sound of the engine was as familiar as the man who drove it.

"Lily. Stop."

I shook my head and kept going. I couldn't stop. If I did, the numbness might disappear. And that meant I wouldn't be able to keep myself moving. I wasn't on crutches anymore. At least I had one thing going for me.

A truck door slammed and footsteps pounded behind me. He caught up with me before I had taken half a dozen steps away from the truck.

"Lily."

I couldn't find my voice, my throat was so tight from bottling up my emotions.

Edge reached out and grabbed my elbow. "Hey, stop. Lily, I heard what happened. We're going to fix this. The Triple C's are talking to Marie right now."

I pulled away and shook my head. "Please don't try—" Of all the times for that numbness to wear off . . .

"This is bullshit." Edge's angry outburst was so uncharacteristic that I forgot my own misery. His nostrils flared and his eyes caught the afternoon sunlight, making them gleam like ice in a blazing sun. I couldn't stand to see his usual smile turn to this.

"It's all right. I should have guessed this would happen."

"No, it's not all right. Aubrey is trying to get back at me. She hates Truhart. So does Reeba Sweeney, for that matter."

"Even if she did, it doesn't change all the crazy things I've let happen since I came to Truhart."

"The arm-wrestling match was just a Friday-night norm for Lori's. The whole thing was blown out of proportion."

"What about the fitness class that broke through a loose board in the gym last week when they tried to do the running man? And the nutrition group that made Twinkies-flavored granola bars? That was ridiculous."

"I thought they were great. I offered to sell them at the Dairy Cow."

I stomped my good foot. He didn't understand. I had lost control. The fitness program was a joke. "They were right. Things are bad, Edge. The Walkie Talkies do more garage-sale shopping than walking. They should have called themselves the Shopper Stoppers."

"I can't believe you are joking about something so important." Was this really him talking? How strange that we were suddenly playing opposite roles.

"I'm just pointing out that this whole thing has been less than orthodox. And I let it get out of control."

His eyes narrowed. "Are you giving up?"

"No. There is nothing to give up. I am done. Fired." I switched my duffel bag to the other hand and stepped around Edge. "Time to pack up."

"Not yet. We have to fight this."

"Fight the gym closing. That is important. The grant is over for me. I've lost. But that doesn't mean that Truhart needs to lose. They need to keep challenging themselves to get fit. Keep fighting."

"You're right!' Edge grabbed my bag out of my grasp and marched to the truck.

"Wait! Give that back." I chased after him in a half run, half hobble.

He opened the door of the truck and threw it behind the seat. Then he turned to me and lifted me off my feet.

"Put me down!"

"Not until you come back to the gym and listen to what the Triple C's and I have to say to Marie."

He dumped me in the passenger seat and slammed the door. I could have jumped out, walked back to the Callahans' without my bag, and caught the next bus to the airport. But I didn't. Something about the intensity in Edge's voice made me stay. I wanted him to make everything better. Even though I doubted he could.

"Aubrey has already taken over my job. I don't see how anything anyone says is going to matter. This is a bad idea," I warned him.

He made a U-turn and headed back toward town. "You know what a bad idea is?"

I crossed my arms.

He continued. "A bad idea is losing you. You're the best thing that has happened to Truhart and to m—" He stopped himself. I smiled despite my low spirits. "Another bad idea is moving the gym out of Truhart to Harrisburg. No one will come. Having Andrew Vanderbeek lead the Walkie Talkies is the worst. One look at Andrew and they'll turn into stress eaters."

I couldn't argue with his logic.

We pulled up in front of the community center and I wimped out. "You go in."

Edge sighed and unhooked his seat belt. He leaned over and planted his lips on mine. He tasted like chocolate and mint.

When he finished, he leaned back with a satisfied smile on his face. "Come inside."

I blinked. There must be a good reason why I should stay in the truck. But my mind wasn't working. How did he do that to me?

When Edge opened my door and held out his hand, there was no other option. I would have followed him into the fires of teddy-bear hell at this point. I placed my hand in his and let him lead me to the door of the gym.

I heard the sound of angry voices before we stepped inside. Marva O'Shea was pointing her finger at Aubrey and yelling something about Halloween costumes and pawn-shop dealers.

"Is that your left hand that is in a sling, Vanderbeek? Aren't you right-handed?" Edge's voice was biting.

Andrew clutched his sling to his chest. "The table fell on my pinky."

Edge snorted and pulled me to the center of the room. But I held back, reluctant to face Aubrey and Andrew again.

"You are all just a bunch of losers. You can't even equip your own gym," Andrew said with a sneer.

"We don't need a fancy gym," Corinne said.

"No gym? How in the world do you think you can get your town in shape?"

"We use creative ways!" said Addie Adler.

"Creative? Are you going to tell me that coffin is a weight bench and that Santa's butt is a balancing ball?"

Marva stomped her feet. "You're just trying to—"

Elizabeth Lively stepped between Aubrey and the group of angry ladies. "Look, everybody. Let's calm down."

Aubrey threw up her hands. "Calm down? I'm being attacked by a fat lady who can't keep her garters up."

Everyone looked toward Addie Adler's ankles, where a thing that must be a garter drooped below her knee.

Not to be outdone, Addie stepped out of her shoe and pulled off her garter with more deftness than I had ever thought possible for a woman her age. "This may be a garter to you, but to me it is an exercise band!"

Marva nodded. "That's the creative part of our workout."

Elizabeth focused on Marie. "Just because it isn't pretty doesn't mean it won't work. And I would like to point out that Andrew and Aubrey's attitude toward their future clients is completely unprofessional. How are you going to work with people you make fun of?"

She had a great point. Even Marie had been taken aback by the way Aubrey made fun of Aunt Addie.

Edge let go of my hand and moved into the center of the room next to Elizabeth. "Did you get specific orders from the grant committee to shut down the gym, or was that just pressure from Reeba Sweeney and Aubrey?"

Marie looked down at her paperwork. "The instructions were that I should visit the site and evaluate its effectiveness based on the criteria set forth by the grant."

"And what were those criteria?"

"The participants should show progress in all of the following areas: knowledge of health and nutrition, reduction in overall BMI, and improved strength and agility."

"What makes you think we aren't making progress?" Edge asked.

Marie sputtered, but Aubrey stepped forward. "It's obvious. From the fried-food fest I saw at Lori's to the pancake breakfasts this town gorges on every weekend."

"They served turkey sausage and fruit last Sunday. That was new for the pancake breakfast." The sound of my own voice surprised me.

Aubrey waved her hand, dismissing me. "My dieters are drinking protein shakes and cutting out carbs."

"That isn't sustainable for most people, and you know it." I moved away from where I was holding up the wall.

Aubrey refused to look at me. She turned to Marie. "Harrisburg has a combined running and walking mileage of five hundred miles on our treadmills. I doubt Truhart has even gone a single mile yet."

I raised my voice. "Of course they have. And they have done it in the real world, outside of the gym."

Andrew snorted. "Because there isn't anything in this place except for Santa's ass!"

"Who's to say that just because you spend thousands of dollars on gym equipment it's better?" The ladies stepped aside and made room for me right in front of Marie. Andrew could make fun of me and the gym. But Santa's ass was the last straw. "Just because we choose unorthodox ways to keep fit doesn't mean we are going to be any less successful."

Marie bit her lip. "Lily, you have a point. But I need more than that to take back to the grant committee. Your program isn't quite what they were expecting."

"It's better. And we can prove it," said Edge.

Aubrey grabbed Marie's arm. "This is pitiful. Come on. Let's go before they convince you that Truhart is the Paris of the Midwest, like the festival they were planning last summer."

Regina turned purple. "It was a nice idea. Our trees are like the Eiffel Tower and our lake is like the Seine."

Andrew snorted. "Oh my God! Do you see what I mean? They're all batty."

Marie stepped away from Aubrey and gazed around the room at the Triple C's. "How are you going to prove your program is as good or better?"

"A challenge!" Edge declared.

"Yeah!" the ladies said, nodding their heads.

"What? That's crazy!" Aubrey said.

I almost agreed with Aubrey. While I was completely supportive of our methods in getting fit, there was no way we could compete with the professionals in Harrisburg.

"The Great Warrior Memorial Day Weekend Challenge," Edge said with his finger in the air.

Elizabeth added, "It will be a perfect way to start the summer."

Marie looked doubtful and slumped over her clipboard. "That gives you less than a month to get ready."

"We'll be fine," Addie assured her. "Nobody loves a good last-minute scramble like Truhart. Remember how we planned the Truhart Timberfest in practically one month last summer? And how all the Halloween decorations were ruined by that storm right before the House of Horrors opened in October?"

"And Charlotte's wedding. Don't forget that!" said Addie Adler.

Corinne put her arm around Addie. "It'll be like old times."

"Umm, exactly what are we challenging here?" I didn't mean to dampen their enthusiasm. But I couldn't imagine how a warrior challenge would play out.

"We'll have an obstacle course just like *American Ninja Warrior*."

Marie clapped her hands. "Oh, I love that show." For the first time since she walked in the door earlier, she looked excited.

"And we can have a nutrition quiz of some sort," Elizabeth said.

"Yeah. With a cook-off," said Marva.

Andrew was sweating the way he had during the arm-wrestling match. "This is ridiculous. Your chef would serve chili fries while ours would make kale and quinoa."

Regina narrowed her eyes. "We know about quinoa, Aubrey. For goodness' sake. And where to find it at the Family Fare, thanks to Lily!"

"You could have the same ingredients available to both chefs and see who cooks the most delicious meal," Corinne said with a sparkle in her eye.

Aubrey snorted. "I can see it now. Your chef would probably throw everything in a blender and call it a smoothie."

Marie's face dropped. "Maybe this isn't such a good idea."

Corinne put her hands on her hips. "Our chef can do vegan!"

Marie made a note on her clipboard. "Warrior chef. I like it."

Andrew wiped his forehead with his good hand. He really needed to get that gland issue checked out. "If we are having a competition, you need to make it about weight loss."

"Fine." Edge spoke with amazing confidence.

As a fitness instructor, I knew that wasn't the point of any competition. "It shouldn't be based on weight loss. It should be about lowering your BMI," I said.

"Weight loss, BMI. Either way, we'll win," said Aubrey. For the first time, I wondered if she truly had the skills to be a fitness trainer. She was rude and a bully. And she also didn't respect the importance of "good" weight loss.

Marie looked like she had just been saved from a root canal. "I think this is a great idea. I'll take it back to the grant board for approval. I don't think it will be a problem."

Edge put his arm around my shoulder. "So Lily stays."

"For now."

Andrew mumbled something to Aubrey. It sounded like, "Now they'll lose for sure . . ."

Edge marched to the front door and tore off the sheet of paper announcing the closing of the gym. He threw it across the room toward the trash, and Andrew jumped out of the way to keep his precious pinky from being smashed.

"No changing your mind, Marie. Without Lily we are lost." I loved how sure he sounded. I wished I had the same type of confidence.

"Where are we going to have this competition?" I asked. Was I the only one who was concerned with the details of this crazy challenge?

"Memorial Day weekend at the county fairground," suggested Edge.

"Aren't a lot of people gone then?" asked Marie.

"Not in Truhart. This is where tourists from downstate come on Memorial Day weekend. A Warrior Weekend Challenge will give them even more reason to head to the great north," said Regina.

Aubrey nodded. "Fine with us. We get twice as many tourists on that weekend."

Addie Adler finished putting her garter on and stepped back in her shoe. "What does the winner of the competition get?"

"Money?" Corinne asked hopefully.

"I'm afraid we don't have that kind of budget," Marie said.

"A prize!"

"Ha! Maybe the loser has to put Santa's ass in the center of their town with the words *kick me* across it," jeered Andrew.

Marva shook her finger at him. "That's not nice. Even we wouldn't do something like that to the kids. Imagine seeing people kick Santa. You are a very rude young man."

Trying to keep another confrontation from happening, Marie ushered Aubrey and Andrew out the door before he broke his other fingers on Marva's tongue-lashing that followed him out the door.

LESSON SIXTEEN

Vary Activities

There were a lot of reasons why the challenge was a bad idea. I ignored them all.

Instead I focused on the upside of things. With the change in the weather and the newly issued challenge, my walkers were motivated to move. They walked and walked and walked. They still stopped at garage sales, but they were obsessed with finding old workout equipment. Infomercials must be all the rage in Truhart, because every exercise fad that was featured in the past twenty years became the hottest garage-sale pick around. Two ladies drove to Harrisburg for their walk. They found a Bowflex at a yard sale. Corinne Scott bought a second ThighMaster at a church rubbage sale in Gaylord. Not to be outdone by the "latest trends" of the past twenty years, Gladys Stubbs fished two sets of Shake Weights out of the landfill.

But Addie Adler took the prize. She had Edge pull her old vibrating belt out of the attic of the Amble Inn. When I told her that vibrating belts were a fitness fad that had proven to be useless in losing weight, she disagreed. She insisted that she had lost twenty pounds using that equipment when her nieces and nephews were young.

"It's true, Lily. I remember her using it when she babysat us." Edge shook his body back and forth. "I just wish she had put us all down on the ground before she used it!"

Edge made himself the official chief of the obstacle-course team. Instead of calling themselves ninjas, they called themselves after an old term for lumberjack, the River Hogs. They held "tryouts" in order to choose the four women and four men who would compete. East Elementary School's playground became the center of the obstacle course, with a warning from the principal that if they broke the equipment they had to pay for it.

Hopeful participants gathered for the tryouts, attracting quite a crowd of kids in town. Edge hung ropes from the swing set and demonstrated stepping from swing to swing without falling off. Many locals I had never met showed off their upper body strength on the monkey bars. They climbed to the top of the super-dome climbing structure as fast as they could and then leaped across the sloped stepping stones that Edge built. Corinne's brother, who owned Auto Doc, had promised to make log rolls out of PVC pipes and old casters. All in all, the course was quite impressive.

I sat on a bench, clutching my fleece around me, and watched as people competed for a spot on the team. It was a brisk day, but you would never know it watching the warriors. They tossed off their sweatshirts and were covered with a sheen of sweat within the first half hour.

Elizabeth Lively ended up being quite agile on the rope climbs. When she finished her run-through, her fiancé, J.D., gave her a proud high five.

"Are you sure you don't want to try out?" she asked him.

He shook his head. "It wouldn't be fair since I work for the county sheriff's department. I feel I should be a neutral party in this challenge."

"Do you think any of the officers who live in Harrisburg feel the same way, J.D? Come on. You live in Truhart," Edge griped.

But J.D. wouldn't budge.

"At least help us train, J.D. You had to do some of this stuff at the police academy."

J.D. agreed, but Edge was still bitter that his friend would not join the team. "Be careful on the rollers," I called out. The last thing we needed was someone else with an ACL tear in Truhart. Edge had just finished showing everyone how the makeshift course should be navigated at a faster time, and came to stand next to my bench. "This stuff will be easy for them by the end of next week."

"I don't care so much about that. I just don't want anyone to get hurt."

"Nahh. They'll be fine."

"Are you sure you know what the course is going to look like?"

"Marie gave me a list of the obstacles. She got a local contractor to build it in return for free advertising. This is as close as we can get to training without using the real deal. We should be fine."

Edge held out his arm until it was right under my nose. "Check out these muscles."

I waved my hand under my nose. "Are you trying to win the BO competition?"

He looked insulted. "You know you want me. Take a look at these biceps."

I caught sight of Rocky Stone straining on the monkey bars. "Come on, Rocky. You can do it!"

Rocky had lost almost ten pounds since he started "working" at the gym. I was so proud of him. So was his mother. She and I had spoken on the phone several times and she told me she had never seen Rocky so determined to lose weight. He claimed he had more energy and more motivation than ever.

"Look at this, Ms. Shue! I can do a chin-up!"

I wasn't the only one cheering him on. The new principal at the high school had come out to watch. We both agreed that we needed to find a way to combat the bullying and help reach kids who wanted to lose weight like Rocky.

On the other side of the course, Edge was making notes as he watched two of his friends race across the balance beams. Edge had barely looked Rocky's way. I wandered over and glanced at the notes he was making.

He pulled them closer to his chest. "Are you peeking at my notes?"

"I'm just wondering how you're picking the team. There are a lot of people here. Are you going to have to make many cuts?"

He swept his gaze around the playground. "A few of the guys aren't sure they have the time to train. So, I might add them as alternates. Otherwise I think I know my team."

"Is Rocky on your list?"

He straightened his baseball hat and lowered his voice. "You know he can't really compete, don't you?"

"I know he isn't in shape yet, Edge. But look at him. He is working so hard. The experience of moving toward a goal with a team would be so good for him."

Edge cast me a sideways glance. In the sunlight, I could see the red in his beard. His T-shirt was molded to his chest by the layer of sweat he had worked up demonstrating the equipment. He looked quite different from the first day I met him. Flannel shirts were man camouflage, and should be outlawed for single men. How had I ever thought he was anything but hot?

"I just don't want to see him get hurt. And I have to be fair about it."

I pulled out a feminine tool I had never used before. I lowered my chin and pressed myself against him. "Please. Can you make him an alternate? As a favor to me."

He let out a long, tortured breath. "What are you going to do for me?" he asked in a gruff voice.

I pulled his head down and whispered exactly what I would do for him.

"Can we do it now? We can use the backseat of the truck."

I pushed him away. "Go back to your notes, Coach."

"What notes?" He readjusted his sweatpants.

I walked away, letting my hips sway, which was possible now that my knee was healing. Finally! My leg brace was off today. Doctor's clearance. Thank God!

Before I was out of earshot, Edge called out, "Hey, Lily!"

When I turned around, he winked. Then, in a schmaltzy macho gesture, he formed his fingers into a V and pointed them back and forth at his eyes and mine. "You and me at my place later."

I walked past Elizabeth, avoiding her speculating gaze. We weren't much of a secret. No one seemed to care. In fact, everyone seemed happy for us.

Just yesterday, Louise had stopped me at breakfast.

"Lily, you're an adult. So is Edge. I'm a light sleeper."

I wanted to bury my head in my eggs.

She pinched her lips and put a hand on my shoulder. "I would hate to see you hurt. Turn on the driveway lights when you sneak over to Edge's."

When I told Edge, he practically rolled on the ground with laughter.

This morning after he escorted me back across and the street, he looked up and waved at his mom, who stood at the window. I collapsed on his childhood bed and put the pillow over my head. As I recovered from my embarrassment, I thought about my life before coming to Truhart. Up at dawn. The rigid workout schedule. Coming home to a lonely meal and falling asleep to the sound of the television in the background, spending my one day off each week at my mother's house, listening to her tell me how wonderful my brothers' lives were. Even the times I had made it out to an event that might include a celebrity or two, were dim compared to my life now.

It made absolutely no sense.

But, like the way our secret was no longer a secret, I was learning not to care about logic or what anyone else thought.

"Are you sure you didn't pull a muscle, Edge?"

He grunted from where he lay across my lap on his new couch. "It's just a little sore."

Little sore? The man had winced every time he used his fork at dinner. It was only the first week of practice for the new team. I couldn't help worrying about injury. I dug my thumb into a spot on his neck and kneaded away the knot. "Maybe you should ease into this a bit. Give your muscles time to recover."

"Nope. We're warriors. No pain, no gain, as the saying goes, right?"

"Actually, Edge, that isn't a very good saying. I want you and the River Hogs to go a little slower. You need to work up to the obstacle course. You should be rolling with the foam rollers before the workout, and strength training in the gym to supplement your training at the playground."

"Rolling is for wimps."

"You are absolutely wrong. What do you think I am doing right now? A roller is a poor man's massage."

He leaned his head back and kissed me. "Then I must be a rich man."

I pulled my lips away. "I have to insist that you slow things down a bit. I don't want anyone hurt."

He sat up and turned to face me. "We have like three weeks to do this, Lily. We don't have time to work up to it." He made air quotes with his fingers when he said the word *work*. I didn't like the way he was ignoring me.

I poked him in the chest. "Hey! The last time I checked, I was still the trainer in this town. I want you to hold your next practice at the gym so you can train in a safe environment."

"And when would you have us practice on a real obstacle course? The day before the challenge?"

I stood up and made my way into the kitchen. He was getting very pushy for a man with no greater ambition than scooping ice cream. When I first met him, I thought his only form of exercise came from lifting a bowl of chips. Now I realized he had the propensity to be a fitness maniac. I wasn't sure I liked it, to be honest. Part of me wanted the lazy buffoon back. Even the whipped cream was gone from his refrigerator.

He must have sensed my mood because he got up gingerly from the couch and came over to me. "Sorry, Coach. You're in charge here. I get it. I just can't stand the thought of Aubrey Vanderbeek holding this over my head."

"What is it with you two? Was your high school fling a bigger deal than you told me?"

He grabbed an apple and leaned back against the counter, shuddering. "I told you, our dating was only in her dreams."

"You could have fooled me." I stole his apple and took a bite. "Are you sure she wasn't your first love or something?" The apple tasted like sawdust at the thought of Aubrey and Edge together.

"God no! We went to senior prom in high school. It was the worst date of my life. We were supposed to be friends and she was all over me." He ran his hand over his eyes. "Keep the apple. You just made me lose my appetite."

"Me too." I put the apple on the counter. "I'm still missing something."

"Aubrey ended up being good friends with someone I was with for a while."

The person whose name had been mentioned at the dinner table one night. A skier. "Julie . . . Jane . . . Jackie?"

His lips lost all color as they pressed together. "Jackie. Jackie Durham."

My jaw dropped.

"Heard of her, have you?" he said sarcastically.

"Olympic gold-medal winner?"

"Two golds and a silver so far."

"You and Jackie Durham were together?"

"Engaged."

A moment ago I was trying to hold my stomach at the thought of Edge and Aubrey. Now I was trying to resist the overwhelming feeling of awe. A man I slept with had been engaged to an Olympic medalist. It was like one degree of separation between me and the sports hall of fame.

"Feel free to wipe that look of surprise off your face. I know it seems like a crazy thing. But back in the day when we were on the skiing circuit, we were both in line for glory on the slopes." He leaned against the counter. "At least that's what I thought. Aubrey Vanderbeek told Jackie I would never amount to anything. It didn't bother me then. She was like an annoying mosquito, always hovering in the background, trying to break us up."

"She wanted you for herself."

"Jackie was pretty close with her for a while. Then even she started to think Aubrey was crazy."

I was still caught up in the one degree of separation thing. But now a sense of inadequacy trickled down my spine. Edge went from a superstar lover to a fitness trainer with a bad knee. No wonder he wanted to beat Aubrey.

"So . . ." I cleared my throat. "What exactly happened between you and Jackie?"

He looked out the window at the gray lake that was churning up in the spring wind.

Why was I dredging this up? I was with Edge now. He didn't need a reminder of a long lost Olympic-star girlfriend.

"On second thought, never mind."

"Lily—"

"No really. I mean it. Just because I am sleeping with you doesn't mean I have to know your whole history."

He twisted toward me and winced at the sudden movement. "It doesn't? Don't you think you have the right to know?"

"No. I mean, we use condoms . . . except that time in the shower . . . But you know . . . the timing was safe and . . ."

He rubbed his neck and sent me a pained look that was either from his neck or the conversation. "Lily, you should stop selling yourself like a low bid on eBay."

"I'm not—"

He stepped closer. "Shut up. You have every right to ask me about Jackie."

"I do?" Did that mean we were more than just convenient sex? I wanted to ask him to spell it out.

He pulled me back to the couch. "Maybe you need to check my body for muscle tears."

"Wait. I'll switch sides so I can look at you properly without you straining your sore neck." I scrambled to the other side of his lap and tried not to act as eager as I felt.

The corners of his mouth turned up. "You know, you aren't as tough as you think you are."

"Yes, I am."

He ignored my denial and lifted my hand to the side of his neck that hurt. I took the hint and started rubbing while he talked.

"Aubrey introduced me to Jackie when we were competing in our region at the Juniors in Marquette. We were seventeen and getting ready to make the leap to the next level. We shared a love for skiing and an excitement over the amount of attention we were given by the coaches who came to watch us. We both went on to train in Colorado under the same team of coaches. We were away from home for the first time and saw more of each other than we did our own families."

I knew exactly how young and fresh Edge looked at that age. I wasn't proud of being a stalker, but I had Googled him after Tracy told me about his concussion. The picture I saw was at the finish line of a race. He was pink-faced and heartbreakingly young, with panda eyes on his face from ski goggles and sunshine. He was laughing at the camera in a victory celebration that had made me smile. He was thinner. And his face was free of whiskers.

I kept working that knot, hoping he wouldn't stop his story. "So you two became engaged?"

"Not right away. We were young. Traveling together from event to event. We were together so much that people started commenting on what a great couple we would be."

"It sounds like a natural fit for both of you."

"Yeah, well, then it all came apart."

"When you got your concussion?" I traced the scar on his temple.

"Who told you, by the way?"

"Tracy."

He closed his eyes. "Geez. Sisters have big mouths."

"I wouldn't know," I said. "But for the record, so do brothers."

"True. Peter hasn't been able to keep a secret his entire life." I made a mental note not to say anything private around his sibling if I ever met him.

I smoothed my finger over his temple and was glad I had never seen the accident happen. Poor Louise. It must have been awful. The scar was almost invisible after all these years. "So, Jackie just dumped you after your concussion?"

"No. She was nicer than that. She stuck with me during the first two concussions, you know. Did Tracy mention those?"

"Yes. She said they were mild. But the third wasn't."

"It wasn't. I spent months in a dark, quiet room. Can you imagine what that was like for a twenty-two-year-old? I couldn't read. Listen to music. Even the television bothered me."

"I'm sorry." I thought of his truck. Led Zeppelin at an ear-blowing volume must be like heaven after that horrible year of silence.

"A year is like a decade when you're young, you know. When I finally started recovering, she was already off to her first Olympic games."

I played with his hair and he rested his head on my shoulder. "We tried to make it work. But it was pointless when we weren't anywhere near each other. We ended up realizing we had nothing in common. We broke the engagement."

"You never went back to skiing."

"You know what, Lily?" He stared at the ceiling and picked up my hand, matching our fingers together and then shifting them so they interlocked. "When I lay in my damn bedroom for all those weeks, I didn't miss skiing half as much as everything else. The music. The food. ESPN."

I laughed. "No ESPN would have been tough."

"I heard my family upstairs at mealtimes and would have done anything to be with them. I missed the laughing, the conversation, hell, even the arguing. I missed my grandpa's last few months.

"I do ski sometimes. I train kids at the junior ski school every winter. But my brain and my life here are more important to me than competitive skiing."

I kissed his temple. "Good choice."

"Hmmm." He was relaxing now. "I think I'm a little sore in other places besides my neck." He looked at me out of the corner of his eye.

"Poor baby. I'll make you feel better."

He sighed. "If you don't mind."

I leaned down and kissed his pouting lips. He tasted like apple. I was getting used to the way his beard brushed my face. It was softer than it was coarse. Last night I'd dreamed I was kissing a teddy bear, and now I made the connection. Edge was a giant teddy bear. A big animal that was supposed to be fierce and scary but ended up being cuddly and sweet. Every time I was with him I wanted to hug.

I smoothed my hand across his chest and unbuttoned his shirt, making my way down until it was open. He moaned as I trailed my fingers down farther. I wanted to make him want me. And a part of me, the insecure part, wanted to make him forget Jackie Durham. My experience as the seducer was very limited. Sex had been predictable and swift for me in the past. I enjoyed it just fine. But it followed the logical path. Touching the sensitive spots and then seeking release. With Edge the path was a meandering mess. Never, ever boring. I was learning to be adventurous.

When I was frustrated by the limits imposed on me by my knee, Edge found a way to make things right. We ended up better than right. Our lovemaking was inventive and creative and fun. I never worried he would laugh at me, or think I was odd. Mainly because he was so willing to let himself be the comic relief in any situation. A man who laughed at life and didn't mind if it laughed right back at him wasn't the kind of man who looked down on my own bumbling foreplay.

I took the lead, determined to make my mark on him. Except for his moans and the way he involuntarily bucked, Edge was all too happy to lie back and let me lead our lovemaking.

"Are you sore here too?"

Edge groaned. "This is the ultimate massage."

I used both hands now. "And this?"

"It hurts like the devil." He grinned. "Make it better."

I repeated the motion several times. It was so new to be in control. For the first time since my surgery, my body was in charge. Edge lay back in my lap now, watching me as if it were the most erotic thing in the world. It was heady to have this kind of power. I forgot about the challenge, the gym, and even my knee. The whole world had shrunk to a small set of nerves and erogenous zones. And Edge, who existed for me.

We reached our peak together. Panting and talking to each other in harsh, seductive whispers that I would never remember afterward. The words belonged to the moment and were lost soon after, like debris on the side of the road after a frantic road race.

When we finally caught our breath, and I raised my head from Edge's chest, damp with sweat, I wanted to say the words I really felt. But suddenly, I was too shy.

Instead I asked, "Still sore?"

He propped open one eye. "No. But ask me again in an hour."

I tucked my head in his shoulder and enjoyed the rise and fall of his chest as he fell asleep.

When I first met Edge, I was full of purpose and determination. Somehow Edge had lightened the burden of my failure. Now he had given me another gift. He had given me back the most personal part of my identity and let me govern my own pleasure and demand his. Our lovemaking had had nothing to do with making his sore muscles better or finding funny ways to make love.

The limitations of my own body and mind were fading.

In a way, losing control had given me back myself.

At least for now.

LESSON SEVENTEEN

Include the Whole Family

I spent the following afternoon at Cookee's Diner, going over the details of the cook-off with Ambrose Macallister, aka Mac. He was a large man who favored white T-shirts and aprons with funny sayings. I liked him when I met him a several weeks ago, and I liked him even more when he explained his philosophy of fresh organic ingredients and vegan fare.

"I still serve burgers and fries for my meat-loving customers. I make a mean pot roast and an even better chili. But since last autumn, I've been caught up in the new food culture. Learning about grains and legumes, and all the substitutes for protein that vegetarians and vegans use in their food has completely changed the way I cook."

I watched him flip a burger as he explained his philosophy and marveled at the fact that this man still chose to work at a diner.

"Mind you, I work at the Grande Lucerne twice a week now. They have a clientele that appreciates gourmet fare that stretches the boundaries of meat and potatoes. They offered me a full-time job in their kitchen. I couldn't take it, though."

"Really?" I took a bite of his mushroom risotto and closed my eyes. "Delicious," I said with my mouth full.

Mac sent me a satisfied smile. "Glad to hear you like it. You know, I would rather flip burgers for friends than spend my entire week locked in the kitchen preparing plates for strangers. Cooking is about more than the food. It needs to be shared. So maybe folks around here aren't always into kale and Swiss chard; they still appreciate something new once in a while. This way I get the best of both worlds."

Edge walked in the door just as Mac was finishing his explanation. "Mac thinks he's going to convert all of us before the year is up."

"Don't act so tough there, Edge. I saw you gobble up the tuna, avocado, and quinoa salad the other day."

Edge patted his stomach. "As an athlete in training I am forcing myself to eat more than chili fries."

Mac raised his spatula. "Don't give me that BS. You liked the stuff."

Edge leaned over my shoulder. "Just taking my job as official taste-tester for the cook-off seriously." He held his mouth open. "Bring it on, Lil."

I spooned the risotto into his mouth and he stepped back, pretending to savor the flavor like a real connoisseur. "Slightly salty and a hint of sweetness. It's the perfect umami on my tongue . . ."

Mac chuckled. "Umami! You crack me up, Edge. Where'd you learn chef lingo like that?"

"I wouldn't know."

But I did. Last night, Edge had told me stories about life on the circuit. He went into great detail about his favorite meals on the road. He was more than just a homegrown boy. Surprisingly, Edge was a closet foodie. He had traveled all over the world by the time he was twenty-two. It was strange to think that in some ways he was more worldly than I was. A man who drove a teddy bear truck, was a part-time bartender, was a ski bum half the winter, and owned an ice cream parlor and putt-putt golf course. What other layers lay beneath that beard?

As if he knew I was thinking about him, he cocked his head to the side and grabbed my trainer bag. "Ready to go?"

"Hang on, I have to pay."

Edge reached for his wallet. "I'll get it."

Mac waved us both off. "This one is on me. I'm in training today."

Before I could protest, Edge put his arm around my shoulders and led me out. "She's a great guinea pig, isn't she? Thanks, Mac."

"Guinea pig?" I asked, raising my eyebrow as he helped me into his pickup truck.

"You do have a certain usefulness when it comes to testing new ways to do things." He was referring to some rather creative ways we had made love last night. Lord, I still couldn't believe I could be so dexterous, even with my knee.

"I have to stop by Lakeview for a sing-along. It's a half day at school, so Justin and Jason are there and I promised Tracy I would take them home," Edge said.

"No problem." I quite liked watching Edge light up the adult day care with his charm and silly banter. In fact, I liked the way he lit up every room he walked into.

He tapped the steering wheel and my heart did a funny flip-flop.

I looked away. A shiver of heat passed down my spine and once again I felt the words bubble to the surface. I put a hand to my mouth and forced them back.

I love you.

I wanted to shout it out loud.

I fanned the air in front of me and fought back a wave of panic. No. No. No.

If anyone had told me that cold March day that I would be head over heels in love with this man, I would have taken the first bus to nowhere.

Now I was terrified that I wasn't worthy of such a man.

Saying the words was one risk I wasn't ready to take. If I told him I loved him, he would probably hug me and let me down gently. Because he was that kind of guy. One of the good ones.

"Are you sure you don't mind going to Lakeview? I can just drop you off at home if you don't want to go."

"No," I croaked. "It's fine. Really."

He turned up the driveway of the day care center. Before he could come around to help me out, I opened the door of the truck and breathed in the fresh air. Ignoring his quizzical expression, I brushed away his help. The last thing I needed was to let him know my feelings right now. If I bared my soul to him, there was a strong possibility I'd melt right where I was. Nothing would be left of me but a muddy puddle.

I took off my coat and threw it in the truck as if I'd lived in the North Woods my whole life. Fifty degrees was too warm for me today.

When we entered, everyone called out to Edge like they did each time we visited. But this time, several people called out my name, too.

Mr. Frasier was reading a newspaper in the corner of the front lobby. As always, he watched the comings and goings of the center.

"Hi, pretty lady."

"Hello, Mr. Frasier." I tilted my head to see the date of the newspaper in his lap. It was the same issue as the last two times.

I followed Edge into the living area. Justin and Jason were perched on a couch by the window, playing games on their latest Nintendos. They ran across the room when they saw Edge.

He gave them air high fives. "You guys going to help us sing today?"

Their faces fell. "Not karaoke," Justin moaned.

Edge spread a hand on his chest and pretended to be offended. "Fine. Go back to your Mario Brothers. But remember, they can't cook chili like I can."

I took my usual seat in the back. More than a dozen people, mostly ladies, wandered in from the arts and crafts room. Their pleasure at seeing Edge was pasted all over their faces like the flowers on their hats.

"Are you all ready for Karaoke with Callahan, folks? Now put on your dancing shoes, we're going to make you work for your music today." He grabbed the basket of streamers and party maracas, and I helped him pass them around the room.

Once his guitar was tuned, Edge started to sing. "'Oh, give me a home, where the buffalo roam . . .'"

He encouraged everyone to sway to the music. My heart filled with pride. An entire room of people captivated by the man I loved. I stopped myself before that thought continued.

No melting. No melting.

I looked away, hoping I wasn't wearing my feelings on my sleeve. Mrs. Krebbs was pushing her walker out of the arts and crafts room toward us. The bottom of the walker caught on the carpet in the front hallway and she went flying. She landed on the floor with a sickening thud. Everyone scrambled toward her. Louise and the aides were there first. They checked her for injuries and tried to calm her.

"I'm all right," she insisted.

Louise shook her head. "We aren't taking any chances, Mrs. Krebbs."

Louise turned to Edge, who had joined us. "Can you help me get her into the other room, honey? I want to call the doctor."

Campers shifted restlessly as they watched the excitement in the hallway. Justin and Jason craned their necks, hoping for blood and gore, to be sure.

"I'll be right back, everyone!" Edge carefully lifted Mrs. Krebbs as if she were nothing more than a rag doll and followed Louise into the other room. Ivy rolled her wheelchair out of the living room, ready to follow Louise.

Before I thought about what I was doing, I was clapping my hands. "Hey there, everyone. While Edge takes a short break, let's have some fun."

I moved around the couches and chairs and took Edge's place at the front of the room.

"What exactly are we going to do?" asked a skeptical Mr. Galardi.

"Well . . ."

They stared. I knew how to rally people to work out. It didn't matter that most of the people in front of me could barely walk across the room. I could do the same thing here. Maybe.

"Umm, I'm not any good at singing, so we can put this away." I moved the guitar against the wall.

From the couch Justin whispered, "Phew . . . I hear she sings really bad."

A stereo system with a patch cord coming out of it sat on a table in the front of the room. "Maybe we can have a little music. How's that?"

Mr. Galardi grunted and said, "I thought Edge was going to play his music. I don't know any other songs but his."

I pulled my cell phone out of my pocket and opened up my music app. "Sure you do. I'll bet you know lots of songs."

Frantically I scrolled through my music library, looking for something other than rock and roll that might sound familiar to the campers. Most of my songs were little-known alternative songs.

Then I spotted Michael. My all-time favorite.

"Ha. Here we go." I plugged in my phone and turned up the volume. The low techno guitar note started to play the first few notes. The low murmur of Michael's talking filled the room, then the high-pitched "Whoop" and the music started. Michael Jackson's voice urged everyone not to stop until they got enough.

"Come on, everyone. Let's see if you remember your moves."

At first they stared at me like I had lost my head. Disco was a far reach from "On Top of Old Smoky" and "Hello Muddah, Hello Fad-duh." But Michael was special. It was impossible not to move when you heard the beat. One by one, feet started shuffling and hips began rocking. Even hips that hadn't been out of their wheelchairs in years.

A bunch of sad-looking balloons that had lost their "lift" after a birthday party were gathered in the corner like dust bunnies. I untied their strings and tossed them in the air.

Jason and Justin had paused their video games, mildly interested in my attempt to entertain. I called over to them. "Boys, see if you can keep these balloons from falling to the ground."

Someone had stored long foam tubes in a bin against the wall. They had been used to make the gigantic flowers in the arts and crafts room. I grabbed them and gave them to people who were confined to chairs. "Use these to reach the balloons if you need to. But don't injure Jason and Justin here. Ivy might get mad if you hurt her great-grandsons."

Of course, one bright-eyed man purposely smacked Jason on the head, and Jason promptly pretended to die. But then he jumped back up to catch a balloon.

Some of the campers had amazing rhythm. More than that, the smiles around the room were contagious. I moved among the chairs and helped keep the balloons aloft, laughing when I lost and they dropped to the floor.

"Sorry. I've got a bad knee."

One man patted me on the back and told me, "Watch yourself and don't worry about saving the balloons, honey. Safety always comes first."

When the next song came on and Michael told everyone to just beat it, I let the balloons drop and moved to the front of the room where everyone could see me. Getting the seniors to move wasn't that different than coaching a fitness class. They needed direction and encouragement to make moving fun. Instinct told me to keep up the energy.

I punched the air, one hand at a time, and then crossed my arms in front of me. "See if you can follow me."

It was as easy as that. Without asking questions they imitated my moves. Some were a little slower than the beat. And several people were unable to do the actual motion. But what they did do was good enough. Catching on to the music, Justin did a pretty good moonwalk.

"Is Jason as good?" I asked Justin, peering back at Jason.

The campers turned around to see Jason responding to the challenge in the back of the room. I did the same so it would be easier to follow.

Mrs. Jackowski, one of the more nimble seniors, changed moves. "Try this."

We followed her until Mr. Galardi tried his moves. I looked toward the back of the room and spotted Ivy. Her head was bobbing to the disco beat. Her toe was tapping. And her right wrist was waving back and forth. Better than any of her moves, however, was the smile on her face. It was as if she remembered a moment in the past when she had strutted to the catchy sound of "Beat It" or "Thriller," and it was all coming back to her. I didn't bring attention to her like I did some of the other campers when they showed off their moves. I left her where she was in time. At the party.

Two songs later, Jason and Justin were turning red from exertion. I changed the song to Gladys Knight & the Pips, letting the midnight train slow us down on our way to Georgia. "If you aren't already sitting down, find a seat and tap your feet to the beat."

Mrs. Fleetwood had such a look of happiness on her face that I asked, "Do you remember this song?"

"It was the first song I danced to after my husband asked me to marry him," she said over the music.

"Now that's a song that would make anyone say yes," I said.

Mr. Frasier called out, "Marry me!"

"I just might." Everyone laughed. I was just about to change up the moves when I looked up.

Edge stood in the back of the room, leaning against the door frame with his arms crossed. He stared at me in a way that made me wiggle my toes to keep from doing a victory dance. The gleam in his eyes had nothing to do with Mr. Frasier's outburst or the way the rest of the room was swaying to the beat.

Crap. My melting heart had started to boil. I was in big trouble.

It took me a moment to realize the music had stopped. Jason mocked my dreamy eyes and Justin rolled on the floor in glee. Edge moved off the wall, pretending he was going to step on Justin, and said, "Who needs 'The Hokey Pokey' when we can have 'The Hustle'?"

"Yeah!" the boys cheered, trying to trip him up. He snatched them both and held them fast.

"Lily, will you come back every week and dance with us?" Louise asked before we left.

Jason and Justin asked if they could come, too. How could I say no?

Later, Edge told me how things had gone with Mrs. Krebbs while they were waiting for the doctor.

"She heard your music from the living room and we had a hell of a time keeping her from getting up and boogying."

LESSON EIGHTEEN

Create Balance

"Couldn't we just celebrate Mother's Day like everyone else and go to brunch at the Gas 'N' Go Café?" Olivia asked Louise as we drove out of the church parking lot.

"The Triple C's have been working hard on this," Louise reminded her.

A special brunch for mothers was being held at the Amble Inn, down Winding Road. The brunch had been organized by the Triple C's, with help from Edge and the Adler family, who owned the inn.

We made our way to the table reserved for "Callahan." The centerpieces were made up of beautiful bowls of strawberries, grapes, blueberries, and melon. Salads decorated with sliced grapefruit and poppyseed dressing were already placed at each setting.

"I can't believe how healthy this looks," Tracy said as she plucked a grape from the plate in the middle of the table. I pulled off a card that displayed the menu for the buffet and the calorie count for each item. No chili fries. No donuts. Just healthy banana-nut waffles, crustless quiche, and even made-to-order smoothies. Was this the same town I had arrived in just a couple of months ago?

We had just taken our seats when a handsome man came over and sat down between Louise and Ivy. I was about to explain that the seat was taken when Louise turned and gasped.

Ivy laughed and said, "Mine!"

He leaned over and kissed her on the cheek. "Happy Mother's Day, Grandma."

Louise clapped her hands and laughed. "What have you done with my son?"

Edge smoothed a hand over his face. "Don't you like it?"

"I forgot how good-looking you are under that beard." She put both hands on either side of his face. "You silly man!! Why have you been hiding all these years?"

"I can't promise it won't be back. But I figured all that hair was taking a few seconds off my obstacle-course time. The less wind resistance the better!"

I struggled to pick my jaw up from the table.

Ever since I had met him, I wondered why Edge had been hiding his face behind a beard. I had speculated about all sorts of things, including the possibility of a weak jaw and a bad lower lip. None of those things were true. His jaw was square and chiseled. His lips were the perfect fullness.

And those dimples. Good Lord.

Even more surprising, a tiny indentation in the center of his chin.

He caught me staring at him. "Like it?"

I nodded and looked toward the centerpiece. No way was he going to catch me drooling. "It's nice."

"Just nice, Lily?" Tracy was amused.

Louise patted her hand. The kids knew nothing about Edge and me. We were still careful to keep quiet when we tiptoed back and forth. I hadn't woken a soul, except for one time when I tripped on a plastic superhero figure one of the twins had left out. When she came to investigate, Sarah believed me when I said I was checking my coat pocket for notes. Later, I had heard Edge warning both boys to clean up before they went to bed the next night.

I twisted my napkin into shreds, trying not to leap across the table to stroke Edge's smooth chin.

We waited for the tables to be called, one by one, for the buffet. Even without all the fatty foods, the buffet managed to look decadent. If I hadn't seen the calorie count I never would have believed how healthy the food was. When we sat back down, Addie's gracious niece who ran the Inn, Virginia Adler, stopped by our table and greeted everyone.

"Edge has been a big help, Louise. He's been quite the taskmaster about the menu, and we are very grateful," she said.

Justin asked if a taskmaster was one of the rulers of the universe.

"Yes!" Edge said, pointing at both boys. "You are under my control!"

Virginia laughed and pointed to an older man with a long nose standing behind the buffet. "Nestor is back from the Keys and he whipped up his usual magic in the kitchen." Then she inclined her head to a table in the corner of the room where a dark-haired family sat. "The Kreapps helped us with all the produce."

"I remember them. They owned the grocery store before it became the community center." Tracy said.

"That's right."

When Virginia left, Jason stared at his plate. "Where's the bacon?"

"No bacon for us," Edge said. "We're warriors now!"

"I'm not," spoke up Justin. "I'm just a hungry kid and I like French fries."

Tracy hushed them both.

With the exception of the boys, everyone was happy with the food. The fact that the Kreapps were able to share their organic food with us and we were enjoying a healthy alternative to fried food and loaded pancakes was more than I could ever have expected. The feeling of frustration I had felt when I first tried to make changes was gone.

Almost.

A little part of me was disappointed that I hadn't been able to motivate people on my own. It had taken the warrior challenge to get the town motivated. Before Andrew and Edge faced off in the arm-wrestling match at Lori's, Edge was practically taunting me with his ice cream and Uncle Pete's candy. Now he was taunting anybody who wasn't interested in eating healthy and helping Truhart win the challenge.

"The Kreapps have given me all sorts of inspiration. I'm thinking of starting an organic ice cream line," Edge said.

He was officially becoming a health nut.

Why did the thought bother me? I should be happy. Here I was, eating healthy food, enjoying Mother's Day with the Callahans, enjoying the view of Edge's unobstructed smile. Suddenly it changed to a frown when he spied something over my shoulder.

"I can't believe she's here!"

I turned around. "Who?"

"Reeba Sweeney."

Sitting at a table by the buffet was Regina Bloodworth; her husband, the mayor; and Reeba Sweeney.

Edge stood up so fast his chair almost fell over. "The spy!"

"Edgar, calm down," Louise whispered.

He sat back down but kept his eye on Reeba. "She's trying to see what we're up to so she can go back to Aubrey and tell her all about it."

I leaned across the table and tried to catch his eye. I had worn a dress for the first time since coming to town. The gray jersey knit covered my scarred knees and clung to the rest of my body. Edge hadn't even noticed. Even worse, now he was staring at Reeba.

"It's not like it's a secret that we're trying to eat healthy, Edge," I said.

The mayor motioned over the older man who had helped prepare the brunch. Nestor Nagel. Then Nestor waved over a man from the Kreapps' table.

"Damn, I can't believe it. She's talking to the Kreapps."

"So what?" Tracy said.

"So what? It's like stealing. The Kreapps are ours."

"Oh, for God's sake, Edge, give it up. You sound like you're still on the ski slopes," Tracy said.

That shut Edge up. He clamped his lips together and barely touched his food. For the rest of the meal we made a point of talking about other things besides the challenge. The weather. The garden that Ivy used to love. The funny personalities at the day care.

When we finished, Edge caught Elizabeth's elbow as she passed our table and nodded toward Reeba. "She's spying."

Elizabeth hesitated. "She isn't—"

"I don't trust anyone from Harrisburg. We've got to anticipate those scammers."

"Actually—"

"We need an extra practice this week." Then he turned to me. "Lily. It's Sunday. Tell the Walkie Talkies they need to up their game. After this meal today, they need to push for an extra mile."

"It's Mother's Day. I'm not going to tell them anything."

"What?!" His eyes were wide.

"You're being ridiculous."

Edge wasn't listening. He focused on Reeba like a laser beam. "Look at that. The mayor is bringing her this way." He crossed his arms and prepared to give Reeba Sweeney a piece of his mind. His newly visible jaw clenched. I suddenly wanted his beard back.

"How was I supposed to remember that Reeba Sweeney had a twin sister?" Edge followed me out of the Amble Inn. Everyone had gone home and we had stayed to help clean up.

I was too angered by his rudeness to give him an inch. "She was a nice woman. And a judge!" Alice Sweeney pretended as if nothing was wrong after Edge confronted her with accusations of espionage. I wouldn't have been so generous.

"Well, it's not completely my fault. Elizabeth could have told me."

"She tried, you numbskull. But you were too busy with your big conspiracy theory to listen."

"It was a natural reaction."

I rounded on him. "You're lucky she was so nice to you."

"With a sister like Reeba, she's probably used to being confused with the devil."

"You're getting too caught up in this challenge thing, Edge. You need to calm down."

"I thought this was what you wanted. Just a few weeks ago you were telling us all how to eat healthier. It's supposed to be a good thing."

It was a good thing. I had been ecstatic to see so many people embrace the idea of a healthy brunch. Louise had thoroughly enjoyed her meal. And Ivy had enjoyed her smoothie. But the end of the meal was enough to give a person indigestion.

We reached Edge's pickup truck. "Come on, Lily. Don't let this ruin your day." Edge opened the car door for me.

I refused to meet his eye. When I was seated he leaned down. "Aren't you curious what kissing me without my beard will be like?"

I pulled on my seat belt and stared straight ahead.

"Come on. You know you want to plant one right here." He blocked my view and pointed to his chin.

I hated how he melted away my anger with humor. I reached across and put my finger on his cheek. Soft. Smooth. "It isn't fair. Why wasn't I born with your sex appeal?"

"You don't think you're sexy?"

I dismissed him with a puff of air.

He lowered his head and I inhaled the musky aftershave he had used this morning, letting it go to my head. "Besides the way you taste with chocolate drizzled on your skin, you're cute even when you are mad at me. And your dancing makes me want to disco all night long. And I have a confession . . . I hate disco." He kissed me every time he paused. "And your mouth fits me perfectly with or without a beard . . . And most of all, you look sexy in a dress."

He had me at chocolate.

While Louise and Ivy watched an old Cary Grant movie, and Edge worked at the Dairy Cow, I sat on the floor of Edge's bedroom talking on the phone and playing with the carpet fibers.

"Happy Mother's Day, Mom!"

"Oh, thank you, honey! Chip is here and we just face-clocked Ned."

Mom's English was perfect, but she mixed up words sometimes. "You mean face-timed?"

"Yeah, I looked pretty good in that little square."

I heard Chip laughing in the background. Of course Chip was the one to fly in for Mother's Day. He was a suck-up. While Ned probably sent two dozen roses and a new appliance for the kitchen, Chip had flown in and taken Mom out to a buffet, Mom's version of a five-star restaurant.

"Did Chip take you out to eat, Mom?"

"Oh yeah. All you can eat crab for fourteen ninety-five. Can you believe it? What's the price of crab out there?"

"We don't really have an all-you-can-eat seafood buffet in town, Mom."

"That's too bad."

"Did you get the new tennis shirt I ordered you?" Mom was a good athlete for an older woman. My brothers took after her side of the family.

"Yeah. Thanks, honey. Then Chip took me shopping for a new warm-up suit and a new tennis racquet to match it. The ladies are going to be so jealous of my new graphite. How is your knee?"

"Fine. I have all my range of motion and I've graduated to unlimited walking without a brace."

Chip grabbed the phone. "Just be careful you don't fall off the sidewalk, hippo legs." Oh God, I hadn't heard that nickname in at least ten years.

"So how is that little town—what's the name of it again?"

"Truhart."

"Are you getting them to touch their toes yet, or is that too much for them?"

"Actually, they are doing really well."

"Oh yeah? Are they wrestling pigs and playing cornhole now?"

Smart ass. Chip was the last one to talk about cornhole. At our last family gathering he had not only won the cornhole toss, but he had managed to drink the most beers in the process.

"Ha ha. You should see it. They're taking to the fitness training very well, Chip. In fact, we have a whole Memorial Day Weekend Warrior Challenge going on with the other half of the county. There's a weight-loss challenge and a cook-off, and even a ninja warrior challenge on an obstacle course. Everyone's really excited, and it's getting quite a bit of press around here." It took up the entire left-hand column of the local *Harrison County Courier* last week.

"Sounds fun. Maybe I should enter."

"You couldn't do half the obstacle course my team is training for. I've even got a gourmet chef. The food is going to be phenomenal."

He whistled. "Impressive, Lily. Send us more information when you get time."

I promised him I would. And I made a vow to conveniently forget. Then I caught up on all the news in his life. The whirlwind of conferences and recognition events. And, of course, there was the part that had to do with saving the world. It was amazing that Chip could fit so much into a single lifetime. He even managed a girlfriend. Although he hadn't introduced her to Mom yet. Chicken.

I heard about Ned and his beautiful wife. His career. And the fact that Chip and Ned had managed to meet for dinner in Florence a week ago. "The Chianti was absolutely amazing, Lil. You would have thought you'd died and gone to heaven."

Lite beer was more my style these days.

It had been weeks since I let myself wallow in self-pity. I had forgotten that sense of failure that overwhelmed me when I spoke with my family.

By the time I hung up, I realized I had drawn hundreds of tiny circles in Edge's bedroom carpet with my hands. I rubbed my fingers back and forth, covering the tracks of my frustration.

LESSON NINETEEN

Monitor Your Progress

One of my younger Lollipa-Losers, the name the weight-loss participants had officially christened themselves, stepped on the scale and held her breath. I peeked over her shoulder and wrote down her weight. "A pound down, Amber. That is fantastic."

She stepped off and her eyes welled with tears. "I can't believe I didn't lose more. I've been eating right all week."

I hugged her. "You have been working out a great deal this week. Remember, muscle weighs more than fat."

"Why bother to lose the fat weight if I gain the muscle weight right back?"

"Your real goal is health. Just remember that and don't worry about the weight. It will all work out in the end."

Her lower lip puffed out. "It will all work out? I hate that saying. My aunt says it to me whenever I don't have a date on a Friday night." She walked to the other side of the partition, her shoulders sagging and her head down.

I made a note on my clipboard. This was one of the hardest parts of weight loss. Everyone measured the scale as if it were the holy grail of progress. But the real goal was muscle tone and loss of fat. With Dr. Manning's supervision, I had recorded each participant's weight when I first came to Truhart. The added pressure to beat Harrisburg was not helping my team lose weight in a slow and steady manner. I reminded every participant over and over that the real game was over a lifetime. Not just a few short weeks.

Edge appeared at my side. "Amber looked upset. Isn't she losing weight?"

"Everyone loses weight at a different rate."

He tilted his head to read the clipboard and I hugged it to my chest. "This is private. No games this time."

"It's a competition. We need to know where we stand. Besides, we have more participants than the required number. If they aren't losing weight, we can remove them from the team with no penalty."

"Do you hear what you're saying? That's ridiculous." I walked around the partition and waved the next person forward. There was only one person left. "Step back behind the partition, Edge."

"Oh, come on. It's me. I'm a team captain."

"I don't care if you're the flippin' president. This information is confidential."

Edge stomped off and I heard the door to the gym slam on his way out. What a baby. Last night Louise had tried to explain to me how competitive Edge used to be during his skiing days. "I thought he had outgrown it. I should have known it was still inside him."

Tracy had added, "Yeah, like a dormant disease, waiting to take over his body. Seriously, Mom. Someone's got to stop him."

Louise had raised an eyebrow at me. "Maybe someone can give him a few gentle reminders what this challenge is all about."

I thought about what she said now. Gentle? No way. Someone had to whack Edge upside the head with a long pole. Then I frowned at the direction of my thoughts. What a terrible thing to think about a man who had suffered from a concussion. My brothers were competitive. My colleagues in fitness were competitive, although they covered it up by talking "health" talk, like I had just done with Amber. But the fact was that we all were competitive to some extent. Some of us just did a better job of covering it up than others.

Marva O'Shea walked around the partition. "I sure hope I have a good weigh-in today, Lily. Last week we celebrated Jenny Scott's birthday and I couldn't help myself. I had two pieces of cake."

She stepped up on the scale and refused to look down. "If I weigh more I'm just going to quit this stupid challenge. I try and try, but every time I lose one pound I gain two. Last night Corinne and I got into it because she tried to stop me from eating the second serving of lasagna at dinner. I don't know what happened to me. I just went off on her." I thought about my conversation with Corinne several weeks ago. What had she called it? Blovering? This new disagreement sounded more serious than bickering. "Corinne never gains weight. She eats and eats all day long and she still looks like a skinny old stick. All I have to do is look at a Twinkie and it's on my butt. It's not fair. She has it so easy—"

She stepped off the scale and covered her face with her hands. "Oh Lord. I can't believe I said that . . ."

I put my arms around Marva's shoulders and let her cry it out. Weight loss was such an emotional issue. In a culture that is so focused on looks and body shape, being overweight was almost paralyzing. I held Marva in my arms and thought about how long it had been since I had experienced the agony of long-term weight gain. My own struggle as an adolescent had motivated me to become a fitness trainer. Then the impact of my father's death had taken a toll that I remembered too well. It was one of the reasons I had been excited to work on *Just Lose It*. But as soon as I was on the set, the lights and cameras made me more focused on my own success rather than my client's gritty anguish over trying to lose weight.

Maybe L.A. and Hollywood weren't where I had ever belonged.

I tucked that thought away and put Marva out of her misery. "You lost three pounds."

She jumped back. "I did?"

"You did."

"Even with the two pieces of cake?"

I nodded. "Yup."

She jumped back on the scale to make sure. "Oh my God. I did! Wait until I tell Corinne. Imagine what I would have weighed if I hadn't had the cake."

Marva ran out the front door and left me alone in the gym, grateful to witness a victory that had nothing to do with winning.

Our first meeting for high school students struggling with weight issues went very well. At first the kids were shy. When Rocky, of all kids, revealed his own embarrassment over his body, however, the floodgates opened. We talked about very small changes we could make until next week's meeting, and the students walked out carrying more energy and optimism than when they arrived.

Afterwards, Rocky dropped me at Lakeview Adult Day Care. "Ms. Shue, I can't tell you how much fun I am having practicing the obstacle course with the River Hogs. They've all been super nice and I can do all the obstacles. Can you believe it?"

"Yes, I can believe it, Rocky. Not only is the weight coming off, but you are strong now. Getting stronger every day."

He gave me a spontaneous hug before driving off. I was so proud of him. Proud of so many people in town. I couldn't remember the last time I had enjoyed this kind of satisfaction in my career.

The campers at Lakeview loved dancing with me to "Call Me Maybe." We replayed it three times at their insistence, and now I couldn't get it out of my head.

After Louise brought me home, I walked across the street, looking for Edge. I wanted to tell him about my amazing day. The garage door was open, but Edge's truck wasn't there. Edge had been so busy with his obstacle-course team and working at the Dairy Cow that he hadn't worked on the ranch all week. Last night he had been late getting home. I had fallen asleep without sneaking across the street to be with him.

Now I wandered around the house trying to figure out where he had gone. The ice on the lake had melted. But the water was still frigid. Next to the shoreline was the large patch of land that made up Ivy's garden. It was just beginning to show signs of life. I stared at the clumped-up dirt and the sprouting perennials that poked out of the soil and wondered when people planted in this part of the world. Surely it was time to tend the soil and plant the first seedlings. I leaned down and surveyed the rose bushes near the house. Tiny buds were visible on the stems. Good. They survived the winter.

The garden needed tending to, before the weather warmed up. Especially around the perennials.

I went to the garage, where the garden tools were hanging on a rack, and pulled out a hoe. For the next half hour, I worked the soil loose and evened out some of the areas that the winter wind had eroded. I grabbed some shears that had been lying on a shelf in the garage and cut away the burlap on the rose bushes. Edge should have done that weeks ago. They needed light. I clipped a few dead branches so that the plant's energy would go to the new growth.

I would come back when I had time and bring a few hardy annuals to brighten up the borders. I leaned the hoe against the side of the garage when a movement in the picture window of the Callahans' living room caught my eye.

Ivy sat in her wheelchair gazing at me. She raised her hand and waved. It was the first time I had ever seen her do that.

I waved back. One gardener to another.

LESSON TWENTY

Stay Positive on Bad Days

"She likes it, Lily. You are a genius." Louise captured me in her arms and kissed my cheek.

"It wasn't that big a deal." I sat down next to Ivy and watched her drink the smoothie I had prepared for her. Yogurt, strawberries, bananas, almond milk, and my protein powder. I had grown tired of watching Ivy feed her toast to the dogs and scowl at her eggs. This morning I had asked Louise if I could make Ivy breakfast.

"I should get one of these for the day care. I can't tell you how many seniors have trouble eating hard food and meat."

"The best part is you can customize it, Louise. Protein and vegetables, fruit or yogurt. There are all sorts of recipes you can modify."

A horn honked from the driveway, "Oops, gotta go."

"Tell my son to come in and share a cup of coffee next time, will you? He's hardly been around all week."

I felt her pain. Edge was running himself ragged. I kept telling him to take it easy. But some sort of virus had taken over him. It was called the Warrior Weekend Challenge.

When I climbed into his pickup, I said, "I missed you yesterday."

He leaned across and gave me a kiss. "Busy again. Sorry. I got home late and crashed as soon as I walked in the door."

I wanted to talk to him about the garden, but he was more interested in talking about the challenge. "We're in countdown time. Less than a week to go. How are things going with the walkers?"

"Great. If we were to map it, they would have made it all the way to Chicago on foot by now. They're really pleased."

"Chicago? That's all?" He scraped a hand over his eyes and turned onto the main road. With his clean face and hard jaw, he should look great this morning. But his eyes had tiny coils of red circling the irises and he had dark circles under his eyes.

I stared at his profile. "What do you mean *that's all*? That's pretty darn good. You can practically see the progress on their worn shoes."

"I just—" He shook his head. "Never mind. We'll beat them at the obstacle course."

"Never mind? We can beat them on the road, too. Who knows how far Harrisburg has walked so far?"

He grunted. "What about the Lollipa-Losers? Any progress there? Aunt Addie says she's lost twenty pounds so far."

More like fourteen. But I didn't want to correct her testimony. It was important for her to feel good regardless of the details. If the rounded-up number of twenty made her happy, then so be it.

"Our Lollipa-Losers are still losing, and I'm really proud of them."

"Their BMIs—Do you think we stand a chance if Harrisburg has, say, lost . . . I don't know, an average of twenty-five pounds per person?"

I sighed. "I don't know, Edge. I would have to crunch the numbers. We'll just have to wait for the weigh-in on Saturday."

He tapped the steering wheel. I got the fact that his dormant competitive nature was coming out. But I wanted to make him understand that everyone was a winner. No matter what happened. I opened my mouth to explain and stopped. Mentioning the competition seemed to do nothing but add tension to our relationship.

I reached for the knob on the dashboard and searched for classic rock on the radio. I passed a sports-talk radio station and he said, "Wait, I want to hear how the Wings did last night."

"They won." I was surprised he didn't know that. The NHL playoffs were a big deal around here, and last night the twins and I had watched the game in the recreation room. By the third quarter we were practically throwing our popcorn at the officials, who kept giving us penalties that resulted in a power play by the opponents, the Colorado Avalanche. We screamed so loud during the shoot-out that Louise yelled at us to quiet down.

I was just about to tell him to stop working so hard on the challenge and enjoy the finer things in life, when his phone rang. The caller information read "Uncle Pete." The elusive uncle I had yet to meet.

Edge took the call on the speaker system. "Hey, Edge. Any chance you can take the truck Friday? I've got a meeting with a guy in Pinconning who thinks he can sell my candy at his cheese store. It might be pretty lucrative if I clinch it."

"Sorry, Uncle Pete. The challenge is Saturday. Remember? I've got a lot to do to get ready. Maybe next time."

"It's really an important opportunity. What if you just take the morning for a couple of hours? I should be able to make it back by then."

"Can't do it. I'm reviewing some of the finer points of the rope climb with my team at noon. Besides, I can't risk overworking myself before the big day. "

Pete tried all sorts of incentives to persuade Edge to take a shift, but Edge wasn't budging. Uncle Pete sounded so disappointed by the time he hung up that I almost volunteered myself.

"I can help go over the rope tactics with the team if you want to change your mind and help Uncle Pete."

Edge had the audacity to laugh. "God no, Lily. Ropes are hard to explain. I'll do it."

My whole body tensed. "I am a trainer, you know."

"Yeah, but this is obstacle-course work. It's different. We're in the home stretch here. Uncle Pete will have to understand. Trash and chocolates can wait."

I crossed my arms in front of me and turned my head to watch the landscape out my side window. It had rained last night and there was more drizzle in the forecast. The grass was greener every day now. The buds on the trees were opening up and silvery-green leaves rustled in the wind. With the promise of summer around the corner, the landscape was far prettier than it had been when I first came to Truhart. I couldn't wait. Not just for summer, but for things to get back to normal. Whatever that was. Edge was obsessed with winning. So was the whole town, for that matter. A twinge of anger flared deep down, and I pushed it back, not wanting to give in to the emotions that threatened to ruin my new feelings for Edge.

We listened to sports radio and I stared out the window, practically counting the minutes until the challenge was over.

* * *

The Lollipa-Losers met at the Amble Inn to eat a healthy breakfast the day before the Warrior Weekend Challenge. They discussed
ways they were going to refrain from eating for the rest of the day. I
interrupted their discussion and reminded them that fasting was not
only against the rules, but not in the spirit of healthy weight loss.

"A liquid diet is perfectly acceptable today," Marva reminded me.

"As long as you keep nutrients in your smoothies," I reminded
them.

I heard Addie Adler whisper across her table, "I'm going to load
up my plate with pancakes as soon as we're done with this challenge
weekend."

"Stay steady, everyone. The last thing you want is yo-yo dieting,"
I said loudly. I reminded everyone that weight loss was a long-term
project that was a challenge all its own. I made a note in my planner.
I was going to speak with Marie about this when I had the chance.
There needed to be a strong follow-up after the event.

After the breakfast, Edge drove me to the gym.

A shiny black BMW with a rental sticker on it was parked in
front. My mouth went dry when I spotted the two figures in the front
seat.

"Lily?" I sat unmoving, ignoring the fact that Edge was talking to
me. He came around to my side of the tuck and opened my door.
"Are you okay?"

How could I explain he was about to be confronted with a fellow
comedian and a fast-talking Korean mother?

"Do you know them?" Edge said, looking back and forth between
me and the car in front of us.

"You could say that."

He helped me out of the truck, keeping a hand on my elbow to
steady me.

The BMW doors flew open and two figures jumped out. One
short, dark-haired woman dressed in a white quilted jacket, and one
tall, dark-haired man wearing a cashmere turtleneck and a wool sports
coat.

"Lily! No brace!"

"Hi, Mom."

"Lilibutt!"

212 • *Cynthia Tennent*

"Hi, Chip."

They hugged me, Mom rocking me back and Chip pulling me off my feet.

When my athletic shoes were back on the concrete, I asked, "What are you doing here?"

"A speaker at a medical conference in Traverse City canceled at the last minute and Chip took his place so we could see you," Mom said in her speedy, accented English. "I made him fly me out, too."

"We flew to Traverse City this morning and drove straight here."

"We know you have that big Warrior Challenge and we thought we would come and cheer."

Without waiting for me to introduce him, Chip held his hand out to Edge. "Chip Shue. And this is my mother, Jan."

"Edge Callahan. It's so nice to meet you, Mrs. Shue." Edge sent them a killer smile I hadn't seen for days.

My mother's eyes lit up as she looked back and forth from me to Edge.

Over the years, Mom greeted any man I introduced her to with the narrowed eyes of a potential mother-in-law. I could always tell by the way she greeted them whether she was happy or dismissive of a man's potential. It was embarrassing. Ninety-nine percent of the time the men had been colleagues, or my friends' boyfriends. One had even been my boss's boss, the owner of the company with gyms up and down the West Coast. He was good-looking and his clothes were very expensive. Her eyes had lit up with dollar signs until I introduced his husband. Later, I had been forced to endure a rant about the injustices in the world for women in search of rich, good-looking straight men.

I saw the gleam in her eye now and knew she was glad she made the trip. While the three of them exchanged pleasantries, I noted how Edge laid on the charm. The way he complimented Mom on her young appearance. And how Chip stood straighter next to Edge. The love affair was so mutual I was almost jealous. Part of me wished Edge had driven up in the cuddly garbage truck with a scraggly beard, just to throw them both off.

"We can't wait to see your new gym. Is this it?" Mom asked.

I took a deep breath. There was no avoiding the embarrassing reality of my new job. I unlocked the gym and ushered everyone inside.

A stunned silence filled the room.

Edge moved to the center of the room. "Lily is a master at turning a tiny budget into an efficient workout room." He showed them the PVC rollers, the foam-coated step boxes, and the sand-filled soccer balls. He picked up one of the gallon milk jugs with pebbles that we used as kettle weights.

"They've been talking about this all over the county. Even the gyms with a huge budget are amazed."

My mother, the queen of saving money—her own, not her sons'—was enormously impressed. "My kids call me cheap. Ha! I knew all my talk of being frugal was going to rub off someday."

Chip took another tactic. "I didn't know you were pressed for cash on this job. I would have been happy to make a donation."

Before I could say anything, Edge handled it. "We could have raised the money ourselves. But that's beside the point. Working out and getting fit shouldn't be an economic issue. Everyone can do it on a shoestring. Even our little town. That's the whole point."

He moved next to me and put his arm around me. A point that wasn't lost on my mother's excited face.

"Lily has single-handedly modified the way we think about nutrition and fitness, as illustrated by the charts in the room. Her walkers would have forged a trail all the way to Chicago had they been making a contiguous trek."

I lifted my brow at his speech. Fancy language. How did Edge know that would impress Chip?

Chip pointed at my knee. "And she did all this as a gimp?"

Edge's eyes grew dark. "A gimp? Your sister is a wounded warrior of the fitness world. She's our hero."

I held up my hands. "Okay, you're laying it on way too heavy, Edge."

He just smiled and stared at Chip. Something passed between the two of them.

Chip raised an eyebrow. "Well, well . . ."

I didn't know what he meant by that. Fortunately, I was interrupted by the first of the walkers, who were ready to chart their final day's mileage.

After Edge left, Chip and Mom stayed around for an hour, meeting several walkers, reading the large posters around the room. If they were disappointed by the community center, they didn't show it.

Chip even took a few pictures of the room and sent them to Ned. Finally, he said, "We'll get out of your hair for a while, Lil. I am going to take Mom to lunch and head back to the Grande Lucerne, where we are staying. We can't meet you tonight, but we'll be here tomorrow for the big day! Dinner after that?"

"Sure." Hopefully I didn't look as dazed as I felt. Having my family here was like an odd mash-up of classical jazz and rock music. It shouldn't fit. But it was working anyway. Thanks to Edge.

"Bring that nice man tomorrow night, too," Mom said with a wide smile. She elbowed me in the gut. "He's straight, right?"

"Yes, Mom."

"He likes you, I can tell," she said with a wink. "Don't screw it up!"

That night, I was late getting to the ranch. When I walked in the door, Edge pulled me into his arms and we stumbled to the bedroom. This time there was no foreplay. We didn't talk. Or laugh. Or tease each other with food. We came together in a silent explosion that left us both drained.

Afterward I lay in the crook of his arm and traced my hand across his chest. "Aren't you supposed to abstain from sexual intercourse before the big day?" I teased.

"Yeah, well, that's an old wives' tale. Mostly." He kissed my forehead. "Your family seems really nice."

"Oh my God. I can't believe they came." I rolled to my back and groaned.

"What's wrong?"

"You think your family is spirited? When my family is together we live the Warrior Challenge every day."

"I haven't met your other brother, but they didn't seem that bad."

"It's just that Chip and Ned are, like, über successful. Everything they touch is gold. Mom loves it."

"Then you fit right in."

"What are you talking about? I'm the everlasting loser in the Shue family."

He rolled over until he was on both elbows above me. "From the moment I first met you, I was awed by your tenacity. You worked harder than an athlete training for the Olympics. And I should know. You were relentless the way you tried to keep the town on track for the fitness grant. Lily, your passion and dedication amaze me."

"Wait a minute . . . I thought you said I took everything too seriously."

"I did. But then I realized you weren't serious at all. You just care deeply."

I took a deep breath and let his words sink in. "But I always feel like the straight man in the comedy routine when I'm around you. The Abbott to your Costello. The boring one." How strange to think he had admired me all along.

"Your humor is there, just below the surface. You just like to play it straight. Which is perfect for me. No ego problems, because I get the punch lines." He grinned and kissed my brow.

"I understand egos. My family is one gigantic one." Having Mom and Chip in town had doubled the intensity of my dread for the Warrior Challenge tomorrow. I wished more than anything that the silly challenge had never happened. There was no way to make him understand the pressure I felt when I was around my family.

Then he said something that had me thinking the rest of the night. "Don't fool yourself, Lily. Your ego is alive and well, just like your humor. Unfortunately, it isn't as strong as the way you second-guess yourself."

I drifted off to sleep in Edge's arms and woke up in the middle of the night feeling chilled. Beside me, the bed was empty. I got up to investigate. But Edge was nowhere to be found. His truck was gone. I shivered as I looked down the lake road and searched for the glow of headlights.

The night had turned cold. The moon cast a silvery glow on the rose bushes in Ivy's garden. Maybe I had removed the burlap from the roses too soon. It looked like we might have a frost tonight.

LESSON TWENTY-ONE

Avoid Injury

The Triple C's organized a caravan of cars to take us to the county fairgrounds. There must have been over fifty minivans, SUVs, and trucks in a line as we made our way west. I sat in the backseat of Ivy's old Ford Taurus, wedged between Louise and Olivia. Sarah drove and Ivy sat in the front seat.

Ivy's face was a mixture of happiness and excitement to be riding in her old car.

"Mine," she said every few minutes.

Edge was driving his truck, stuffed with banners and chairs and fold-out tables that the Triple C's had decided we would need.

"Is it going to warm up at all?" I seemed to be the only one concerned about the weather. I worried about the effects of the temperature on the cook-off and the obstacle course.

"This is pretty normal this time of year," Louise said, patting my leg. "The temperature goes all spastic on us for a few weeks before it settles down in the summer. We're used to it. Heck, Joe O'Shea considers anything over freezing Bermuda-shorts weather."

When we pulled up into the field bordering the county fairgrounds, we were swarmed by a sea of olive green. Harrisburg had taken the warrior theme to the extreme. Green tents, green flags, green long-sleeved technical shirts that must have cost a fortune. Camouflage dotted the fairgrounds as the professional-looking banners declared the Harrisburg Warriors the mightiest contestant of the games.

We sat stunned for a full thirty seconds before Louise said, "That's a tacky shade."

We laughed halfheartedly and parked near the side of the field. Sarah and Olivia were going to take turns watching Ivy until Tracy arrived later with the boys.

Marva unfurled her handwritten banners and planted them in the ground with metal stakes. "Those things took nothing but a printer to make. Our banners took heart. Right?" she said to anyone who would listen.

Mac was already at the field, standing by the large tent where the cook-off would be held. He was trading jokes with the other chef and thankfully didn't look like he was worried at all about his part of the challenge. When I greeted him, he introduced me to his friend and rival, the chef from the Grande Lucerne, Gaston Lapin.

Marie Joiner stood nearby, her usual clipboard in her hands, a worried expression on her face. I walked over and shook her hand. She introduced me to the panel of judges, many whose names I recognized. They had authorized the Fit4You grant. They looked at me with curiosity. I was the trainer with the unorthodox methods and the knee injury. The one whose job hung by a thread, even though no one would admit it. Marie and I never discussed the outcome if Truhart lost today. I somehow managed to keep my smile glued to my face as I shook each hand and tried not to break down and beg them to leave the gym open.

Aubrey and Andrew Vanderbeek, wearing full camouflage, joined us. They had painted wide stripes under their eyes that added to their warrior visage. They looked me up and down as if they couldn't believe what they were seeing. Underneath my white puffy winter coat, I wore the yellow T-Shirt that the Truhart team had decided to use as their uniform.

AIM HIGH,
WORK HARD,
DON'T QUIT!
—LILY SHUE

Aubrey stared at it and laughed. "Sweet shirt." The sarcasm froze the air between us.

I bit my lip and willed the sun to go down soon. This day could not be done fast enough.

"Lily!"

I turned around to see my mother and brother. I redirected them away from the Vanderbeeks to the chefs and introduced them to Mac and Gaston.

Chip shook Chef Gaston's hand. "We had the pleasure of eating at the Grande Lucerne last night, and I can't tell you how delicious the meal was."

My mother nodded. "But you needed more miso on the sea bass. Not enough flavor."

The Frenchman raised his eyebrows and took the comment with grace.

While Mom and Chip settled near a space heater that had been brought by the judges, I made my way over to the River Hogs to see how they were doing.

Edge stood beside a group of huddled figures, his hands in his pockets. Next to him, J.D. Hardy's face was thunderous.

Something was wrong.

Before I could ask what had happened, Edge stepped aside. Elizabeth Lively sat on a bench, shaking her head and talking to one of the warriors. Her arm was in a sling.

"What happened?!" I asked.

J.D. glowered. "There was a little accident last night." People around us scattered, nervously aware of J.D.'s mood.

"What happened?"

"It seems the obstacle-course team did a little late-night reconnaissance."

"Reconnaissance?"

J.D. narrowed his eyes at Edge. "Late-night drills on the 'real' course. Here. Evidently, they have been doing it off and on for the last few weeks. Along with their midnight spy missions to see how the Harrisburg team was doing."

I couldn't believe what I was hearing. I looked from Edge, who stared down at his feet, to Elizabeth, who held her arm in pain.

Elizabeth raised her chin. "I don't care what you say, J.D. It was fun. And besides, it helped to even the playing field between Harrisburg and Truhart. You know they were probably doing the same thing to us."

"You think so?" His tone was sarcastic. "I got the impression they were working hard to beat you. Not cheat. And no one over there looks injured."

"Whose idea was this? And why didn't I know?" I stared at Edge, who looked as comfortable as a lion tamer without a whip.

Elizabeth and Edge exchanged looks. It was obvious there were two ringleaders.

Elizabeth reached for J.D.'s hand. "Can we argue about this later? I really hurt right now and we have to get you ready to take my spot on the obstacle course."

J.D. scowled. "I didn't say I would do it!" As angry as he looked, he hovered by Elizabeth's side and pulled her coat closer around her shoulders to keep her warm.

Elizabeth leveled J.D. with her blue eyes and said, "Please. I need a hero right now." It was some kind of code word because J.D.'s eyes darkened at her as if she weren't playing fair.

I grabbed Edge's arm and pulled him off to the side for my own conversation.

"Is this what you were doing last night?"

He held his hands up. "It was just a silly game."

"Silly enough to risk someone getting hurt? Why would you practice on the obstacle course in the dark? That was an accident waiting to happen." My chest felt so tight I could barely breathe.

"We aimed our car headlights on the course. It was as bright as day."

He started walking away from me and I grabbed his arm and turned him to face me. "This whole thing has gone too far."

"Lily, we'll talk later. I have to go make sure the judges put J.D. on our new roster."

Suddenly the day turned even more sour. "You promised Rocky he could be your alternate."

"Well, yeah, but he will understand when I tell him J.D. stepped forward."

I searched for Rocky. He stood with the other warriors, his eyes bright with excitement at the upcoming competition.

I pointed. "Look at him, Edge. He's been training with you since the start of this challenge. What are you going to tell him? He's not good enough?"

Edge's jaw contracted and his eyes wavered. "Don't . . ."

"Don't what? Remind you that decency is more important than this challenge?" I stepped forward until we were inches apart and no one could hear our conversation. "What would have happened if this challenge had never been made?"

"What are you talking about?"

"Would anyone be working so hard getting fit and eating right if we hadn't started this challenge?"

He searched my face as if he wasn't sure he recognized me. "Sure they would. You had people at the gym before all this started. You are the one who wanted to motivate everyone."

I shook my head. "You didn't care, though. You were pushing ice cream and Uncle Pete's candy to my walkers."

"I was just trying to market my product."

I crossed my arms. "No. You wanted to beat me."

"There was no competition."

"Wasn't there?"

He blinked. "I just thought you were going overboard with the fitness talk."

He didn't understand. "You aren't an Olympic racer anymore, Edge. You quit competition a long time ago."

His gray eyes turned into ice. "Thanks for reminding me."

I swallowed. "What I mean is, stop treating everything as if it's a game to win. You don't have to prove anything to anybody. Even today's challenge."

"We're doing this for you. And you care about winning just as much as I do." Edge pointed at my T-shirt. "'Aim high. Work hard. Don't quit.' Isn't that your motto?"

I put my hand on my chest, wishing I had never coined the phrase.

"You better make up your mind what you want, Lily. Because you can't have it both ways."

I struggled to make him understand. Things had changed for me. I captured my T-shirt with my fist and held it out. "You were right about my ego and my insecurity. But . . . they feed off each other. Don't they? You feel it, too?"

"Insecurity? Me? I'm the guy who drives a teddy bear truck, sells frozen treats to little kids, and sings stupid songs to old people."

I bit my lip. "I liked that Edge."

"No you didn't."

I was so mad I couldn't stop myself. "I loved that Edge."

I couldn't believe I said it out loud.

He stepped back. A dazed look in his eyes. "Lily—"

"I don't even care if you don't feel the same way about me. I'll deal with my own wounded heart."

He grabbed my arm. "But I—"

"And something else. We might lose. No, let's not fool ourselves. We *will* lose. And I am going to be fired for good. So, there goes my insecurity and my ego. In the garbage in a single day! But I don't care about any of it. I would rather lose this whole battle and my own pride than risk hurting a boy like Rocky."

The boulder that weighed down my chest had been dropped. I was out of energy. Exhausted from the Warrior Weekend Challenge before it started.

I turned and walked away, sweating in the cold breeze that blew across the county fairgrounds.

By the time everyone was settled, and the cook-off was set to begin, my head was pounding. I watched as Mac and Gaston took the ingredients given to them and fired up the grills. They had two hours to prepare the meal, and a crowd gathered around to watch them work. A team of amateur sous-chefs gathered to prepare copies of what they made. The food would be sold for lunch, and the money raised was going to be split evenly among both communities.

In the meantime, Marie Joiner announced over the microphone that it was time for the weigh-ins. With a feeling of nausea, which may have been related to my own empty stomach, I handed over my files to Marie and the panel of judges. One by one, participants entered a tent where a doctor and nurse weighed them, marking their BMIs on a chart. I waited outside the tent with Aubrey, and we gave everyone who came out a sticker proclaiming their success.

At one point Aubrey said to me, "Truhart doesn't stand a chance."

I ignored her. Many people walked out of the weigh-in happy. They pumped the air with their fists and proclaimed that they met their goals. But not everyone was pleased. Instead of wearing their stickers like badges of honor, a few participants tore them off after they passed us.

Aubrey didn't seem concerned. She said to one of her disappointed team members, "I told you to watch those carbs, Linda."

I was dumbfounded by her insensitivity. I followed after the dejected woman and told her she should be proud of herself. "This is just the beginning of your journey. Don't stop. You'll reach your goal if you stay motivated."

She smiled politely and moved away.

I pulled Aubrey and Marie aside. "We need to be mindful of the people who didn't make their target goal. This is a really difficult and public thing for people to go through. We shouldn't let them feel humiliated or like they let their teams down."

Aubrey pretended to agree. "After the competition I'll send an email."

"No." The sound of my strong objection surprised even me. "We need to spend the time now. This is important!"

Marie looked at me sideways and made a mark on her ever-present clipboard. I wanted to rip it out of her hands and stomp on it.

"Dr. Manning will announce the weight-loss-challenge results after lunch. It's time for the walking teams to submit their results now," Marie said.

The walkers stood excitedly in the middle of the field, where a long table of judges had been set up. I kept a smile plastered on my face as the leaders of the two groups spoke into a microphone and introduced each member of their team. Marva was the presenter of the Truhart Walkie Talkies and she included a plug for the Family Fare in her speech. The applause was equal if not louder from the Truhart fans, who had cowbells and horns that made my ears ring as they cheered.

When the announcements were finished, the walking teams presented their mileage to the judges.

The crowd waited, talking in hushed whispers as the judges deliberated with calculators. After several minutes the results were announced.

Harrisburg had won by more than three hundred miles.

Aubrey raised the trophy—a golden, spray-painted tennis shoe—above her head.

Edge was huddled by the River Hogs and our eyes met. I gazed past him. After my confession of love, I didn't want to see his discomfort.

He had predicted the defeat a few days ago. Of course, now I understood how he had known. His late-night spy maneuvers into enemy territory had already told him Truhart was going to lose.

The walkers moved off the field with sagging shoulders and I did my best to console them. "You have nothing to feel bad about. You walked for better health and fitness. The victory is in that accomplishment. Not beating someone else."

People were already talking conspiracy theories. "They totally inflated their numbers," and "My cousin says they didn't walk more than two miles a week," were just some of the comments from the Truhart sideline.

Addie Adler, wearing bright-colored sweatpants and a headband that made her look like she belonged on the Jane Fonda workout videos, shook her head. "I just hate losing to Harrisburg . . . again."

The nutrition quiz was next. My team was made up of four of my best, including Nestor Nagel, the older gentleman who had recently returned from the Keys and had helped at the Mother's Day brunch. He didn't look like someone who would know his food groups, but he was the shining star of the show. With bright blue eyes that sparkled and a thin, crooked nose that made him look like a funny-man from an old vaudeville show, he answered question after question. The final score was Harrisburg 24 and Truhart 32. The sidelines erupted in bell ringing and cheers as Nestor held the nutrition trophy, a golden apple, over his head.

Everyone broke for lunch, the meals prepared by Mac and Gaston. The judges enjoyed the grilled chicken and salads so much they ended up going back for seconds. Those who were competing in the obstacle race after lunch only nibbled. Twice, Edge headed toward me and I dodged away from his path. I couldn't eat anything, but I squeezed into the tent with Mom and Chip, doing my best to avoid Edge. Louise joined us with Ivy, and when Chip saw Ivy, he knelt in front of her and took her hand. He talked to her for a good ten minutes, even though she wasn't able to say much. I reminded myself he had a medical degree, after all. And a soft heart that I forgot about way too often. Maybe I needed to rethink my own warrior challenge.

After we finished, Louise said she was going to take Ivy back to the car to warm up.

I hovered by the edge of the food tent and waited for the results of the cook-off. Mac and Gaston stood beside each other as the judges declared the cook-off a dead heat. They each took a corner of the golden cookbook trophy and held it over their heads for photographs.

The Truhart crowd wasn't pleased. Corinne Scott waved her granddaughter's pom-pom. "Come on! You know Mac's chicken quinoa sliders were far better than that silly chicken kabob ragout thing!"

Someone handed her a bowl of the chicken ragout and she took a bite. She took another bite. Then she sat down to finish the rest. Her speech forgotten.

In the middle of the afternoon, Aubrey and I were called to the center of the field to hear Dr. Manning announce the results of the weigh-in.

Aubrey stood confidently next to me in her T-shirt, looking like she could withstand a blizzard. I unzipped my coat to reveal the yellow T-shirt with my words written across it. The weather hadn't changed. Goose bumps swept over me and I cursed my thin L.A. blood.

Marie held the microphone and asked, "Would you like to say something before the results, ladies?"

Aubrey took the microphone first. "I just want to say how proud I am of my team. Harrisburg has been incredibly motivated and disciplined and they are all winners in my book!" She held up her finger and pumped the air with a number one sign. What a fraud she was. When I was fired, I was going to write a letter to the grant board with my observations of her lack of professionalism. They probably wouldn't listen to me, but what did I have to lose?

Marie passed the microphone to me. I hesitated, thinking about the important message I had for everyone.

"We are not always winners, Aubrey." I took a breath, and my low voice gained strength. "In Truhart we call our weight-loss group the Lollipa-Losers. Sometimes we all feel like losers."

Aubrey mumbled, "Speak for yourself."

I caught a glimpse of Edge standing with the River Hogs. He had hardly smiled since I bared my heart.

"We haven't always done things in the conventional way on our side of town. No excuses. Anyone who has seen our gym knows what I mean."

Aubrey laughed. "It's a disaster."

A chant started across her side of the field. "Harrisburg! Harrisburg!"

I raised my voice to be heard. "But we stuck with it because we were motivated by something other than winning. Remember, everyone, it doesn't matter if you got on the scale today and were a pound up or a pound down. Whether your team wins or loses. It's about supporting each other." Corinne and Marva stood together, arm in arm, at the edge of the field. Mom and Chip were beside them . . . supporting me. It wouldn't hurt me to remember my own words more often.

The yellow side of the field was kicking up. "Truhart! Truhart is number one!"

I held up my hand. "I know this is a competition, but we should rally round each other. Even those across the field—" The chanting was too loud now. The cowbells and horns had added to the noise, and the clamor was deafening.

"We are all—" I couldn't even hear my own voice.

I handed the microphone to Marie with a tight smile. Who was I fooling? No one cared what I had to say. Marie held up her hands and tried to quiet the noisemakers.

When that failed, Aubrey grabbed the microphone and put her fingers to her lips and whistled. "Shut up! Let's hear the results."

I clenched my fists so hard my fingernails cut into my palms. Sadly, I didn't feel a thing.

Marie opened the envelope and said, "Harrisburg wins the weight-loss challenge."

The camouflage sideline went crazy and rushed the field, picking Aubrey up in a victory lap.

I stumbled away from the celebration. It didn't matter if the River Hogs won the obstacle course after this. I couldn't face the thought of Rocky standing on the sidelines, knowing he had been passed over. Everything about the challenge had gone wrong. As far as I was concerned, my defeat was complete.

LESSON TWENTY-TWO

Make Sacrifices

I walked down the county road, making my way back to Reply Lake and the Callahans'. I had no idea how far I had gone. Or how much farther I had to go.

After the weight-loss-challenge winner was announced, I left the warrior games. I walked away as the Harrisburg crowd swarmed the field and celebrated.

In all the commotion, no one saw me leave the competition.

Now the only thing I heard was the wind rustling through the trees at the side of the road, and the faint hum of cars on the highway several miles away.

I looked down at my shirt.

AIM HIGH,
WORK HARD,
DON'T QUIT!

I erupted into hysterical laughter. How ironic was that?

Lily Shue had just quit.

Thank God I left my phone in my bag on the field. At least that was one blessing. I didn't have to hear Mom pleading for me to come back home with her to Santa Monica. Or Chip's teasing. *Couldn't even handle a Podunk town in the middle of nowhere without screwing up?*

That wasn't fair of me. They were being supportive in their own way. What was I going to do now? I couldn't even think about going back to fitness training in another gym somewhere. Not because I was too embarrassed to show my face after my multiple failures. But because I didn't want to leave Truhart.

I don't know why I wanted to stay in a town that didn't even have the decency to listen to my pep talk. Or to face Edge, who had acted like a Boy Scout on a mission to sabotage the neighboring camp last night.

Maybe I was taking it all too seriously. Maybe I had lost all perspective.

I pictured Edge and Elizabeth with their other team members, dressed in black, holding flashlights in their mouths and breaking into the gym in Harrisburg. It was pretty funny to think of the two of them tiptoeing around in the middle of the night and spying on their neighbors. Like a scene out of *Animal House*. I almost wished I had been there to see their silly antics.

A truck came up behind me. A dingy purplish stuffed animal with yellow beady eyes laughed at me from the front bumper.

"Hey there, little lady. Can I offer you a ride?"

Déjà vu was so strong I wondered if I was experiencing some weird form of PTSD. But instead of a hunky bearded man behind the wheel, a square-jawed man with white hair and a blue baseball hat with a navy veterans' seal on it leaned out the window. He was surprisingly handsome. Like his nephew.

"Uncle Pete?"

He narrowed his eyes. "Now I know my brothers and sisters aren't the purest of kin, but I don't think there are any illegitimate nieces or nephews wandering around the county that I've never met."

I held out my hand. "I'm the fitness nut. Lily Shue."

"Holy cow! I've heard all about you from Edge. He wasn't lying. You're a fine-looking lady."

I smoothed my hair back. He probably wouldn't be talking about me anymore after today. "Can I take you up on the offer for a ride?"

"Of course." He started out of the cab to help me.

I held up my hand. "You know what? I'm pretty sure I can get in myself now."

"That's a good thing. My back is going out even as we speak."

It was a personal victory to be able to climb in on my own. At least it was one thing I had been able to accomplish lately.

When I was settled in the seat, Uncle Pete asked me, "Where to?"

"Home." Before he could ask, I added, "The Callahans'."

It seemed like the logical place to start. Later, I could go to the apartment I was originally supposed to stay in, something I had put off thinking about for weeks. Even if I wasn't the fitness instructor in town, the Triple C's might let me stay there anyway.

"So isn't today that big challenge? How did it all go?"

I opened my mouth to tell him, and was shocked when I broke down. The wall of tears I had been holding back all day collapsed.

Uncle Pete must have wished he had never stopped the truck to talk to me. In between gulps and broken explanations that probably made no sense, he handed me tissues and patted my back.

"Now, now . . . This will all seem better in a day. You can't blame yourself for anything." He consoled me as if he was used to women sobbing in his truck.

"But it's all wrong. Rocky is going to feel like a loser again. The losers are going to gain weight . . ." I sniffled and blew my nose. "And Edge is never going to be ticklish again."

He raised his eyebrow at that comment. "Uh, I don't know nothing about Edge being ticklish. But I do know about Truhart. It's a funny little town. Everyone thinks they know better than everybody else and nobody stops to listen to a soul. Winning isn't everything. and eventually they'll figure it out."

He handed me another tissue. I blew my nose and took a deep breath.

Desperate to change the subject from my embarrassing day, I took a deep breath and asked Uncle Pete the one question I had been dying to ask since the day I arrived in Truhart. "Uncle Pete, why do you decorate your truck with stuffed animals?"

"Ha. You should hear the mayor go on about it. For years he threatened to fire me if I didn't remove every last little bear. At first I took them off to please him, but eventually they found their way back." He chuckled. "Edge told me you thought he was some kind of serial killer when he picked you up."

"Well . . ." What could I say?

"You know, Lily, I used to hate my job. Every day I hauled smelly trash and wanted something else for my life. Then one day I found the cutest white teddy bear in a trash can. I thought to myself, Who could throw out such an adorable little guy? I put the bear on the truck and it made me happier. Then the next little stuffed animal came along. I did the same thing again."

I was beginning to understand.

"You know, there are a lot of tough things in life. Lord knows I've seen some pretty bad stuff." The veterans cap and the tone of his voice told me more than he was willing to say. "Now I've got friends along for the ride. People around town leave stuffed animals out for me. It makes them happy to know I am taking care of their little guys. There's something nice about changing something unpleasant into something nice. Even if it's just a little gesture. It's like my candy. A little sweet to go with all the sour stuff people deal with."

He told me all about the display he was going to have at the cheese shop in Pinconning and how he was going to make it big in the candy business. I was pretty sure he exaggerated quite a bit for my benefit. His chatter worked. By the time we arrived at the Callahans' I was feeling better.

Uncle Pete shook my hand and held it. "My nephew is very special to me, Lily. He cares a lot about you."

I swallowed and tried not to cry again at the thought of Edge. "I told him some things about the way I feel today, Uncle Pete. I don't think he feels as strongly as you think."

"You're wrong there, my dear." He handed me a bag of candy. "You'll feel better soon."

Impulsively I gave him a hug. "Thank you so much, Uncle Pete."

After he drove away, I put the candy in my pocket and walked toward the house. What would have happened if Uncle Pete had been driving the truck the day I arrived in Truhart? Would things have been different? Would I have ended up staying somewhere other than the Callahans'?

I had just pulled the key out of my pocket when I heard the sound of tires screeching on the road behind me.

I turned around and what I saw made my blood run cold. Ivy's hunched figure sat behind the wheel of her white Ford Taurus. The car careened back and forth in a zig-zag. Then it picked up speed as if she had forgotten the difference between the brake and the accelerator. It veered off the road and plowed through the mud and grass, knocking down perennials as it bounded straight through the garden and into Reply Lake.

"Ivy!"

I ran across the road, my heart beating out of my chest, terrified that the car would sink before I could get to it. It floated on the lake surface, bobbing away from the shore like a ship without a rudder.

How had Ivy gotten behind the wheel? Then I remembered, Louise had taken her to warm up.

I kicked off my shoes and tore off my coat. I was just about to jump, when I stopped.

I had to be smart about this. The nose of the car was sinking slowly. There was no way Ivy would be able to open a door or even the window herself. I wouldn't be strong enough to open it with the water pressure from the outside.

I spun back toward the ranch. Thankfully, the hoe I had used to work in the garden the other day was still propped against the house. I grabbed it and rushed to the shore.

I jumped over the low timber edge that ran along the shoreline and into the frigid water. Adrenaline took over. I didn't even feel the cold after the initial shock. I ran through the shallow water until it was too deep. Then I swam toward the Taurus with one hand holding the hoe, making painfully slow progress.

When I reached the car, I could see Ivy inside. Her hands were on the wheel as if she were still attempting to drive the car. Her face was a mixture of terror and confusion.

"Move back!" I yelled.

I didn't have time to wait for her to understand. I raised the hoe and hit the driver's side window. Ivy instinctively leaned away from the window. Good. I didn't want her hurt.

I slammed the hoe again, this time aiming the sharpest edge of the hoe at the window. It smashed through the safety glass, leaving a gaping hole. I raised the hoe several more times to clear the glass.

"Stay calm, Ivy. I'm going to get you out."

Water lapped over the side and into the car. I ran the hoe over the sill to make a wide opening and dropped it. Making a fist, I cleared the rest of the jagged glass on the edge of the window, ignoring my bloody hand.

"Come on, Ivy. We have to get you—" I swallowed a mouthful of water and choked. Thankfully, she had her seat belt on when she went in the water. Now, however, it made it difficult to unbuckle. I held on to the door and reached in, yanking her toward me with all my strength. I lost my footing and felt the strain on my knee. The water was rushing into the car now. The car was sinking. The water made Ivy lighter, more buoyant, as I finally pulled her out.

Swimming in the frigid water was a nightmare. I had been trained long ago in lifesaving and I held Ivy's chin up with one hand and crawled slowly to shore. The importance of keeping her head above the water was paramount. If the cold didn't kill her at her age, swallowing water and catching pneumonia might.

The last part of the rescue was the hardest. My strength was almost gone and I struggled to pull Ivy through the shallow water near the shore without hurting her. For all her frailty, she was heavy in her wet clothes, and I had trouble holding on to her. Her eyes were barely open and I was worried about hypothermia.

With one last heave, I lifted her out of the water and over the timber edging onto shore.

She fell toward me. I twisted to cushion her fall.

And felt a horrible and familiar *pop*.

Together, we collapsed in the dirt of Ivy's garden, a shivering mess.

When I regained my breath I gazed over at Ivy. She lay on her side, facing me. Her lips were blue. Her body was cold. I sure as hell wasn't going to lose her now.

My coat was a few feet away, right where I had thrown it off before jumping in the water. I grabbed it and covered her head and her chest, rubbing her arms to keep the circulation going. I tried to feel a pulse but my hands were too numb. Streaks of blood stained the white coat, and I panicked until I realized it was my own.

"Come on, Ivy. Come on. Edge and Tracy and Louise . . . they all still need you. Don't give up. They'll be here soon."

Someone would pass by. Wouldn't they? I was so tired. And cold. My knee was alarmingly numb and I couldn't feel my lips.

I tried to drag myself to my feet, but Ivy was lying on my leg. Even if I could get her off me, I didn't think I was strong enough to make it to the ranch or the road. I doubted my knee would hold me.

"It's going to be all right, Ivy. Someone will drive by soon." I kept rubbing the coat over her upper body.

I felt a lump in the pocket and remembered what Uncle Pete had given me. Sugar would help prevent hypothermia.

I reached into the coat pocket. "Ivy. I have something for you."

I fumbled with the bag's twist tie and managed to take out a chocolate. Lifting the coat so I could reach her mouth, I begged her to take the candy. "Try this, Ivy. It will help you."

It took several attempts, but she finally opened her mouth and let me place the candy on her tongue.

I talked to Ivy and plied her with candy for what seemed like hours. But I was almost out of strength. I was just about to close my eyes when I saw Ivy staring at something beyond my head.

"Mine," she croaked.

"What?" I turned slowly to see what she was looking at.

Behind my head was a single flower, sprouting out of the soil. Its three petals were white and at its center was a little yellow stamen. I hadn't seen it the other day. A robin landed not far from us. Another bird called in the distance.

"Now," Ivy said, stronger this time. "Good."

Was she talking to me or the flower? I turned my head again. Her eyes were closed. But she was smiling.

I looked back at the flower. It was like a lily, but it was different.

Dad would know what kind of flower it was. He was always telling me about spring bulbs. The hardest part wasn't the sun or the water or even the planting. The hardest part was being patient. They broke through on their own time.

I felt the collar of my wet T-shirt. The necklace he had given me was still there.

My mind drifted and I started to shiver, even though I didn't feel anything but numb.

What was it Dad used to say? *You can't force a bloom. They'll come when they are ready. Just be patient, Lily Bud.*

Mom used to tell me I was a lot like my dad. I never understood how that could be.

But now it made sense. People were easier to coax than to push. They were fragile, like a flower, and needed careful attention. Why had I never understood?

Helping people get fit wasn't a sport.

It wasn't about winning.

In so many ways, what I did was more like gardening. It was about being patient and nurturing.

It didn't matter to Dad that I missed that stupid soccer goal all those years ago. Nobody ever thought that was important but me. I don't know why I never understood.

The sound of a siren woke me up from my strange half dream. The noise grew closer until I heard a car door slam and the soft sound of running feet on sod.

J.D. was suddenly next to me, kneeling in the dirt. "I found them," he said into a radio. "At the Callahans'. Call Edge."

He ran to his SUV and returned with a blanket. He placed a blanket over Ivy and started to put his coat around me.

I pushed it away. "Put . . . it on . . . Ivy."

While he examined Ivy, he said, "We've been searching all over for Ivy ever since Sarah realized her car was gone."

Ivy said something, and J.D. calmed her down. "Shhh . . . save your strength, Ivy. Your family will be here soon."

Another car engine. A familiar and very, very dear voice. "Grandma! . . . Lily?"

I raised my head as Edge dropped down beside us. I tried to explain. "Ivy drove the car . . . into th-th-the lake."

He looked at the water and then turned his gaze sharply back to me. "Jesus . . ."

"An ambulance is on its way," J.D. said. "I think it's okay to move her off Lily."

Together they carefully lifted Ivy off my leg. I couldn't seem to stop shaking. My California blood was making me feel like I was in a block of ice. Something warm covered me and I realized it was another blanket. Edge moved me gently onto his lap and I felt so silly to be shivering so much.

I tried to speak. "I g-gave her . . ."

Edge reassured me in a low, soothing voice. "It's okay, honey. You don't have to talk."

"B-but how is . . . she?" I asked.

"Her pulse is strong. Her lips are losing some of the blue shade they had a moment ago. You did good, Lily," J.D. said.

"T-t-tried."

J.D. reached over and placed his hand on my neck, feeling my pulse. "Ivy is in better shape than Lily," J.D. said quietly.

"I'm f-f-ine."

"Shh. Don't talk." Edge wrapped something around my hand. Pain was slowly returning, and I winced. He rubbed my arms briskly, trying to get my blood flowing, sending tiny needles up my spine.

I heard the crinkle of the bag. "I g-gave her P-Pete's Treats."

J.D. handed me a piece of candy. "Eat some yourself." The sweet chocolate melted on my tongue.

Things were blurry and out of order for a while. More cars and people arrived. And an ambulance. Louise was frantic "Mom! Oh my God! Mom, are you all right?"

I closed my eyes, and the next thing I heard was Chip directing paramedics and my mom's sharp tone, slipping into Korean. When I raised my head, Ivy was already being loaded into the ambulance.

Louise tried to get in the back of the ambulance, but the paramedic wouldn't let her. "It's all right, ma'am. We'll take good care of her."

Edge pulled another blanket over me. "I don't have h-hypotherm . . . Just cold."

The corners of his mouth drew up in a tiny smile and he kissed my forehead. "I'm so sorry about today . . . I tried to find you. I should have told you weeks ago. I love—"

"Don't." I squeezed his arm, only I was so weak it was just a tap.

He looked pained. "You were right about everything."

"I-I . . ." I had trouble finishing my sentence. What I originally thought were shivers had turned to a sudden urge to laugh. I thought about the fact that Pete's stupid treats and all those calories I had complained about had probably saved Ivy's life. And the irony of landing in the middle of a garden. Dad would be amused.

From deep in my chest a rumbling started and I couldn't stop myself.

"Lily?" Edge's voice sounded distressed. He leaned down and examined my face, afraid he had missed something.

My mood grew lighter by the second. Ivy was alive. It was wonderful.

"Lily? Are you all right?" His smooth face hovered over me in a strange blur.

I could barely speak in between my giggles. Attempting made me laugh even harder. "Edge . . ."

"What?" He was looking back and forth from me to J.D. with alarm on his face. "She never laughs like this."

I threw back my head, letting the hilarity mix with the tears. "I think I t-tore my ACL again . . ."

"Awww shit . . ."

LESSON TWENTY-THREE

Be Patient—Lily Shue
(New Triple C's T-Shirt)

A month later I lay in the preoperative holding area in a Traverse City hospital. My hair was in a cap and I wore a ridiculously unflattering blue hospital gown. I had an IV in my arm, and an X on my right knee where the surgeon was going to cut.

Edge was beside me. Holding my hand. A beloved beard back on his face.

"Don't let me cry when I wake up," I begged him for the third time.

"I'll tell you a joke." Poor Edge. Turns out he is quite a softie. After I told him I tore my ACL, he couldn't stop wiping away his own tears.

"Do you have my ring?"

He patted his pocket. It was going to be a short engagement. Just until I could walk down the aisle without a leg brace.

So much had happened in the last month. After I was checked out at the hospital and cleared by the doctor to go home, Edge had insisted that I return to his bed at the ranch. As soon as Chip made sure Ivy was being treated and would recover, he and Mom seemed perfectly fine with Edge nursing me back to health.

"I'll send kimchi and *dduk-guk*," Mom promised when she left. Edge's refrigerator would never be the same.

That first night after the accident, nothing warmed me as much as when Edge told me how much he loved me. When I asked how long he'd felt that way, he said it started somewhere between the moment I stubbornly insisted I could get in the garbage truck on my own, and the way I knew my NCAA basketball rules.

"You seriously fell in love with me because I understood a traveling call?"

"Then there was Jimi Hendrix."

"Yeah, but I like Michael more."

"I'll get used to it," he said. He even played "Baby Be Mine" for me.

It was a tender night, despite my pain. The last thing I could do was make love. But I was patient. So was Edge.

The June sun was like heaven when it finally poked through the clouds. The summer was in full swing. Edge had started a line of smoothies at the Dairy Cow, using my protein powder. It was all the rage with the tourists from downstate.

Ivy's garden was beautiful, thanks to Edge and the rest of the Callahans.

Best of all, Ivy was remarkably unscathed by her little drive into Reply Lake. On a warm Saturday night last week, we set her wheelchair by the garden and Edge played silly songs on his guitar. It was a lovely night.

A nurse came and added an anesthetic to my IV. I would be sleepy soon.

"Your mom and brothers want to come in before the surgery," Edge said. They flew in two days earlier. I suspected the real reason was because Ned wanted to check Edge out. Of course the three of them got along famously. I never doubted it. They were like the Three Stooges. The comedy and the slapstick never stopped. Even I couldn't stop laughing.

I was growing sleepy. The nurse was waiting for Edge to leave. "I'll see everyone after surgery. Just don't let Chip show me a fake leg and tell me they cut mine off."

"He told me about that. Good joke. I should have tried that on Peter." He kissed me tenderly. "Half the town is in the waiting room."

After saving Ivy, I had suddenly become the town hero.

"I hope there's healthy food in the cafeteria, then."

"They wanted me to give you this before you went into surgery."

He reached into a bag and held up a golden knee brace. "Since you get a new one after this, they spray-painted your old one for you."

Another prize was already with the Triple C's. It was a new grant for gym equipment. The prize for winning the Warrior Weekend Challenge.

Aubrey Vanderbeek still thought we had cheated. But the judges saw something they liked in the Truhart team. With one team member left to go, and only a tie needed to win the obstacle course's final race, Edge had put Rocky into the competition. As he struggled to complete the challenge, yards behind his competitor, he had been surrounded by a sea of yellow T-shirts. The town of Truhart had cheered him on, drowning out the Harrisburg team's victory dance as Rocky crossed the finish line behind him. Instead of dejected moans of defeat, Truhart raised Rocky up on their shoulders and paraded him around the field like a champion.

Not only did Rocky get extra points for effort, but the judges saw the way the citizens from Truhart crossed the field and shook Harrisburg's hands. Several bonus points for sportsmanlike conduct put Truhart over the top.

"I love you, Lily." The drugs were starting. It was time for me to go to sleep. "One more thing. Uncle Pete sent you this."

He reached into the bag and pulled out a teddy bear with a little Velcro strap on its knee.

I couldn't stop smiling at the sight of the burly, handsome, bearded love of my life clutching a teddy bear. It reminded me of that first day. "I wish I could take it into surgery."

Edge tucked it under his arm and gave me a kiss as the nurse wheeled me away.

"We'll both be waiting for you when you wake up."

Did you miss Elizabeth and J.D.'s story? Keep reading for a special excerpt of *Skinny Dipping Season,* and a summer that changes everything.

Chapter 1

Iloved everything about my grandmother's house, including the
creepy garden gnome who stood like a sentinel by the front door.
Even though it had been years since I last saw him, he still leered at
me with his one remaining eye and dared me to enter the cinder-
block house in the middle of the woods. I carried the box I had so
carefully color coded and marked as fragile past him on my way to
the front door.

"You need to end this farce now."

For a crazy moment I thought the gnome had spoken to me. But
the comment came from my father, the Honorable Thomas Lively,
who stood inside the doorway with his hands on his hips.

"Your mother says if we don't get her out of here soon her mi-
graine will start up again." He removed his glasses and gazed at me
with the same no-nonsense, flinty expression that had helped him
win reelection to the U.S. Congress six times.

I didn't have to turn around to know that a rigid figure sat in the
front seat of the Lincoln Town Car. My mother hadn't left the car
since it had pulled between my Honda and a drainage ditch an hour
ago. Some things never changed.

After I left a message with my parents telling them I was moving
to Grandma's vacant house in the north woods, my cell phone
erupted with a stream of incoming calls. Mom and Dad thought the
idea was ridiculous. I hadn't expected them to drop everything and
rush away from their vacation home in Harbor Springs with my little
brother Elliot in tow. But here they were, not a half hour after I arrived.

Readjusting the weight in my arms, I stepped past my dad and
tripped over a fake fern. I lost my grip and the box somersaulted

across the room with a jarring crash. As a tightness spread across my chest, I had an irrational thought: If I never opened it, maybe nothing inside would be broken. I could just keep the packing tape on it and imagine that all the pieces were whole.

I shoved the box behind the fake fern and turned to my dad. "I'm not changing my mind."

"I know the situation is bad, but people have short memories, Elizabeth. You don't have to move here," he said, running his palm across his thick gray hair. His eyes darted back and forth like they did when he was getting ready to outmaneuver a political opponent.

"Even the lawyers said I need to disappear for a while, Dad. You're just lucky that you won't have to resign because of me." I hugged my arms across my middle and tried to avoid touching the nicotine-stained walls. "You agreed that I should get away before the national press targets me. And being here will give me the one thing I need: A quiet town where nobody knows me and nobody cares."

My little brother Elliot stomped through the door, dumping one last box in the middle of the living-room floor. A cloud of dust rose from the dingy carpet and caught the day's last rays of sunlight.

"This crap is heavy," he muttered, lifting his black T-shirt and scratching his pale, hairless stomach as he looked around the stark room. "*Jeee-sus.* I can't get over the fact that this place hasn't changed since Grandma lived here. Shi—"

"Don't talk like that, Elliot. And why are you helping her unload her car? We're trying to convince her to come back with us."

"She wants to stay. I would too if everyone in Ohio thought I was a bitch."

Disappointment from my parents I was used to, but Elliot's words knocked me off balance.

Like I had done a dozen times since March, I studied him for signs that he was hiding something. But he wasn't looking at me as he continued to scratch his belly button. He was gazing up at a crack on the ceiling. "This place is a shit hole."

"I said, watch your tongue young man," Dad said as he started to sit down. He lost his footing and sank into the springless interior of Grandma's orange plaid couch. He landed between the two couch cushions and they made a V from his weight. "What the hell—?"

Elliot snickered. "Watch your tongue, Congressman."

My father reacted the way he always did when Elliot challenged him. He zeroed in on me. "Since your bank account has been wiped out and you have no job anymore, how are you going to get by?"

"I actually have some cash that wasn't used to pay off legal fees."

Dad's face turned red with the effort of extricating himself from the couch. Elliot laughed out loud and I offered my hand, but he waved me away. When his feet were finally underneath him and he was free, Dad looked back at the couch and frowned. "Cracks in the walls, peeling paint. What a mess! No wonder we can't find someone to buy this place. We should have bulldozed the house and sold the property."

The horn of the Lincoln blared from the driveway. Dad ignored it and kept talking. "Listen, I know you don't spend like your sister and mother, but even you would hate to go without your fancy haircuts and yoga classes. I doubt they have a Starbucks near the bait shop."

"Maybe I'll live like everyone else."

Dad leaned down and scrutinized me as if I were still ten years old. "They don't use hand sanitizer and three different kinds of soap around here. I'm not paying for more therapy."

I took a suggestion from my psychotherapist and pictured his words rolling off me like water on wax. "I am staying, Dad."

He disregarded me as usual. "I've been thinking and I don't believe this is quite as drastic as we thought. I know a family in South Africa who needs an au pair. They owe me a favor or two and would be happy to take you in."

That sounded just like my father. It was always about favors and money. "Are they serious? Besides the fact that I'm twenty-seven and too old, what kind of person would take on an au pair with a criminal record as a favor?"

"No, no, Elizabeth. They aren't from Ohio. They would never even have to know about the incident. And remember, the lawyers have said that because it was a first-time offense, it was a misdemeanor. They used that logic to persuade the judge to let you keep your driver's license. The probationary period is over, so whether you are out of state or out of the country, the incident is no longer an issue."

The *incident*.

I hated how the family called it that. Sometimes I wished they would just come out with it: drug possession.

It was my first offense. Marijuana. In my father's car. The same

Lincoln Town Car that sat in the driveway. The one subsidized by the good people of Ohio.

I was innocent.

"It has been almost a full week since the local newspaper printed a story about you. Except for that one parasite, reporters have all but disappeared from my office and my staff only fielded one call from the media yesterday afternoon. Given the circumstances and my position, that is a very hopeful sign. I've even been advised by my public-relations staff that in another year or so my name might be at the top of a short list for the Energy and Commerce Committee."

As my father rambled on about his political plans, my attention drifted out the window to the gnome in the front yard.

How old had I been when I bought my first gnome? Seven? Eight? My father was a newly elected state congressman from the 9th district back then. He and Mom were spending the summer meeting constituents and glad-handing donors. I had just been kicked out of summer camp for repeatedly ignoring the rules and feeding the raccoons that raided the trash bins each night. It was decided that I would stay with Grandma. On my first day in Truhart, Grandma took one look at my long face and declared that it was time that I started a collection like every self-respecting Michigander. She drove me to an antiques store on the edge of town and let me choose anything I wanted. It didn't take long before I had planted myself in front of a cluster of strange little people frolicking on the shelf. I could have chosen the pretty lady figurines with billowing dresses and graceful white necks next to them. But the funny little gnomes enchanted me. I began my collection that summer.

Years later, my little sister, Alexa, and her friends snuck into my room and drew obscenely graphic pictures of body parts all over them with permanent markers. Mom told me I was silly to cry over my tacky collection and threw them in the trash.

Dad was now on to my least favorite subject. "—things with Colin can be worked out. The pressure of all the publicity surrounding your arrest and the media frenzy in Ohio after that was really hard on him. But he is a reasonable man, and once he sees that the fury has settled down he'll be ready to take you back."

Take me back? Everyone assumed we broke up because of my arrest. If Dad knew the truth, he would stop bothering me about Colin.

Alexa didn't deserve my protection. The only reason I had never told anyone that I caught my sister in bed with my boyfriend was that by the time I had recovered from the shock of my arrest, I realized that the family didn't need another "incident" to deal with. It wouldn't have helped my case. And as Colin pointed out, it would probably have just given a judge more reason to think I was using drugs to escape my problems.

"You and Colin can work out a long-distance relationship, but it is more likely he would want to visit you overseas or on the east coast rather than Truhart. You and Elliot were the only ones who could ever stand it here."

"I know you hate Truhart, but this is the perfect place for me right now, Dad."

"I'll admit you have to get away from the public eye. But you don't have to do anything this drastic. You'll hate it."

"Grandma lived here and she loved it."

"You just proved my point." A bitter grunt escaped his lips. "You won't last a week!"

I hated it when he talked that way. I didn't stand up to him very often, but being in this house gave me courage. I stepped in front of him and steadied my voice. "Try me!"

Dad straightened and raised his eyebrows. If I didn't know better, I would have thought I saw respect reflected in his blue eyes. But I must have been mistaken. That was something Dad saved for campaign donors.

I didn't have long to savor my triumph. Dad turned toward the door and shrugged his shoulders. "At least come say good-bye to your mother."

Following him outside, with Elliot trailing behind me, I picked up an overturned plastic chair on my way to the Town Car. The gravel driveway bit into the thin soles of my shoes and combined with the sharp sting of the cool air to clear the numbness that had set in.

I smoothed my hair behind my ears and straightened my sweatshirt as I paused beside the passenger door and waited for my mother to roll down the window. When nothing happened, I opened the car door to reach her rigid cheek.

"I'm sorry you came all this way for nothing, Mom. I'll call you to let you know how I'm doing."

My mother, once known in Truhart as Becky Blodget—but now

referred to only as Mrs. Thomas Lively—barely shifted as my lips touched her icy skin. I could smell the familiar odor of alcohol on her breath.

"I'm trying to ignore the irony that you are ending up in the very place I spent my life trying to escape," Mom said. Her sunglasses were slightly askew on her face and her dark lipstick was crusting on her lower lip. Other than that, she was perfect.

"Grandma liked it here."

"Ask your father to get my medication out of the trunk."

I looked down at the travel mug cradled in her hand. At least Grandma had never been afraid to leave her alcohol at home.

Dad opened the driver's door and leaned in. "Your medication is right here," he said, handing her a small container. "Do you want to come in and get a glass of water before we hit the road, Rebecca?"

"I'd rather buy water at the gas station than set foot in there."

Elliot snorted. "God, Mom, you need therapy."

"In the car!" Dad ordered.

Elliot ignored him and walked over to me. He stood with his hands in his jeans, caught somewhere between boyhood and manhood, trying to look like he didn't care about good-byes. Where was the little boy I used to make Mickey Mouse pancakes with? His shaggy hair hid the beautiful blue eyes and long lashes that made him look girlish when he was young. I missed his blond locks that curled ever so slightly when they were short and clean.

My father started the car and the headlights flashed on, illuminating the peeling paint on the front door of the little house. For a moment a band of panic tightened in my chest.

"Stay out of trouble, Elliot," I said, reaching out for him.

He stepped backwards. "Me? Mom and Dad wouldn't have overreacted about my grades and I wouldn't have to go to summer school if you hadn't screwed up like you did. Thanks to you, my whole summer is going to suck!"

I smoothed a strand of hair that caught the evening breeze.

"Elliot, just try to be good and make Dad happy."

"That will never happen. You of all people should know that."

He was right, of course. Instead of arguing, I pulled him into an embrace despite his resistance.

"I love you," I said.

He said nothing, but I felt the touch of his hands on my back and swallowed past the boulder in my throat. Elliot ducked his head out of my arms and yanked open the back door of the sedan. He folded his gangly form inside and slammed the door.

I walked around to the driver's side as my father rolled down his window. "I'd tell you to come back to the condo in Harbor Springs with us and get a job there this summer, but I guess that would be expecting too much."

"I'm sorry I'm such a disappointment." How many times had I said that in the past few weeks? He avoided my eyes and shifted the car into reverse. I stood next to the gnome with my fists balled at my sides, my fingernails cutting into my palms.

At the end of the gravel drive, the car paused and Dad rolled down his window. "Clean this dump up while you're doing nothing, will you? Maybe then we can finally sell it." The tires spun on the gravel and kicked up a murky cloud of dust.

I stood for a long time, watching the tail lights fade to nothing.

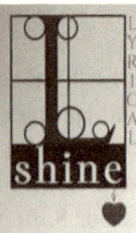

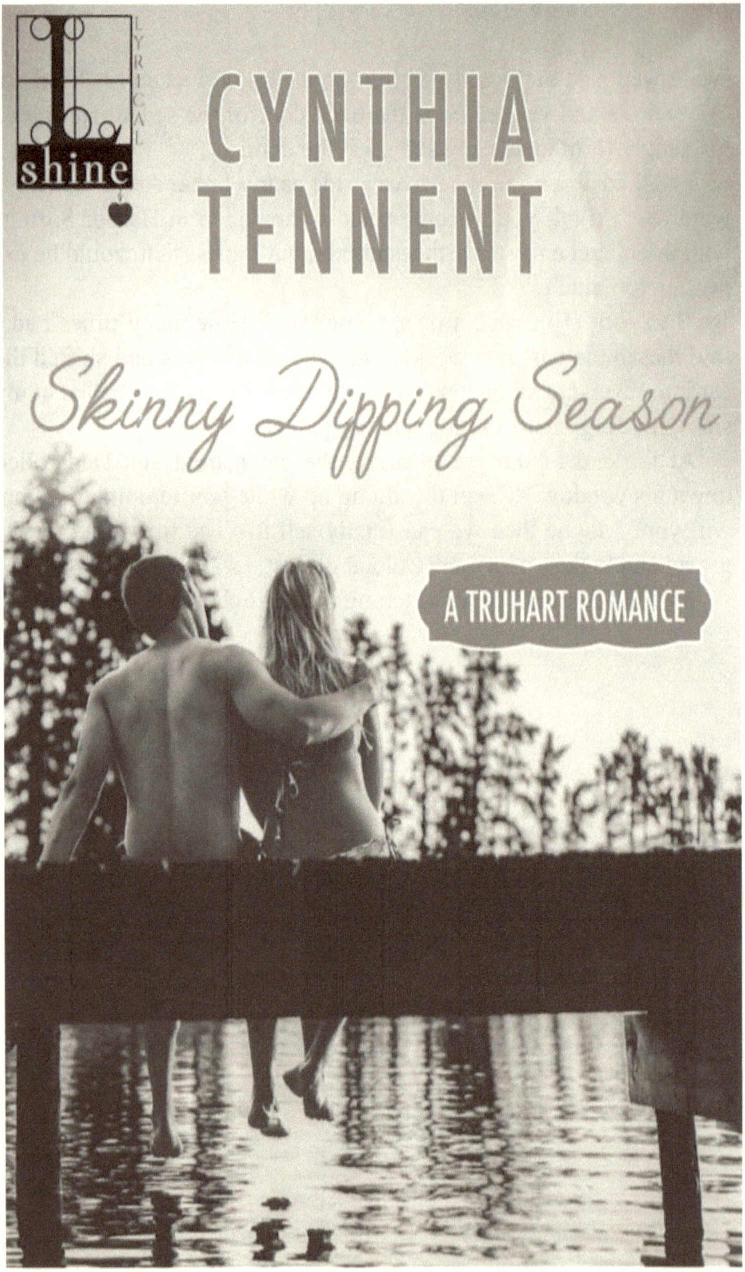
LYRICAL
shine
CYNTHIA
TENNENT
Skinny Dipping Season
A TRUHART ROMANCE

shine
LYRICAL

CYNTHIA TENNENT

"Charm, humor, loyalty, and love."
— Cindy Myers, author of
The View From Here

A TRUHART ROMANCE

A Wedding in Truhart

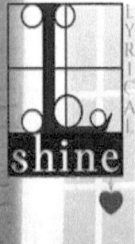

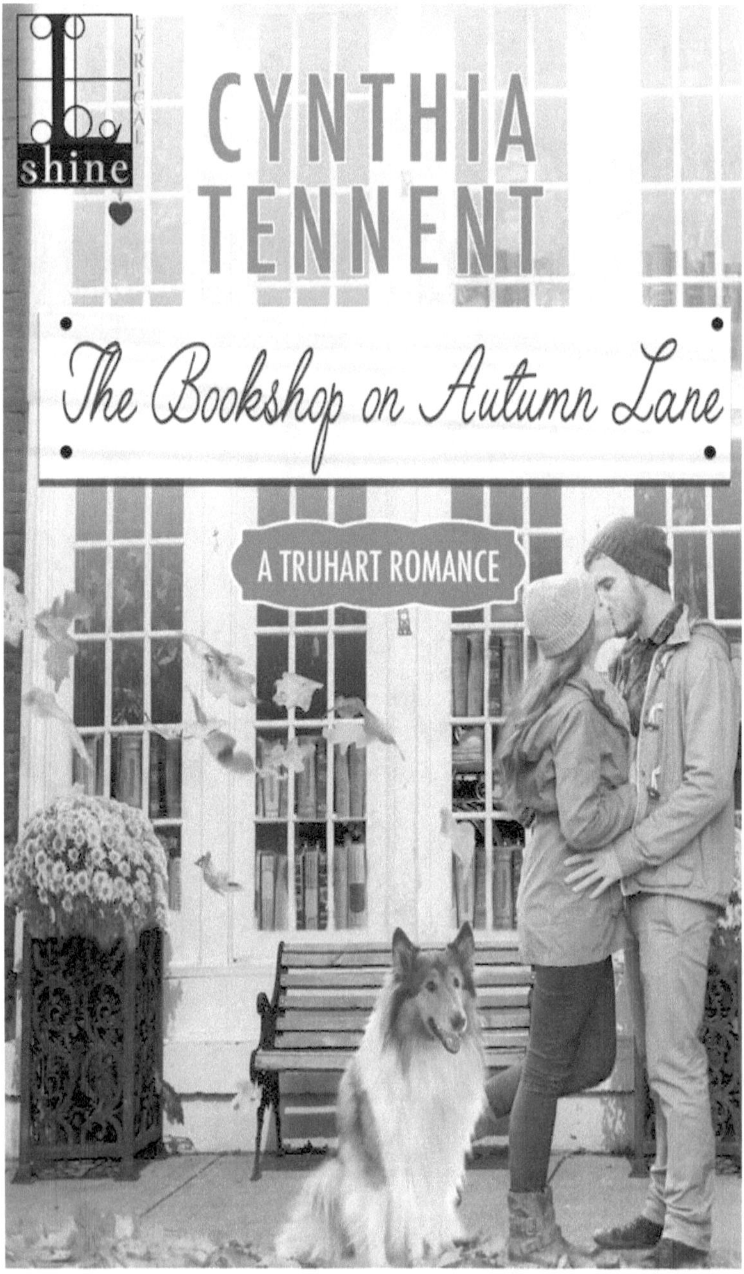
LYRICAL
shine
CYNTHIA
TENNENT
The Bookshop on Autumn Lane
A TRUHART ROMANCE

Cynthia Tennent believes that when life gets tough, the tough should pick up a book. She is especially partial to stories in which a girl can be a hero and her trusty sidekick can be good-looking. In her Truhart Series, she writes about life in a small town, where love is plentiful and all dirt roads lead to happy endings.

Cynthia lives in Michigan with her patient husband, their three strong-willed daughters, and her collie dog, Jack. When she isn't writing, Cynthia volunteers, pretends to exercise, laughs with her friends, and tries to understand technology.

Visit her at www.cynthiatennent.com

www.ingramcontent.com/pod-product-compliance
Lightning Source LLC
Chambersburg PA
CBHW020750250626
47155CB00003B/1013